ART MAGES OF LURE

BOOK ON'

CURSE PAINTER

JORDAN RIVET

Contact the author at Jordan@JordanRivet.com

To receive an exclusive short story and discounts on new releases, join Jordan Rivet's mailing list.

Book cover design by www.ebooklaunch.com

Editing suggestions provided by Red Adept Editing

Map by Jordan Rivet

Curse Painter, Art Mages of Lure Book 1/ Jordan Rivet – First Edition: September 2020

❀ Created with Vellum

For Mom,
who taught me to love books
And for Dad,
who got me hooked on fantasy

T HIS STORY BEGINS WITH A CURSE. It was a little curse, not strong enough to maim an enemy or destroy a livelihood. It wasn't the type of curse the authorities would bother to prosecute once they'd met their quota for the month. It wasn't even the type of curse to keep its creator up at night in a cold sweat after inflicting a little more evil on the world. Or at least, it wasn't supposed to be that type of curse.

Unfortunately, in the business of adding tiny bits of evil to the world, even with the best intentions, sometimes things could go terribly awry.

CHAPTER 1

Rough bark scratched Briar's legs as she climbed the maple tree next to the finest house in Sparrow Village. Her paint satchel swung against her hip, the jars inside jingling faintly. She tried not to look down. The ground was too far away already.

Afternoon shadows advanced from the woods behind the property, swallowing up the stable and creeping toward the whitewashed house. Briar held her breath as she climbed past the expensive glass windows. The house's inhabitants, servants included, should still be away at the summer fair. Hopefully, the place was empty—and would stay empty until Briar finished the job.

She edged along a stubby branch jutting toward the second floor of the house. The limb creaked, and the leafy canopy rustled threateningly. Trying to ignore the sounds, Briar wrapped her legs around the end of the branch, opened a jar of brown-ochre paint, and selected a long-handled brush from the bundle in her satchel. Then she braced herself against the clay-shingled roof and began the painstaking work of painting a curse.

Stroke by stroke, the image of a fine house with a peaked roof took shape. The oil paint glistened as it spread from the horsehair brush, brown ochre standing out against the white-washed boards. The familiar smell of linseed oil soothed Briar's nerves, and she relaxed into her task. She'd practiced the complex design on canvas to prevent mistakes. Each brush-stroke required precision and a steady hand, though that got harder the longer she balanced precariously between earth and sky.

She hadn't planned on climbing any trees for the job. She'd spotted a ladder when she'd scouted the place a few days ago and had designed the curse for a shadowy spot beneath the eaves. If she painted it too close to the ground, the gardeners would notice and wipe away the paint before the jinx took effect. More importantly, they would know who was responsible. Briar had already given the local authorities too many reasons to distrust her. Unfortunately, the ladder had been missing when she'd arrived to carry out the job, and the maple tree leaning aggressively toward the house had been her only alternative.

As Briar painted, knots jabbed her thighs through her green wool skirt, and twigs poked into her thick hair. She clutched the clay shingles, trying to ignore the dizzying drop below. Painting curses took concentration. This one wasn't nearly as dangerous as some she knew, but she couldn't afford any errors.

She finished the shape of the house and used blue smalt to add windows, their placement roughly the same as the windows on the real house. Cursing objects was always simpler than cursing people. To affect a human, Briar had to paint an item of clothing they wore often or touch a cursed canvas or stone to their skin long enough for the spell to stick. Getting caught was all too easy, but many curses could be painted right onto inanimate targets—assuming she could reach them without breaking her neck.

This particular curse wouldn't hurt anyone, and it was the most interesting piece of magic Briar had executed in months, her perilous position making it all the more stimulating. Her blood heated in her veins, and her fingers tingled with magic, with the sizzling rush of creation. It was going to be a good one. She could feel it.

The local blacksmith had doubted her abilities when he'd hired her for the job. Her clients rarely believed she could live up to her reputation at the sight of her paint-smudged hands and humble clothes.

"I've heard downright perplexing things about you and your ... profession, but you look awful young," the blacksmith had said at their furtive meeting in his smithy the week before. "Can you really help?"

"Possibly." Briar pushed her dark, frizzy hair out of her eyes, poised to flee at any hint that it was a setup. It wouldn't be the first. "I hear you want to curse Master Winton."

"Aye, the merchant. Five weeks I spent on a bleedin' suit of armor at his bidding, and he refused to pay fair wage. Claimed it wasn't ornate enough. I have young'uns to feed."

"Have you gone to the sheriff?"

"That loiter-sack?" The blacksmith spit in the dirt beside his anvil. "He and Winton are close personal friends."

Briar took a horsehair paintbrush out of her satchel and twirled it between her fingers, the bristles tickling her damp palm. "Where is the armor now?"

"On display in Lord Barden's manor." The blacksmith eyed the paintbrush nervously. "Winton claimed it wasn't worth the price then gave it to his lordship himself as a bleedin' present. Now I'm out the coin and the steel."

"And you want revenge?"

The blacksmith glanced at the summer-bright path outside his smithy and lowered his voice. "It's not just for me, you see. I have daughters. I want to show them we don't take abuse from rich bastards what think they can get away with it."

Briar noted the blacksmith's frayed trousers, the patches on his boots. A wreath of wildflowers hung on the smithy door, the petals wilting in the heat. She imagined the little girls collecting the blooms and clumsily tying them together to brighten their father's workplace. The blacksmith's daughters would have less to eat that winter because of Winton's greed. Briar liked jobs that brought a little justice for ordinary folks— or at least payback.

She tucked her paintbrush behind her ear and stuck out a hand. "I'm in. Tell me about Master Winton's house."

The blacksmith had described the property situated on a spacious lot at the edge of Mere Woods—two stories tall, expensive clay shingles, clear glass windows. And no ladders, apparently.

Perching in the maple tree was becoming less comfortable by the minute. Briar switched from blue smalt to malachite green and began adding vines to the image. She would twine them around the painted house as thick as ivy and add colorful flowers at key points along their lengths. The curse would make the pitch sealing the house against moisture slowly disintegrate. By the coldest months of winter, the roof would leak, and wind would howl through the cracks. She would make Master Winton pay, though he would never know his ill fortune was a result of his cheating ways.

Briar was proud of the curse's subtlety, but the intricate vines were taking too long. She should have prepared an easier design. Her arms ached from bracing herself against the roof, and the distance between the tree and the wall seemed to grow with each stroke. She began to sweat, the paintbrush slipping in her grasp.

As she paused to open a jar of yellow ochre, she detected

movement out of the corner of her eye and froze. Someone was there.

No. Not now. She held her breath, struggling against a powerful urge to run. She couldn't be caught, but she couldn't leave the curse as it was either. Without the final stroke, the little image beneath the eaves would be no more than a pretty picture.

She peered through the thick maple leaves, hardly daring to blink. The grassy expanse between the house and the woods was deserted except for the creeping afternoon shadows. Yet she felt someone watching her.

A horse snorted inside the stable, and magpies chattered in the trees, but she detected no movement, no other sound.

Telling herself she was jumping at shadows, Briar resumed her work. The jars rattled in her satchel as she switched between yellow ochre and vermilion, adding flowers to the vines. Curse painting required a strict stroke order, and she couldn't rush the process, but her brush kept slipping as she juggled two colors and her awkward position. She put the paintbrush in her teeth and clenched her legs tighter around the branch so she could grip the vermilion jar with both hands. The lid was stuck. Knots dug deeper into her thighs as she teetered on the stubby tree branch.

Movement again, a flicker of blue. This time, the shadows took on shape and substance. She wasn't imagining it after all. Someone was standing next to Winton's stable. She could just make him out through the leaves—a tall man in an indigo coat looking right at her.

Briar's heartbeat spiked, and her limbs quivered, making it harder than ever to keep her perch. She wanted to scramble out of the tree and run for it, but she didn't know what the stranger would do if she tried. She stared at him, as motionless as a sparrow facing a tree snake.

Seconds ticked past. The tall man didn't leave the shelter of the stable. His shock of blond hair was visible even in the shadows, and he held something long and thin in his hand.

Could he be Master Winton's gardener? The merchant was a nasty fellow, according to the blacksmith, but would his man really stand back and allow him to be hexed? Briar could be planning to burn the house to the ground with the family inside, for all the gardener knew.

Her legs shook hard enough to rustle the branches. She would attract the attention of passersby if she kept on like that. She couldn't do anything about the stranger. She had to finish the job.

The jar of vermilion popped open at last. Briar rushed the last few strokes of the curse and messed up two flowers. She repaired them with a few quick flicks of the hard edge of the paintbrush, sweat dropping from her forehead to the earth below. One more petal, and the curse would be complete.

She dipped the brush in the jar and brought it, dripping red, to the wall. The branch groaned beneath her as she stretched toward the farthest corner of the painting for the final stroke.

Suddenly, the stranger stepped out of the shadows. He held a longbow, an arrow already nocked. The action startled her, and her hand slipped, leaving a long red slash down the curse painting. Briar gasped and scrambled for more paint to counteract the slash. Before she could fix it, there was a loud *crack*, and the branch gave way beneath her. Leaves and twigs lashed Briar's face as she tumbled from the tree and hit the ground hard. Paint jars crunched beneath her.

She stared up at the shivering branches, winded and shocked. She had fallen. She had actually fallen. Leaves drifted above her, floating on the late-summer breeze.

Don't just lie there! You'll be caught for sure.

She sucked in a breath and forced herself to sit up. Paint and shards of glass covered her shirt. As she brushed them away, pain shot through her wrist. Her left arm had taken the brunt of the impact. She tried to rotate her wrist, and agony lanced through her. She clenched her teeth to keep from vomiting, black spots dancing before her eyes.

If her arm was broken, she wouldn't be able to work for months. She couldn't afford such an injury. She would lose her home, everything she'd built from the remnants of her old life. She should have abandoned the job at the first sign of trouble.

A creaking sound reminded her of the precise curse marred with a broad slash of vermilion. The house gave a deep, ominous groan. She sifted through her curse painting knowledge, trying to work out what that slash was likely to do—and how soon. Every stroke had meaning, and that one ...

The creaking came again, loud and insistent. Briar realized what was about to happen and leapt to her feet. She didn't have much time. She snatched up as many broken jars as she could, shoveling the oily glass into her satchel with her good hand, then bolted away from the house. Running jostled her injured arm, and tears filled her eyes.

The stranger in the indigo coat retreated into the shadows as she darted past. He looked young, with a high forehead, sharp mouth, and dark, quirked eyebrows. The longbow remained undrawn, and he didn't try to stop her.

Briar reached the shelter of the woods just as a roaring, squealing sound startled the magpies from their nests. She looked back.

The house teetered, two stories of whitewashed timber and fine clay shingles swaying like laundry in a stiff breeze. Iron nails began to ping out of the boards one by one, disappearing in the long grass around the house.

Don't.

More nails loosened, fell, scattered.

Please, no.

But it was too late. The final nail popped free, and the

house gave a moan like a dying animal. The walls buckled, glass windows bursting, clay shingles cracking and sliding. Then the entire structure collapsed with a thunderous crash.

Dust billowed into the sky, and splinters scattered across the grass. Briar crouched behind a craggy oak tree, horror consuming her. *This can't be happening.* Magpies wheeled overhead, cawing and scolding from a safe distance.

The dust cleared slowly, unveiling the damage from her botched curse. Somewhere beyond the stable, the stranger gave a low whistle. Nothing was left of the house but a pile of rubble beside a triumphant maple tree.

A whimper escaped Briar's lips. She had worked so hard to set up a new life there, a fresh start peddling quiet, nonlethal curses. Yes, her work was illegal, but she tried not to hurt anyone. She'd even dared hope she might make amends for the things she'd done before. This would destroy her efforts, drawing attention she couldn't afford, maybe enough to attract the notice of the people she'd left behind.

No. She refused to contemplate that possibility. She would run again. She would start over as many times as it took to keep them from catching up with her.

Trying not to rub her paint-covered clothes on anything, she pulled her satchel to her chest and fled into the woods.

Archer emerged from the shadows of the stable and admired the splintered ruin.

He had never seen a curse painter work so meticulously—especially from fifteen feet in the air—nor produce such dramatic results. Not a single whitewashed board or pane of glass remained intact. Willem Winton's fine house looked much better bashed into tiny pieces. Archer wondered what the old charlatan had done to make that slip of a girl want to curse the place into oblivion.

"Who cares why she did it?" He slung his bow onto his back at a jaunty angle. "It was brilliant work."

Archer had heard a curse painter lived in those parts, but he hadn't expected to meet her there. He'd just wanted to engage in a little casual burglary while he was in the neighborhood. Instead, he'd stumbled upon a better prize than gold candlesticks and Mistress Winton's jewels. That girl could be the answer to all his problems.

He turned toward the woods and whistled a high, piercing note. A large dog loped through the trees, shadows dappling its short gray fur. Archer knelt beside the dog and scratched the folds on its neck.

"What do you think, Sheriff? Can you follow her for me?"

The dog whined and rubbed his wrinkly head against Archer's knee, smearing slobber on his breeches, then he trotted over to the maple tree to sniff out the girl's scent among the broken paint jars.

Archer picked up a large glass shard covered in green paint and pocketed it. The curse painter had worked with impressive stealth, at least until the end. He only noticed her perched in the tree when her luminous eyes caught the light, and she stared at him like a large, frizzy-haired owl. She had such power.

The dog looked up, ears pointed like arrowheads, awaiting his master's word.

"Ready, Sheriff? Let's go get her."

Sheriff howled and set off into the trees. Archer jogged after him, slipping into the woods before anyone could investigate the commotion at the finest ruin in Sparrow Village.

CHAPTER 2

B riar's heart drummed a frantic beat as she raced through Mere Woods, avoiding the village proper. The forest seemed bent on delaying her. She snagged her skirt in blackberry patches and tumbled over roots snaking across the path. By the time she reached the Brittlewyn River, sweat dampened her collar, and brambles filled her frizzy hair.

She nearly ran straight into the county sheriff and a pair of Lord Barden's retainers on the bridge. They had stopped for a smoke and were jawing about some tavern wench or other, blocking the only route across the Brittlewyn. Briar dove behind an abandoned cart before the men looked her way. Hopefully they couldn't hear her gasps for breath after her mad dash through the woods.

The leisurely murmur of their voices mixed with the babble of the river. Smoke curled above their heads, taunting her with its slow drift. Why weren't those three at the summer fair? Sheriff Flynn never missed a chance to preen for a crowd, and the local baron's retainers were almost as bad, strutting about in their ugly mustard-brown surcoats.

"Come on now," Briar muttered, worrying at her paint-smudged shirt. "Move along." Sweat crawled down her scalp, and her injured wrist throbbed plaintively. Every minute, she expected an uproar from the mess she'd left behind. She needed to keep moving.

When the trio finally knocked the ashes from their pipes and ambled toward the village, Briar tore across the bridge and up the road on the other side of the river. She didn't dare look back until she reached the little cottage in the woods she'd been renting for the past few months. She paused at the garden gate to listen for signs of pursuit. The road behind her remained vacant—no angry merchants, no villagers with pitchforks. A breeze shivered through the trees and lifted thin curls of sawdust from the woodpile. She was safe for now.

Briar crossed the garden to the cottage, a snug dwelling of roughhewn logs with a thatched roof. She unlocked the door, and the familiar aromas of oil paint, wood smoke, and dry thatch welcomed her home. The tension in her body eased a little. Briar loved her cottage. It only had one room, which was sparsely furnished and rough by most standards, but it filled her with a sense of warmth and well-being, unlike the finer chambers she'd occupied growing up. The cottage was the first place where she'd felt she had a chance—not just at a good life but at being a good person. She was heartsick that she might have to abandon it.

Alert for the sound of hoofbeats, Briar hid the broken paint jars and ruined satchel under her bed and stripped off her paint-splattered shirt. Wincing at the pain in her wrist, she bundled the old shirt into the rag basket by the cottage's only chair and pulled on a crisp white blouse, as if to prove she definitely hadn't been wielding destructive paints that afternoon. She wrapped extra rags around her injured wrist and knotted them with her teeth.

Next, she checked her defenses: small jars of paint and finger-sized brushes carefully concealed around the cottage for emergencies—under her lumpy pillow, inside the fireplace, above the lintel. She tugged a few rungs out of the ladderback chair and hid them too. According to the Law of Wholes, the first of the three laws of curse painting, a curse applied to an object would affect that object in its entirety, regardless of whether the pieces were intact at the time of painting. Just as a curse painted on a few siding boards could destroy a whole house, a curse on a detached piece of a chair could affect the chair from a distance, providing the pieces weren't apart long enough to be considered separate wholes. Briar switched out the rungs on her chair regularly, just in case she needed to hurl the whole thing at someone.

She peeked through the curtained window next to the door. The road to the cottage was empty, and the setting sun bathed the forest in red and gold and deep blue. Soon the shadows would blend into the full dark of night.

Could she have escaped the blame for what had happened somehow? Luck rarely worked in her favor, but the stranger in indigo hadn't confronted her, and the authorities wouldn't necessarily connect her to Master Winton or the collapsed house. As long as the blacksmith didn't talk, they might not even think of her. She hadn't destroyed anything bigger than an ale cart within the boundaries of Barden County, and she wasn't the only curse painter powerful enough to bring down a house. Few mages of any kind could do it so efficiently, though. If it hadn't been a complete accident, she would be proud of her work.

Briar dropped the curtain and dragged an easel and a half-finished canvas to the center of the room. She occasionally created benign paintings to give away so no one would question why she bought so much pigment and always had colorful splatters on her sleeves. Some people in Sparrow Village knew what she was by now, but she tried to make it easier for them to pretend otherwise. She wanted so badly to stay in her little cottage, to finally stop running.

Curse painting as a profession wasn't completely illegal, but like all forms of magic, it was carefully regulated. Mages were required to study in expensive schools and register with the Hall of Cloaks in faraway High Lure. If they passed their studies, licensed art mages received tattoos to track every jinx and spell they performed. Curse painters were usually employed for demolition, mining, and warfare. Ambulatory curses and sleep curses could also bring in a respectable income, providing they weren't used to break other laws—which were numerous. With so many restrictions, most mages—curse painters, voice mages, fortune scribes, even the rare stone crafters—preferred to work directly for the crown and the lords of the peerage.

Unlicensed mages of all types still cropped up, performing illegal magic on the cheap and risking prosecution with every job. Voice mages could avoid notice by peddling healing spells and garden-variety transformations, and no one worried too much about fortune-tellers, but curses were negative by nature. Whether reducing a house to splinters or maiming a romantic rival, it was all too easy for painters to push the boundaries of legality. Even unlicensed curse painters could avoid notice in the outer counties, though, which was why Briar had gone there to start over—and to hide.

She checked outside again. Twilight was falling fast. A large dog loped through the fading light and sniffed around her woodpile. It was as big as a wolf, with meaty shoulders and deep wrinkles enveloping a squashed-looking face. No owner joined the dog, and it soon trotted off into the distance.

Briar dropped the curtain and went to hang the kettle over the low-burning coals in her fireplace. A pot of tea would calm her nerves so she could figure out her next steps. Master Winton would give Sheriff Flynn a list of anyone who might wish him ill. She would have to warn the blacksmith in the morning. She couldn't risk crossing the village tonight.

As she stoked the fire, she imagined the din that must surround the place by now. She should have made the curse smaller so botching it wouldn't have done so much damage. She'd felt the magic in her fingertips, the hot urgency of creation, and she'd gotten carried away. Briar had an almost compulsive need to destroy, something that worried her even more than getting caught. She had walked away from her old life, but she carried part of it with her still.

The kettle sang, and she removed it from the flames. Before she could pour her tea, a knock sounded at the door.

Archer tapped his boot on the flagstone step outside the curse painter's cottage. It didn't look like the type of place to house an illegal curse business. It was little more than a hovel. The green-curtained windows on either side of the door looked like two wide eyes, and the thatched roof drooped a bit above the door, a lock of hair falling in front of a squat troll's face.

The well-kept garden beside the neat woodpile suggested the cottage's occupant looked after the place, but she certainly wasn't wealthy. She couldn't refuse Archer's offer. He was about to make this curse painter rich beyond her wildest dreams—if she ever opened the door.

Archer leaned his longbow against the wall and knocked again. Movement fluttered behind the green curtains, a hint of dark hair and white linen.

"Hello in there!" he called. "I know you're home."

The sound of careful footsteps filtered through the door. It occurred to him that the curse painter could be preparing a jinx.

"I mean you no harm," he said quickly. "I'd like a word with you."

Still no response. Did she really think pretending she wasn't home was going to work? Archer had important business to discuss. He had no time for games.

"I could come back later," he called through the door. "Maybe with Sheriff Flynn or some of Lord Barden's oafs. I'm sure they'd be very interested in what I saw at Willem Winton's house this afternoon—or what used to be his house."

A brief silence. Then the door cracked open, and a pair of luminous brown eyes appeared. "What do you want?"

"Good evening." He gave a bow fit for a duchess. "I am called Archer. I'm an accomplished thief and brigand. I serve the blade, the coin, and the open road. I have come to offer you an opportunity to escape your sordid circumstances and embark on the adventure of a dozen lifetimes."

The girl stared at him, blinking her large, shimmering eyes. It was unsettling, being stared at like that.

"Do you always tell people you're a thief?" she asked at last.

"Don't you tell them you're an *unlicensed* curse painter?"

"Please don't say that so loud." Urgency tinged the girl's voice, though no one was around to hear it. The cottage's location on the quieter side of the Brittlewyn River made sure of that.

"I'm not here to hurt you," Archer said. "I have been looking to hire someone with your particular set of skills, and I must say, yours are the most particular I've ever seen."

"I don't work for criminals." She began to shut the door.

Archer jammed the toe of his boot into the doorway. He'd misjudged her strength and winced as the door nearly chopped his foot in half. "I beg your pardon, miss," Archer said, eyes watering from the pain. "But are you not a criminal yourself?"

There was another brief pause in the poorly lit hut. Archer

felt like he was speaking to a pair of disembodied eyes floating in the shadows.

"I only accept clients under special circumstances."

"Wouldn't you like to hear my circumstances, then?"

The girl ground her teeth audibly. "If you'll stop talking about it out here." She released her hold on the door and stepped back. "You'd better come inside."

Archer was surprised. Inviting a stranger into one's home was risky even in this sleepy country town. But as he ducked beneath the low-hanging lintel, he realized the curse painter was holding an iron kettle, the spout steaming faintly. He was lucky she hadn't thrown it in his face when he stuck his foot in her door.

The light from the crackling fireplace gave him a better look at the curse painter. Though rather short, she wasn't quite as young as he had thought, perhaps eighteen or nineteen, only a few years younger than he was. There was a maturity in her bearing that he'd missed when she was clambering around in that maple tree. She wore a white blouse and a green wool skirt, and her dark hair fell around her shoulders in a frizzy cloud.

The cottage consisted of one room, with a quilt-covered bed in the corner, a small table, and a ladderback chair with a few missing rungs. A large easel with a half-finished painting on a stretched canvas occupied the center of the small space. Other paintings leaned against the walls, the images indistinct in the firelight.

Archer strode to the easel. The painting depicted a pastoral scene, a little farmhouse at the edge of a field of wheat. Tame work, considering what he'd seen the girl accomplish earlier that day.

"What does this painting do?" he asked, examining the swaths of green and gold.

"It doesn't *do* anything. It's just a picture."

"Interesting hobby." He glanced around the room, noting a large locked chest by the wall opposite the door and a basket full of rags by the chair. He could usually find the valuables after a few seconds in a room, but precious little there was worth stealing. "I thought you didn't go around telling people what you are."

"It's an excuse to make the paints. Look, Mister Archer, I don't want to be rude, but would you just tell me what you want?"

"In good time. You *are* unlicensed, correct? That wasn't a crown-blessed hit on that house?"

"It was a private commission." The girl moved over to the table, keeping as much distance between them as possible. She set down the steaming kettle, and he noticed her left hand was wrapped in rags. An injury from falling out of the tree, perhaps? He hoped it wouldn't impede her work.

"That's just what I wanted to hear. And you aren't bound to any of the landed gentry in these parts, are you? No fine sir has your loyalty?"

"I am no lord's lackey."

Archer grinned at the ferocity in her tone. "I think you'll do nicely."

"I won't *do* anything until you tell me what this is about, Mister Archer."

"It's just Archer. And what are you called, Miss Painter?"

She paused for a beat. "Briar."

"No family name?"

"No family."

Silence thrummed between them as she lifted her eyes to meet his.

"As I said, I think you'll do very nicely indeed." He gave her a bright smile and spread his hands with a flourish. "Shall we talk business?"

Briar sighed. "Would you like a cup of tea?"

A few minutes later, Archer was settled in the single chair, resting his shiny black boot on his knee. The girl sat cross-legged on the narrow bed, her skirt tucked tightly around her legs. They sipped mint tea from clay cups while Archer explained the mission.

"Lord Barden, the lord and protector of this fair county, has a daughter, the lovely Lady Mae. Several weeks ago, Lady Mae was kidnapped while out riding her favorite pony. Lord Barden has, quite naturally, been frantic to discover his daughter's whereabouts."

"I heard something about that." Briar shifted back to sit against the wall, resting her injured hand at her side. "She's young, isn't she?"

"Young and beautiful. It has caused quite a scandal."

"Someone at the market said she was taken by bandits," Briar said. "Brigands, like you."

"There is no one like me," Archer said with a wink.

Briar didn't react. She seemed exceptionally guarded, on the verge of fight or flight. He couldn't tell which.

"Market rumors may hint at the truth," he said, "but they rarely paint a complete picture. I have it on good authority that the lady fair was taken by none other than Lord Jasper Larke of the neighboring county."

"Larke and Barden have been squabbling for years."

"So they have," Archer said. "It got so bad a few years ago, the king decreed they must settle their differences or forfeit their lands and titles. No threat is worse to a lord than the loss of his title."

"I wouldn't know," Briar said.

"Of course not." Archer glanced around the hovel. The girl had to want to improve her circumstances. She couldn't help but agree to do the job. Hope flared in his chest for the first time since his return to Barden County.

"The two lords have continued to fight since the king's

decree, but they've kept it quiet. Their animosity festers in secret. Lord Larke dealt an unforgivable blow to Lord Barden when he captured Barden's daughter. Barden can't go to the king because he'd risk losing his lands—which would apparently be worse than losing his daughter, but I'm not here to judge—and so he has turned to other means to retrieve Lady Mae."

Briar's forehead wrinkled in a frown. "He hired you to steal her back?"

"Close. He is discreetly offering a reward for her safe return, with a bonus if it can be done without attracting the ire of the king. I intend to collect both the reward and the bonus."

"What makes you think you can do it?"

Archer coughed, trying not to be offended. He had worked up something of a reputation over the past few years, but she didn't seem remotely impressed by him.

"Lady Mae is imprisoned in a tower in Larke Castle up by Shortfall Lake." He waved vaguely toward the north. "I happen to employ someone who used to work in that castle. We have a better chance of retrieving her than most."

"And where do I come in?" Briar asked. "You want me to knock down this tower?"

"That wouldn't do our captive lady much good, would it? We have to bring her back alive to collect the reward."

"And the bonus."

"Exactly." Archer tapped his fingers on his knee. "The tower presents ... challenges. The spells of a powerful mage guard its walls, and I believe only someone with exceptional strength can break through its protections."

Briar pursed her lips. "So, you want me to travel to the other side of Larke County and help you destroy these spells to rescue a damsel from a tower without hurting the tower too badly? Unravelling someone else's magic is not a simple task."

"You would be well paid." Archer straightened, pausing for effect. "I can offer you *one hundred crowns*."

She didn't even blink at the extravagant amount, one that should have made a girl in her circumstances stand up and sing. "I'll have to decline," she said briskly. "I'm sure you can find a more suitable curse painter for the job."

"I doubt that. I need someone with both finesse and power. I'd heard a curse painter in these parts had the former, and I've seen the latter with my own eyes."

Briar tipped back her cup to drain her tea, partially hiding her face. Her cheeks had gone a little pink, as if she were embarrassed by her power. He couldn't imagine why.

"Thank you, but no."

"All right then." Archer shifted in his seat and—though it pained him a little—asked, "How much do you want?"

She set the empty teacup in her lap and rested a hand on her lumpy pillow.

"It's not about the money. I only work for honest men these days, Mister Archer."

"I am an honest man!" Archer lied. "Didn't I tell you up front that I'm a thief? I serve the blade, the coin, and—"

"The open road. I understand, but this job isn't for me."

"Aren't you interested in the adventure? You must be bored in this quiet little cottage."

Briar's eyes flashed. "I like my home very much."

Her sharp tone surprised him, and Archer wondered if he'd missed something about the cottage. What was so great about living in squalor? He examined the place anew, seeking some reason for her to defend it so adamantly, such as a newborn baby or a solid gold floor.

When he looked back, Briar's hands were in her lap, hidden beneath the folds of her skirt. She seemed to be massaging her wrist. Maybe her injury was worse than she wanted to let on. That needn't stop them. The more time he spent in her company, the more certain he became that Briar was the one for the job.

He tried a different tactic. "Don't you want a chance to be part of something great? If we succeed, we will have done what no other merry band of brigands has accomplished. Even if the gold won't sway you, you'd be rescuing a fair maiden. Isn't that as noble as knocking down the house of an evil old swindler?"

She hesitated for a second, and in that moment, he was sure he had her. Everyone liked rescuing maidens, even other maidens.

Then she said, "No. Thank you, Mister Archer, but I'm not interested."

"I don't give up so easily."

He leaned toward her, and Briar stiffened.

"I think it's best if you go." Her voice rang with a gravity that hadn't been there before.

"But if you'll allow me to share my plan—"

"I want you to leave my house."

Something dark flickered in her face, and cold tap-danced down Archer's spine. Something told him the petite young woman wasn't quite what she seemed. She spoke with the solemnity of a Crown Mage. He should go, but he was so close to having everything he needed for his mission. He couldn't give up.

"I could tell the authorities what I saw, you know," he said softly. "Sheriff Flynn and Willem Winton are old pals."

Briar's eyes narrowed. Her hands twitched in her lap, still hidden by her skirt. "Are you threatening me?"

"I am simply making you an offer you can't re—"

The teacup in Archer's hand exploded, the force knocking him back in his chair. His teeth rattled at the impact, and purple lights sparked before his eyes. Then the chair itself rose a foot off the ground and soared across the room, knocking over the easel and canvas on its way to the door.

Archer thought he'd be crushed, but the door flew open at the last instant. The chair lurched across the threshold, came to a violent stop outside, and deposited him in a heap on the ground.

Sheriff the dog bounded to his side and alternated between licking his ear and howling at the cottage, now closed up tight. Archer picked himself up, brushing dust off his coat. His hand stung from the exploding teacup, but all his fingers were intact.

The curse painter appeared at the window, holding a rung from a ladderback chair in her good hand. "You claimed to be an honest man," she called. "If you truly are, you will leave me be and not speak of me to anyone. But know that I can curse the life out of you in a few quick strokes, especially now that you've sat in my chair for so long. Death curses take to wood especially well. I hope you won't give me a reason to use one. Good day, Mister Archer."

Then she was gone.

Archer stared at the green curtains long after they stopped swaying. How in all of Lure had she made the teacup explode from the other side of the room? He'd never seen anything like it. Any lingering doubts that Briar was the one for the job vanished. He would just have to find another way to convince her.

"Quit your howling, Sheriff," he called to the dog. "I'm all right." He patted his friend's wrinkly head and started back to town.

CHAPTER 3

Briar scrubbed at the carmine paint she'd spilled on her quilt when she'd cursed the teacup, hands shaking from the adrenaline rush of working so quickly. She kept paint supplies tucked beneath her pillow for emergencies, but she hadn't been sure that would work. Carmine lake, a bright red made from crushed insects, was an excellent explosive. Transferring the curse to the second cup had been the difficult part.

According to the Law of Resonance, the third law of curse painting, a curse applied to an object of emotional significance could affect a person from a distance. The stronger the emotional connection or the lengthier the contact, the stronger the curse. But a single curse could also affect multiple inanimate objects that regularly came in contact with each other. Some said the same principle was at work.

Briar remembered an early lesson in a stuffy art studio a few blocks from the sea.

"The phenomenon is called Inanimate Resonance by certain third-law theorists," her father had said after using a single curse to set fire to two books that had spent years tucked together on a dusty shelf. "Others believe the effect is a function of the Law of Wholes. The objects become as one, and that's why a single curse can touch them. At least two schisms have occurred in the Hall of Cloaks over this distinction."

"Which theory do you believe?" Briar had asked, more interested in her father's brushwork than his words. His curses *always* worked the first time, something she had struggled with back then.

"The only thing that matters is that it works." The light of the burning books flickered in his large eyes as he turned toward her. "You are learning practical curse painting, Elayna Rose. You must use every tool at your disposal regardless of what some academic from the Hall calls it. Petty schisms have no bearing on *us*."

Briar had opened the studio window to release the smoke from the books while her father extolled his singular approach to curse theory. She could still hear his heated voice, though many years and many miles separated her from the lesson. She had known, even then, that her father and mother's attitudes toward curse painting were different from other mages. But their paintings were prettier and more effective than the work of other mages too. She hadn't yet realized how dangerous it had been for them to ignore the Hall's oversight.

The lesson about resonance had stuck, though. When Archer had threatened her, she'd scrawled an explosive curse onto the teacup in her lap because it was usually stacked on top of the one she'd given to him. With a flick of her brush, the carmine explosion had transferred from one piece of clay to the other. The distraction had given her enough time to paint a more elaborate jinx on the slim wooden chair rung she kept under her pillow, using a mixture of verdigris and malachite. The two shades of green had worked together to hurl the chair across the room—an example of the Law of Wholes at work.

A few drops of paint had seeped into the rags around her injured wrist. Briar dabbed at the red-and-green smudges, trying not to jostle her arm too much. She had always thought the county sheriff or someone from her old life would force her to use her hidden defenses. She hadn't expected a threat in the form of a fast-talking thief. Had Archer stumbled upon Winton's house at the right moment, or was he searching for her specifically? Even if he wasn't connected to her old life, he'd found her too easily.

Briar breathed in the smells of dry thatch and oil paint, the smells of home, to calm herself. The job offer had tempted her more than she liked. She needed the gold, but that wasn't what drew her in, nor was the prospect of rescuing the fair damsel. Lady Mae probably enjoyed just as much comfort in Lord Larke's castle as she did in her father's manor—more than the blacksmith's daughters experienced, certainly.

No, it was the challenge that tugged at Briar, calling like a siren. The thief wanted her to perform serious magic. It was no petty revenge. A sophisticated enough curse to cut through a licensed mage's defenses would take preparation, study, and a great deal of power. It would require picking apart another's magic at the seams and blowing the pieces to bits. The idea of all that destruction lured her, singing to her soul in a way she hadn't experienced since settling in the cottage.

Challenges had enticed Briar's parents too. They'd pursued their destructive magic ardently, disregarding the laws and regulations governing most art mages. They had never accepted limitations, something that had made them exceptional artists. But human decency had fallen by the wayside too often in favor of pursuing their next artistic challenge, the next beautiful curse.

Briar had worked hard to distance herself from that attitude and the actions that accompanied it, actions that still hounded her memories and troubled her sleep. She'd tried to live by a new code since escaping to the outer counties, vowing not to inflict physical harm beyond discomfort—itches and rashes were fine—never to make a poor person poorer, and to seek justice when the king's law failed. But she wasn't immune to the siren call of real curse magic.

Briar scowled at the painting of the wheat field on the easel. This Archer character had a lot of nerve to march into her home and shatter her efforts at a good, calm life with a powerful temptation. It was little wonder she'd cursed him with such violence when threatened.

She returned to the window to make sure Archer and his dog were really gone. Darkness cloaked the street beyond her garden gate, and the woods hummed with evening sounds— rustling branches, crickets, the hoot of a lone owl. Despite his bluster, she didn't think Archer would actually go to the sheriff. He seemed intelligent—and far too confident for his own good. She wondered exactly how he planned to use an illegal curse painter to break into Larke Castle. *It would be a fascinating challenge ...*

"No. Stop," she told herself sternly. "It doesn't matter." She swept up the clay shards from the teacup and began preparing a simple meal of brown bread, hard cheese, and vegetables from her garden. She sliced carrots with her belt knife, the rhythmic chopping sound filling the cottage. "You are not going to get involved." If she was ever going to make her new life worth what it had cost her to start over, she couldn't get anywhere near that kind of scheme.

A knock came at the door again. *He doesn't give up, does he?*

She left her knife on the table and went to peek through the curtains. Instead of Archer, the blacksmith who had hired her to curse Master Winton was standing on her doorstep, twisting a felt hat in his muscular hands.

Briar yanked open the door, planning to pull the large man inside so they wouldn't be seen together, but as the light from her doorway flooded the stoop, she realized he wasn't alone.

Sheriff Flynn stood on one side of the blacksmith, and

Master Winton himself stood on the other. A fourth person lingered in the darkness behind them.

"Evening, ma'am." Sheriff Flynn leaned his hairy forearm on the doorway. His belly bulged over his sword belt and strained at the buttons on his shirt, and his face was just handsome enough to be dangerous. "I understand you've been up to mischief."

Briar forced an innocent smile. "I beg your pardon?"

"Oh, it's pardon she wants now, is it?" Winton exclaimed. "The little witch. Arrest her, Flynn!" Sweat patches spread under the arms of his purple silk coat, and his flaxen hair stood on end above his red forehead, as if he'd worked himself into a fury on the way from the village.

"What's this all about?" Briar asked, playing dumb on the off chance they were fishing for information.

"There's damage been done," said the sheriff. "Up at Master Winton's house."

"What kind of damage?"

Winton gave a wild laugh. "What damage? How dare you!"

"Patience, friend," Sheriff Flynn said. "We have to do right by the king's law. Little lady, you didn't have anything to do with Master Winton's house collapsing, now did you?"

Briar ground her teeth at his condescending tone. *Little lady?* The sheriff leaned on her doorframe like he owned the place, making it impossible for her to reach for her hidden paint supplies above the lintel. Not that she should be cursing anyone right at that moment.

"His house collapsed?" She widened her eyes, hoping she looked concerned and a bit simple rather than deranged. "I don't see how *I* could have anything to do with that, Sheriff."

"I find it hard to believe myself," the sheriff said. "But this ain't the first complaint I've had about your ... line of work." He straightened, tugging up his sword belt. "I can look the other way when it's a man's trousers ripping in the street or a woman's prized flower garden dying, but this is different."

Briar struggled to maintain her innocent expression, surprised the sheriff knew about those little curses. She thought she'd been so subtle.

"Maybe we can work something out," she began. "I don't know anything about Master Winton's house, but for those little—"

"Don't let her get to you with her doe eyes, Flynn," Winton hissed. "I know your kind, witch. We don't need the likes of you in this village, with your larceny and your vandalism."

Briar blinked. She had never engaged in larceny in her life. She wondered how long Archer's merry band had been thieving in that particular county. *Archer.* Had he truly summoned the sheriff, as he'd threatened?

She eased forward so they couldn't cross her threshold, resisting the urge to glance at her hidden paints. "Doesn't the king's law require proof that a crime has been committed?"

"Aye," Sheriff Flynn said. "Is that paint on your wrist there?"

Briar's fingers twitched. "If you're accusing me just because I dabble in the occasional—"

"It's no use, lass," the blacksmith interrupted, looking down at the hat in his calloused hands. "I told Master Winton you were talking about him in the market, about how he charges too much for linseed oil and the like."

She stared at him, stunned. "You what?"

The blacksmith refused to meet her eyes. "I reckon you took it too far."

"Too *far*?" Briar asked indignantly. He was right about that part, as she truly hadn't meant to knock down Winton's house, but she couldn't believe he would betray her. She'd given him a discount and everything.

She wanted to curse the blacksmith halfway to High Lure, no matter how many starving children he had. She wanted to seize those work-roughened hands and cover them with so much carmine he—*enough*. She stamped hard on the destructive urges pulsing through her. It wasn't the time.

She studied the men on her doorstep, assessing her chances. She still hadn't gotten a good look at the fellow lurking behind them. One of Lord Barden's retainers, perhaps?

"What happens now?" she asked, stalling for time. "You'll take me before Lord Barden?"

"Ordinarily, yes," the sheriff said slowly. "But in this case, you hurt a friend of mine. I don't see as how we need to involve his lordship at all."

"That's more like it," Winton said. "She'll just curse her way out of Barden's dungeon. This calls for more permanent measures."

Cold dread crept through Briar's body. "I can leave town," she said. "You'll never hear from me again. I swear it."

"Afraid it's too late for that." Sheriff Flynn rested a hand on his sword and stepped over the threshold.

"But—"

"I don't reckon you have a thousand crowns to pay for Master Winton's new house?"

"A thou—"

"I wouldn't touch her money if it were a million!" Winton said. "I want vengeance not recompense."

Briar backed away from them. Did she have time to grab her hidden paints? Her knife on the table? The men were blocking the only exit from the cottage. *If I can reach the paint chest, I might be able to—*

Then the sheriff stepped aside, revealing the man who'd been behind him. He was middle-aged, with a pinched, narrow face and sleek brown hair. A long, well-worn cloak embroidered with the gold sigil of the Hall of Cloaks hung down his back, and his arms bore the swirling tattoos of a fully licensed voice mage. Briar drew in a sharp breath, her pulse spiking.

No. Not like this.

The sheriff cleared his throat with a wet gurgle. "Mage Radner, you are hereby authorized to execute this woman."

The cloaked mage nodded formally. "It would be a pleasure."

Briar was already moving when the voice mage opened his mouth and spoke the magic words.

She dove for her paints as the first spell shot across the cottage and struck the table, bursting into a shower of sparks. She landed on her knees by her box of supplies, gasping as she jarred her injured wrist.

I'm not going down like this.

The voice mage advanced toward her. Briar fumbled at the clasp on the paint chest. It was stuck. The hair on the back of her neck stood up, and she threw herself out of the way as Mage Radner shouted another incendiary spell. It hit the paint box, which exploded in a riot of color. Vermilion, azurite, yellow ochre, indigo. The paints splattered across the wood floor, mixed with splinters and broken glass. Briar grasped for anything she could use as the mage stalked closer.

"You haven't a whisper of a chance against me," he said hoarsely.

"Then where's the fun in it for you?" Briar asked.

"This isn't about fun," the mage said. "You've an unhealthy attitude toward mayhem."

"So I've heard."

He unleashed a string of phrases unintelligible to any but a voice mage. Briar rolled away from the blast, her palms slipping in the paints. Verdigris, bone black, umber.

Her jars of spare linseed oil ignited, and smoke began to fill the cottage. The flames spread fast, drinking up the oil, licking at the quilt on her bed, rising toward the thatched roof. She gasped, choking on smoke, and scrambled back from the blaze.

Mage Radner remained calm. He didn't laugh as she

crawled away from him. Some mages gloried in their power. They would have loved dominating an injured curse painter as she made her last desperate effort to survive, but this mage was composed, calculating. He terrified her—but she wouldn't let him beat her.

Sheriff Flynn had gone back outside, giving the mage space to work. Winton was laughing in the darkness behind him. Briar crouched by her table, much too far from the door, and faced Mage Radner across the paint-spattered floor. His cloak billowed around him like a storm cloud. She tried to predict which way he'd shout his next spell. Left, right, straight at her heart?

He feinted right, barking a quick syllable, then he shouted directly at her. She rolled forward, the curse singeing her hair as it passed. She scrambled toward him, picking up more paint on her hands, her knees, her skirt. Glass from the broken jars stuck in her palms, and her injured wrist screamed from the effort.

She ducked another curse, still barreling forward, and her fingers closed on the hem of the mage's dark cloak. She began to scrawl a rough image on the fabric with the paint on her hands. Blood mixed with the shades of green and ochre. She had to get the strokes right.

One. Two.

She lurched to the side as the mage kicked at her, forgetting his voice for a moment. She seized the cloak again.

Three. Four.

Radner tried to pull his cloak out of her grasp, dragging her across the floor, coughing at the thickening smoke. She thrust her fingers into a slick of verdigris paint and reached for the cloak.

Five. Six.

It was the ugliest curse she had ever made, and she'd painted some fiends, but it was enough.

Seven.

"What in the—"

The mage's cloak flew upward, hauling him off his feet. He soared toward the thatched roof and banged his head on the exposed rafters. The painted edge of the cloak burrowed into the thatch. Left unchecked, that cloak would continue shooting straight up until it reached the stars. The mage, half-strangled by the smoke, spoke a few gruff words to halt its ascent. The distraction gave Briar just enough time to slip past him. She hurtled out the cottage door, darting past the sheriff, the black-smith, and the spitting-mad Winton—and kept running.

Paint, splinters, and ash covered Briar from head to foot. Behind her, the cozy little cottage was burning. The thatch caught fire in earnest, fueled by the paints as well as the lingering echoes of the mage's power. The dry crackle of burning straw filled the night. Briar felt as if her heart were being seared in a frying pan as the roaring inferno consumed her home.

She chanced a look back. Mage Radner was outlined in the doorway, stalking slowly out of the blaze, his cursed cloak still twitching. She had no time to worry about the dark, menacing figure. Sheriff Flynn and his companions were untying their horses from the woodpile. She had a head start, but she was on foot, and they were mounting up, preparing to run her down.

Briar flew down the path, gasping, her lungs clouded with smoke. She didn't know if she should run into the woods or try to cross the Brittlewyn. In the woods, she could end up trapped against the curve of the river, whereas she could hide in the village across the bridge. But could she trust anyone to shelter her? She had deliberately kept people at arm's length. And if the blacksmith would betray her, could she trust any of the others who had treated her with apparent kindness?

Hooves beat a thunderous warning on the road behind her. Shouts chased her through the dark. She ran, heart thrashing like a panicked hummingbird. *Woods or village?* She had nothing, no money, no food. She wouldn't survive the forest for long. The paint covering her clothes was soaking in, drying fast. She wasn't sure she could paint so much as a headache curse with what she had left.

Her pursuers were getting closer. She was powerless against them now. They would trample her into the dirt and leave her to die. All over a stupid mistake.

The bridge loomed over the river ahead. They would catch her before she reached it. A howl sounded in the night, as if the dogs of the lower realms had come for her. The horses' hooves tolled a death knell behind her. She wasn't even close to making up for what she had done, the damage she had caused. All she had wanted was another chance, a fresh start, a little cottage in the woods that smelled of thatch and oil paint.

Suddenly, a dark shape reared up directly in her path. She gave a strangled cry, looking square into the rolling eyes of a massive horse. They had caught her. She tried to evade the horse's churning hooves as it snorted and pranced before her.

Then a hand reached out of the darkness, seized her arm roughly, and hauled her off her feet. She clawed at the person trying to lift her onto the horse, scratched, twisted. Her arm was being wrenched out of its socket.

"This'll be easier on both of us if you help, Miss Painter."

Briar gasped in recognition and stopped fighting. She clutched reflexively at a familiar indigo sleeve and managed to swing her leg up over the horse's back.

"Looks like your life here is more exciting than I gave you credit for," Archer called over his shoulder.

"They have a voice mage," Briar rasped.

"Say no more." Archer kicked his heels, and she flung her arms around his waist as his horse took off, thundering toward the bridge and over the Brittlewyn.

"Wait!" Briar shouted.

He pulled up sharply, and Briar swung down to scrawl a tiny mark on the bridge with the last dregs of paint skimmed from her clothes and hands.

"That won't keep them for long."

"They can't catch me," Archer said. "Now hold on tight!"

CHAPTER 4

S moke and fury filled the night as they galloped down the path to the village. Archer's heart pounded in time with the hoofbeats as he leaned forward over the neck of his horse.

Well, it wasn't technically *his* horse. He had borrowed it for the occasion. The leggy, spirited animal was already outpacing the sheriff and his goons. Archer hadn't had that much fun in ages.

"What did you do to the bridge?" he called over his shoulder.

"It's an illusion," Briar said in his ear. "The bridge will look like it's washed out. I didn't have time to destroy it."

"Won't the mage see through that?"

"He'll have to break the curse first."

"How long will that take?"

"Don't slow down."

Archer winced. He'd had more than his fair share of run-ins with licensed voice mages. They were a cantankerous bunch. "Some night, eh?"

The curse painter didn't answer. She clung to Archer's coat, her hands smudged with dark paint. She seemed calm, all things considered. Cursing the bridge had taken quick thinking. It was good to know she performed well under pressure.

She had looked afraid when she'd fled the burning cottage, though, eyes wide and rolling. Archer had intended to demand she commit to the mission before he saved her, but he couldn't go through with it when he saw her terror. He'd hauled her onto his horse—well, the one he had stolen—and for a minute there, he'd felt like a hero from a story. It had been a long time since he'd felt like that.

But he had a mission, and he was still a thief—and a leader of thieves. Despite her fear, Briar had kept her head. That told him all he needed to know.

Archer twitched the reins as they passed the first houses in Sparrow Village, and the stolen horse responded eagerly to his guidance. It wasn't long after dark, and people milled in the streets with flowers in their hair, laughing and chatting about the summer fair. Archer galloped the horse up and down and across several of the busier lanes, forcing the villagers to dive out of his way with indignant squawks. No one would be able to tell exactly which direction he had gone when the sheriff questioned them later. He considered retreating to the village's only inn, where he'd taken a room, but they were already pressed for time, and he couldn't risk Briar leaving before morning. He would introduce her to the team and confirm the deal that very night.

After sufficiently muddling their trail, Archer directed the horse toward an overgrown path leading into the woods. Briar didn't ask where they were going. She must have sensed she was safe with Archer for now. They didn't speak as they left the lights and noise of the village behind.

The foliage thickened around them, hiding them from anyone who might try to follow, choking out the starlight. Then it was just Archer and the darkness and the warm figure of the girl pressed against his back. Her hair tickled his neck, and she smelled of linseed oil and ash. Archer couldn't quite relax with her arms around his waist. She had accepted his help when she had no other choice, but that didn't mean she wouldn't try to blow his hands off again. He'd seen what she could do.

As they got farther from the village, the only sounds were the rustle of branches, the thud of their mount's hooves, and the occasional hoot of an owl. The night deepened, the woods wrapping Archer in a familiar embrace. He had spent happy days in Mere Woods, once upon a time.

He slowed the horse to a walk as they neared the hideout so as not to alarm the rest of the team. They had been camped outside Sparrow Village for nearly two weeks while they'd prepared for the mission. No one had ever disturbed that particular hiding place, but they were always ready to bolt at a moment's notice.

Suddenly, Briar spoke. "What happened to your dog?"

"He'll find us," Archer said. "He probably appreciates that you hid the bridge instead of destroying it. He hates swimming."

"Destroying it would have been terrible for the village."

"The look on Sheriff Flynn's face would be spectacular, though."

"Yes ... I guess it would." She loosened her grip on his coat since they were no longer galloping for their lives and put as much space between them as the saddle allowed. "You didn't send those men after me, did you?"

Archer hesitated. Would she believe him after the threats he'd made? "Didn't have time," he said airily. "They didn't wait long to start burning things, and here I thought Flynn was all bark and no bite."

"That cottage was all I had." Her soft voice was almost lost in the nighttime rustle of the forest.

"You can buy a new one." Archer glanced back at her. "I

happen to know a fellow looking to pay a curse painter for a job."

She didn't answer, and the darkness hid her expression. Did she really think he sent those men after her? The loss of the tumbledown cottage appeared to bother her more than he would have expected. He had learned through a few discreet inquiries at her neighbors'—where he had stolen the horse— that she was renting the place and she had only lived there since the end of winter. No one could say where she had come from or if Briar was even her real name.

Archer knew a thing or two about fake names and secret pasts. He was more interested in her future, though. "Look, why don't you meet the team at least? Hear what we have in mind."

"The team?"

"They're a sorry bunch of lowlifes, but they get the job done."

"Who you calling lowlifes?"

Someone spoke in the darkness, and Archer grinned. They were home.

"Only the finest bunch of larcenists and arsonists I ever met," Archer called.

"It's about time you got back." A burly middle-aged man stepped out of the woods, uncovering a lantern. The light revealed his big red beard and curly hair. A coarse brown vest strained over his broad chest. "My wife was about to march into town to start busting heads."

"I have returned unscathed, and I brought a friend."

The curse painter shifted against Archer's back, peeking out at the newcomer.

"Briar, the curse painter, meet Lew of Twickenridge. He's the brawn of this operation."

"A bruiser with a poet's soul." Lew bowed, putting a large freckled hand over his heart.

"I told you *I'm* supposed to be the brawn." Another figure

appeared in the circle of lantern light. Younger even than Archer, the lad was well on the way to being as burly as Lew, but his big shoulders and round face still carried plenty of baby fat. His patchwork coat looked decidedly rumpled.

"This is Nat. Errand boy, all-purpose foot soldier, and yes, future brawn."

"Are you supposed to be the brain?" Briar asked Archer dryly.

"That would be Lew's wife, Jemma," Archer said. "She planned our little quest. I'm the charm."

Nat snickered and whispered something to Lew behind his pudgy hand. The older man chuckled, making the lantern shake.

"About this quest," Briar said. "I haven't agreed to anything yet."

"You have anywhere else to be?" Archer asked. "Some other hovel to attend to?"

Briar stiffened. Then she swung down from the horse, straightened her skirt, and turned deliberately into the woods.

"I meant no offense," Archer called, dismounting too. He'd thought they'd started to build a rapport on their ride through the woods, but apparently the loss of everything she had in the world still smarted.

"I thought you were supposed to be the charm," Nat muttered then ducked the loose fist Archer swung at him.

Briar paused where the pool of lantern light met the trees. "I'm already on the wrong side of the law. I can't afford to fall in with a bunch of criminals. Unless you intend to keep me here against my will?"

Lew bristled at the implication, and Archer raised a soothing hand toward the girl, as if she were a skittish woodland creature. He knew what she was capable of when threatened.

"Of course not, but if you want to leave, you might as well do it with a full belly and sunny skies."

"It's not easy getting back to town in the dark," Nat said. "I twisted my ankle last time I tried it."

Lew snorted. "That's because you're a lubber."

"Yes, but he's a brawny lubber," Archer said. He took a slow step toward the curse painter. "Won't you hear us out at least?"

Briar hesitated, the lantern light flickering in her eyes. Archer feared she would march into the darkness and disappear forever, but she looked at the dry paint on her hands and clothes, useless now, and her shoulders slumped.

"I don't think I'd be welcomed back to this village anyway."

"It's settled, then," Archer said. "You'll eat a hot meal and listen to our plan, and if you don't take the job, you'll be free to go. I'll even give you my horse come morning."

Briar nodded, and Archer felt a surprisingly powerful surge of relief.

He gestured to the path ahead with a flourish. "Shall we?"

The four made their way deeper into the woods, relying on Lew's lantern to avoid the roots choking the path. Branches crackled under their feet, and a sudden rustle suggested they'd startled a deer from its hiding place. The stolen horse snorted contemptuously. Soon they reached a dense thicket, where blackberry bushes grew taller than a man. Two sycamore trees leaned toward each other, marking the spot and creating a spooky, tangled canopy.

Nat hurried forward to pull aside the bundle of branches serving as a door and revealed a tunnel opening directly into the mass of thorny bushes.

"Welcome home," the boy said to the curse painter, attempting a flourish that looked suspiciously like Archer's. An eager smile split his round face, ruining the effect.

Briar glanced at Archer, her expression unreadable, before following Nat into the tunnel.

"Any trouble today?" Archer asked Lew quietly as they walked beneath the sycamore trees, drawing the stolen horse behind them.

The older man shook his head. "A few hunters passed nearby yesterday, but Nat lured them away before they got too near the hideout. The lad can do quite the pheasant impression."

"Excellent."

This was one of their favorite lairs whenever they were in Barden County, and no one but squirrels had ever found it. Archer needed their lucky streak to last just a little while longer.

The smell of burnt stew reached them a second before they exited the tunnel. A blazing campfire, a patch of bare earth, and a dozen horses awaited them at the center of what would look like an impenetrable mass of thorns and brambles to passersby. They'd made a fair bit of noise on their way through the thicket, especially with the horse in tow, and the last two members of Archer's team were expecting them.

"It's about time." Lew's wife, Jemma, faced them across the campfire with her hands on her hips. A red shawl was folded across her chest, and her golden hair threaded with gray was coming loose from her braid in wisps. "I'd need a whole new plan if you got yourself captured again."

"Aw, you'd have rescued me, Jem," Archer said. "Lew says so."

"I have my hands full with one rescue mission as it is." Jemma shot a glance at her husband, who shrugged his burly shoulders. "Stealing gold is a lot easier than stealing people."

"The gold from the reward is ten times our best haul," Archer said. "It'll be worth the extra trouble."

"Plus the bonus," called Nat. The boy sprawled in front of the fire and kicked off his dirty boots.

"You got that right," Archer said.

43

Lew grimaced as Nat began picking at his patched woolen socks. "Do you have to do that by the food?"

Nat shrugged and reached for his boots again.

Lew sighed and took the reins of Archer's new horse. He nodded to Briar and went to tie up the stallion near the other horses.

Archer turned back to Jemma, who was still glowering at him across the fire. "I've brought you a new secret weapon." He tried to usher the curse painter forward with a hand on her shoulder, but she shook him off. He raised his hands apologetically. "Briar, Jemma. Jemma, Briar."

Briar studied the older woman closely. "You're the one in charge?"

Jemma chuckled, her skin creasing around her mouth. "Oh, I like her already."

"Didn't you say—"

"She's the brains, yes, but I'm the boss," Archer said. "Jemma used to work in the castle where our fair maiden is being kept. She's the reason we are going to succeed where other merry bands of outlaws have failed."

"How many?" Briar asked.

"Beg pardon?"

"How many others have attempted this mission and failed?"

"Let's just say, it won't be as easy as it sounds." Archer headed for the cookpot, seeking to fend off further challenges. "Hope you saved some stew for us."

"Esteban almost finished it off," Jemma said. "You shouldn't have taken so long."

"Oh, right, that's Esteban." Archer nodded at the shriveled figure dressed in black sitting at the very edge of the ring of light, giving no further explanation.

Esteban wouldn't respond well to being labeled, even if Archer called him charming and brawny and as handsome as the king himself. In truth, Esteban was none of those things.

Gaunt, gray haired, and surly, he had been with them almost since the beginning, but he hadn't warmed up to anyone. Only Jemma—who was nicer than they all deserved—made much of an effort with him.

The six of them gathered around the campfire, sitting on fallen logs or sprawling in the dirt. Briar perched on a stump, watching the others closely, and Archer was reminded again of a petite owl. But owls had talons, and he couldn't forget she had the power to hurl him across a room when she felt like it.

After scarfing down a few bites of Lew's special squirrel stew, Archer explained the mission to rescue Lady Mae.

"The castle is a ten-day ride from here, deep within the boundaries of Lord Larke's territory. It has a regular garrison of fifty retainers, and their commander is no fool. He won't leave the lady unguarded, even during the most dramatic diversion. This will be a stealth mission. Jemma knows her way around the castle, so we should be able to sneak into the tower, break open the lady's door, incapacitate her guards, and get her out again without anyone realizing we're there. Lord Larke should be away on his annual tax-collecting jaunt, so that'll make our job a little easier."

Briar listened closely, her chin in her hand. "What are the magical protections on the place?"

"Esteban?"

The old man gave a dry cough. "A Nightshade Illusion at the border wall, a few hexed doorways in the tower, and likely a Marin's Lock on her door."

Briar raised an eyebrow. "Why do you need me? You already have a mage."

Lew and Jemma exchanged glances, but Esteban didn't seem surprised Briar had figured out what he was. He watched her sullenly. Truth be told, sullen was his resting state.

"Esteban's power comes with limitations," Archer said. "He's licensed, you see."

"Then why do you need *him*?"

Lew chortled, and Esteban muttered something about disrespectful children.

"Everyone has a part to play in this." Archer thumped Nat on the not-quite-brawny shoulder. "Even him."

Briar was still studying the mage. She was tense, a bird poised for flight. "You have the tattoos?"

Esteban pulled up his sleeve to reveal the faded black ink looping his wiry arms. The spelled marks meant every bit of magic he performed was catalogued in the mysterious Hall of Records in faraway High Lure, the king's city.

"Where did you train?" Briar asked.

"I have studied at *several* of the best art mage schools in Lure," Esteban said. "I won't have my credentials questioned by an illegal—"

"I don't doubt your credentials," Briar said. "When were you last at court?"

Esteban's mouth tightened irritably. "I have been my own man since before you were born, little girl. You ought to show your elders more respect."

"Forgive me," Briar said. "I meant no offense." She adjusted her position on the tree stump, already seeming less nervous.

Interesting. Archer would have to see if Jemma had any theories about why Briar cared whether someone had recently been at court. Jemma was better at reading people than he was. Esteban was easier to figure out than Briar. The older mage begrudged the fact that they'd hired outside magical help for the job. The resentment was practically written on his face among the wrinkles. Archer hoped that wouldn't become a problem.

"Back to business," Archer said. "Can you paint curses that will break those three spells in addition to ones that will open normal doors and knock out guards?"

"With some planning, yes." Briar looked around the campfire at the band of thieves, then her gaze flitted to the tunnel through the thicket, as if she were still thinking about running away. "But if I agree to help you, I'll get a price on my head for my troubles."

"Only if you're seen and somehow recognized. I don't expect that to be an issue, do you?"

Briar touched a lock of her frizzy hair. "Of course not."

Had that been hesitation, a note of falseness? Archer couldn't be certain. Lord Larke's retainers were unlikely to recognize her, especially if Jemma and Archer himself didn't know her. They were acquainted with most of the lawbreakers in Larke and Barden counties, even though they'd spent most of the past year farther afield. She couldn't be that notorious. So who was she worried about?

"We shouldn't discuss any more details until she gives us a straight answer," Esteban muttered. "Are you in or not?"

Briar cast a swift look at the old mage then focused on Archer. She had turned him down flat before, but this time she might actually need the coin. It wouldn't be cheap to restart her business after what had happened back at the cottage. Still, he held his breath. They needed her too.

"I'll do it," Briar said, "but I have a few conditions. First, after this job, I will take my money and go. I am not joining your merry band, and I'm no thief."

Archer released a sigh. "Fair enough." Rescue missions were outside the job descriptions of most thieves anyway, but then, Archer and the others were not most thieves.

"I'll need a few things for my curses," Briar went on. "New paints and brushes, for starters. I lost all of mine when ..." She trailed off, looking into the fire, twin flames dancing in her eyes. She blinked them away. "Do you have money, or will we need to steal them?"

"I've never lifted paints before," Nat said, cracking his stubby fingers. "Sounds like a challenge."

47

"Those we can buy," Archer said. "Discretion is essential from here on out. We have enough coin to purchase whatever you require to get the job done."

"I need a rare shade of purple," Briar said. "It's made from crushed marine snails, and only one supplier has the right kind in this county. He keeps a shop in the Mud Market."

Lew combed his red beard thoughtfully. "That's a little out of our way."

"The curse won't work without it," Briar said. "It's the only paint that will unravel another's magic."

"We can work in a detour," Archer said. "Anything else?"

"I don't want to kill anyone."

Jemma and Lew exchanged quick glances, and Esteban muttered something under his breath. They'd run enough jobs to know casualties weren't always something they could control. They all looked at Archer.

"We're thieves, not murderers," he said. "I can't make any promises, but I'll do everything in my power to see that you don't have to kill anyone, providing it doesn't endanger the mission." He met her gaze across the fire, his voice going cold. "But all bets are off if you allow any of my team to be hurt out of some misguided attempt to be principled."

"Understood," Briar said. "I will not hesitate, if it comes to that."

"See that you don't."

They stared at each other for a beat longer, and Archer remembered the teacup exploding in his hands. The girl was powerful, and he would have to be careful of her in the days to come.

They couldn't afford to fail. Lady Mae's safety was too important. No matter what they said about the reward—and the bonus—the real stakes were much higher. Only Archer among them knew how vital it was that they succeed.

The deal made, they finished their stew and set about cleaning up the campsite and settling the animals for the night. The weather had cooled considerably since the sun had gone down, hinting that the end of summer was drawing near. They retrieved extra blankets from their cache of supplies—a half-buried trunk they replenished whenever they were in the area—and rearranged their bedrolls so everyone could sleep with their feet to the fire.

Briar accepted a bundle of blankets from Nat with a polite nod and lay down at the farthest edge of the clearing, her back to the brambles and her face to the team. Her eyes remained open, her wariness visible from ten feet away.

I guess I'd be nervous around a fearsome band like ours too. Archer deliberately ignored Lew, who was scratching a poem on the notebook he kept in his vest pocket. Esteban had scuttled over to the far side of the clearing to pick blackberries for dessert.

When Nat and Esteban got into a rousing argument over who had the first watch, Archer took the opportunity to pull Jemma aside.

"What do you think of the curse painter?"

"She's hiding something."

Archer laughed. "Aren't we all?"

"Some more successfully than others." Jemma folded her red shawl tighter around her body and peered up at him. She was a head shorter than Archer, but she could still make him feel like a scruffy kid with more energy than sense. "Be careful with her. I'm not sure you know what you're getting yourself into."

"What do you mean?"

"Just don't let a pair of pretty eyes distract you," Jemma said. "That girl is dangerous."

"I know she is." Archer chose to ignore the part about Briar's eyes. He supposed they *were* rather pretty. "She hurled me out of her house in a chair and nearly embedded a teacup in my face."

Jemma's mouth tightened. "I'm more worried about the killing."

"The fact that she doesn't want to? I reckon that's good. Larke's men don't deserve to pay the price for their lord's actions."

"It's not that she doesn't want to kill," Jemma said. "It's that she has done it before and knows how it feels."

Archer blinked. "How could you possibly know that?"

"It's in those pretty eyes of hers," Jemma said. "You'll see it, too, before this is done."

Archer shifted uncomfortably, scraping his boots in the dirt.

"The important thing is that we get Mae back," he said. "Whatever this girl is hiding has nothing to do with us. She's exactly what we've been looking for. With her abilities, the mission will succeed for sure."

"And that's why you're the boss." Jemma reached up to give him a motherly pat on the cheek. "Someone needs to believe we have a chance."

CHAPTER 5

Briar awoke to a large pink tongue licking her face. She yelped and scrambled back. The huge dog followed, anointing her with slobbery kisses and trampling her blankets with his massive paws.

"Go away," she mumbled.

Instead of obeying, the dog turned in a complete circle and planted himself in her lap like an overgrown kitten. He gazed up at her with a plaintive expression. Strings of saliva dripped onto her shirt. Her legs began to go numb from his weight.

"You have to watch out for Sheriff. He's very affectionate."

Briar jolted at the mention of the man who'd ordered her execution, upsetting the dog's position on her lap. Hazy dawn light filled the camp, and the smell of burnt stew and blackberries lingered. She saw no sign of Sheriff Flynn. The dog gave her a reproachful look and retreated with his shoulders hunched.

Archer sat on his heels a few paces from Briar's blankets, a quiver and bow slung across his back. He rubbed the dog's wrinkled face vigorously, making its jowls flap. "Aw, I'm sure she didn't mean it, Sheriff, old boy."

Briar wiped her cheeks with her scratchy blanket. "You named your dog Sheriff?"

"I thought it was clever." Archer stood and clapped his hands briskly. "Up and at 'em, Miss Painter. We have a long ride ahead of us."

Briar scrambled to her feet, groaning as every muscle in her body reminded her she'd fallen out of a tree yesterday. She'd slept poorly, unable to fully relax surrounded by strangers. She took a few tottering steps.

Archer quirked a dark eyebrow in amusement. "I see you're not a morning person."

She grumbled something unintelligible back.

"Ignore him," Jemma said, strolling over with two steaming tin mugs.

Briar caught a whiff of strong tea.

"He's insufferably chipper most of the time, but mornings are especially bad."

Briar accepted the tea gratefully. The lines in Jemma's face looked a tad deeper at dawn than they had in the firelight. Strands of silver threaded her thick ash-blond hair. Briar estimated the woman was in her midforties.

"We have miles to cover, people to rob, and ladies to rescue," Archer said. "What's not to be chipper about? Come on, Sheriff. I can see our charms are wasted on these two."

Briar and Jemma smiled sleepily at each other and sipped their tea as Archer sauntered over to pester Nat and Lew, who were sound asleep by the fire. Briar felt a little shy around the older woman, who looked more like a kindly librarian than the mastermind of a gang of thieves.

"We should be able to find you a spare shirt in Lew's pack," Jemma said, adjusting her red shawl over her shoulders. "Yours is a tad conspicuous at the moment. I can take in one of my skirts for you this evening."

"Thank you." Briar brushed at the paint stains on her

clothes, which had bits of dried leaves sticking to them. The wrap on her arm looked just as bad, but she didn't undo it. She rotated her wrist and winced.

"If you catch him in a good mood, Esteban might fix that for you," Jemma said.

Briar glanced at the gaunt man currently kicking dirt over the campfire with his surprisingly ornate boots, their leather tooled with silver. His black coat sleeves covered his tattoos completely.

"Won't the spell be tracked?"

"We'll be on the move today," Jemma said. "A stray healing spell in the woods shouldn't give away our scheme. He's careful."

"Thanks."

"Don't mention it." Jemma smoothed back her silver-and-blond hair and smiled. "Oh, and don't do anything to hinder this job, or I will personally cut your throat."

Briar froze. "Excuse me?"

"I trust these louts with my life, but I don't know you from the queen." Jemma maintained her pleasant smile. "If you intend to devote anything less than your very best efforts to the team, you'd best leave now, or you will have no other chance. Do I make myself clear?"

Briar stared at Jemma, something dark and destructive rising within her. How dare this woman threaten her after offering tea and healing. She had no idea what Briar was capable of. The most talented curse painters in the kingdom used to speak respectfully to her. Briar was trying to live by a new code, trying not to fill the world with ruin, but she could still make Jemma sorry she'd ever suggested raising a hand against her.

But as Jemma stared back, eyes as cold as iron in her sweet, lined face, Briar remembered that Sheriff Flynn and Mage Radner were still after her. She had nowhere to go, no paints, and no money. Being a curse painter without hurting people was proving more difficult and complicated than she had expected. She would have to create a hundred smaller curses to earn as much coin as these thieves were offering her, adding a hundred little bits of evil to the world. This mission was a chance to help someone and earn enough to start over for good. Briar would do this one job then be done with these people and their threats.

"I understand you perfectly." She returned Jemma's icy smile. "Shall I wash the teacups before we pack up?"

Archer had finished rousing the others from their bedrolls, and they broke camp with much grumbling and swearing about the early hour. Despite their complaints, the outlaws saddled the horses and loaded their supplies onto the pack animals with an efficiency that suggested they relocated often. The sun was barely peeking above the trees when they left the dense thicket, rearranged the branches in front of the entrance, and set off into the woods.

The forest felt far less ominous that morning than it had the night before. Light flooded through the canopy, and birds serenaded overhead. The smell of warm earth, crushed ferns, and summer-dry pine needles rose from their horses' hooves. As they rode, Briar stayed a little apart from the others, ruminating on the challenge ahead. Nightshade Illusions and Marin's Locks were highly advanced magic, and breaking them wouldn't be easy. Someone must really not want Lady Mae to escape.

Curse designs had started taking shape in Briar's mind as soon as the thieves had described Larke Castle's protection spells. She considered the possibilities as they got deeper into Mere Woods, imagining the strokes in slightly different orders, comparing the pictures in her head with memories of long-ago lessons, long-ago assignments. Her fingers tingled at the prospect of such serious magic.

She had studied curses since she was old enough to hold a paintbrush. The magic was second nature to her, and it had actually been difficult to learn to paint something with no magical properties to cover her tracks. Her parents had been so proud of her talents, of how cleverly she could rip the world to shreds. Their encouragement had come at a cost, in the end. Briar shuddered at the memories of the worst curses she'd painted in their service, the ones that had made her realize she wanted no part of their business. The colors stirred and morphed, bone black, lead-tin yellow, indigo, umber. So much destruction and decay. So many nightmares. She wished it were as easy to stop being what she was as it had been to walk away.

Someone cleared their throat beside her. Briar turned. Esteban, the mage, had spurred his scrawny black mare over to join her.

"Jemma says you have an injury."

"Oh, yes."

Briar glanced back, and Jemma gave her a sunny smile. Jemma rode close beside her burly red-bearded husband, Lew, who looked as warm and unassuming as a country innkeeper.

"I sprained my wrist falling out of a tree."

"Give it here."

Briar leaned partway out of her saddle and allowed the old mage to unwrap the grimy rags. Her wrist had swollen overnight, and she bit her lip as he prodded at the puffy flesh and the cuts on her palms. Her wrist jolted in his grasp with every step their horses took.

"Could this wait until we stop?" she asked, eyes watering.

"It's best if we're moving. It weakens the residual link." Esteban lifted his spindly arm, revealing the faded ink.

The trace evidence of any spell he performed would wend its way back to the authorities via the spell on his tattoos.

"You're a voice mage, right? What—"

"Quiet." Esteban concentrated on her wrist, his eyes going

glassy. He poked her flesh, tapping a line down the most swollen parts. Then he took a deep breath and began to sing.

Voice mages didn't always sing. Words held power enough, and many practitioners were content to bark out their instructions and expect the magic to obey. Radner, the sleek-haired fellow who had accompanied Sheriff Flynn to Briar's door, was one such voice mage. He had separated the words from the beauty entirely.

Briar had known voice mages with a wide variety of styles in her former life, but none had had a voice as beautiful or as sad as Esteban's.

The song had no real words, just a rolling ribbon of syllables emitting from the mage's throat in a soothing refrain. Within seconds, the bruises and cuts on Briar's body faded away along with her lingering fatigue. The notes rose and fell in the most beautiful melody she had ever heard. She hardly noticed the torn ligaments in her wrist knitting back together, so entrancing was Esteban's voice.

The entire forest paused to listen, the birds falling silent and even the wind seeming to still. When his voice faded away at last, the others had tranquil smiles on their faces, and Lew's eyes were damp. Briar wasn't the only one who felt the beauty as well as the magic of the song.

"Well? Is that sufficient?" Esteban asked, his speaking voice hoarser than ever.

Briar rotated her wrist without a single twinge. "It's perfect," she said. "That was beautiful work. When did you—"

"Don't get hurt again. We can't leave a trace too close to the target. You'll just have to keep any future injuries." Esteban kicked his ornate boots into his horse's side and left Briar behind.

"Don't mind him," Nat said, taking the space Esteban had vacated beside her. "He gets extra grumpy after he does that. Takes it out of him, he says." The boy took a robust breath of forest air, his patchwork coat straining at his round shoulders, and grinned at her with crooked teeth. "I feel pretty grand, though. Magic, eh?"

The others looked more spirited, too, as if the song had contained too much healing power to waste on just one injury. The bags had disappeared from their eyes, and a scratch she'd noticed yesterday on Archer's cheek was gone too.

Briar couldn't help feeling jealous of the voice mage. No matter how grouchy he was, Esteban had a form of magic so good, it was almost tangible. Why couldn't she have been born with the ability to heal like that or even to write obscure but accurate prophecies, as fortune scribes did? Why could she only destroy?

Nat trotted off to pester Lew, giving Esteban a wide berth. The old mage hunched over in his saddle, an irritated vulture in expensive boots.

"He's good, right?" Archer asked, drawing up beside Briar. His fine indigo coat hung open over a threadbare white shirt, and he rode the same horse as yesterday, a bay stallion with long legs and a star peeking out beneath its forelock.

"I've never heard anything like it," Briar said. "Where did he come from?"

"Picked him up at a tavern in Chalk Port. He'd been wandering for a long time, and I reckon he needed someone to tell him what to do."

"How does he help with the thieving, though?"

Archer winked. "Let's just say he knows more than one song. We have to use his powers carefully on account of his license."

"There's no way to get rid of it?"

"None that I know of." Archer looked over at her, his unruly blond hair stirring in the breeze. "I don't suppose you could curse those tattoos off him?"

Briar frowned. She and her parents had never even considered becoming licensed, and she didn't know that much about the tattoos. Curse painters rarely worked directly on human skin—their victims wouldn't sit still long enough. "I'll think on it. I don't believe it has ever been done before."

"Doesn't sound like that'll stop you." Archer grinned. "You like a challenge, don't you?"

"Depends on the prize."

Archer's grin widened. "Now you're talking. We might get along yet."

The party of six—seven including Sheriff, the dog—proceeded through Mere Woods along a route the outlaws seemed to know well, following hidden pathways and deer runs to avoid notice on the main road. Their destination, Mud Market, was located at the edge of the forest, a three-day journey from Sparrow Village and the Brittlewyn River.

The woods echoed with the chatter of birds and the murmurs of hidden creatures. The muggy heat marking the end of summer occasionally gave way to cooler gusts promising of autumn. Lew sometimes slipped away from the group, a wide-brimmed hat pulled low over his red hair, and returned with squirrels or rabbits to cook at night. He also gathered mushrooms and nuts to supplement their diet, filling a sack hanging on his saddle during the day and emptying it into the cookpot at night. They all took turns keeping watch, both for signs of pursuit and for the larger creatures that lurked in the darkness.

Archer's crew wasn't quite what Briar had expected when he'd first appeared at her door and threatened to report her to the sheriff if she didn't take the job. She watched them closely throughout the three-day journey. They seemed to genuinely enjoy each other's company, chatting amiably as they traveled through the forest.

Briar tried not to be drawn in by their camaraderie. She didn't yet have a single jar of paint to her name, leaving her vulnerable among the strangers. They appeared friendly enough, but she believed they really would cut her throat if she crossed them. She slept at the edge of camp every night and stayed alert for any sign she needed to flee. She figured she had a better chance of avoiding the authorities' notice if she stayed with the group until she acquired new paints.

Briar had been to Mud Market three times since moving to Barden County, always to purchase the same rare pigment. The town was located at a crossroads where two highways met—or what passed for highways in that remote part of the kingdom—and it was within a day's ride of the river separating the Larke and Barden territories. The highways usually had fewer people than the quieter side streets of the city where Briar grew up, but enough traffic passed through there to support a midsize trading outpost—and for highwaymen to ply their trade, apparently.

"Remember when we hit that noblewoman's coach near here last spring?" Nat asked Lew the morning they expected to reach Mud Market. They had camped in a secluded glade near a large, hollowed-out oak tree they'd used as a supply drop. Briar was eating breakfast with the two thick-shouldered fellows, who shared tales of their exploits as the sun rose over the oak.

Lew sighed. "I'd never seen so many fine silks." He adjusted his scratchy brown vest, patting the pocket where he kept his notebook. "That lady screamed like a bobcat when we stole the jewels off her neck, though."

Nat grinned, displaying his crooked teeth. "I reckon she screamed louder than Esteban that time I put a snake in his bedroll."

"Don't remind me." Lew groaned. "My ears are still smarting from that one."

"What did you do with the lady's jewels?" Briar asked.

"Sold 'em and split the profits, except what Archer kept," Nat said.

Lew tipped his hat and strode off to tend to the horses while Nat lingered beside Briar as she finished her tea. The round-shouldered young lad had often ridden beside her over the past few days, and she recognized the signs of a youthful crush. He probably didn't meet many younger ladies in his line of work. Nat was too young for Briar, but she was sensible enough to use his interest to learn more about the crew—and their perplexing leader.

"Nat, what did you mean by 'what Archer kept'? He gets a bigger share than everyone else?"

"We all get a fair share of the take, but Archer saves an extra portion for the team. He's bleedin' organized too, always talking about investments and the like." Nat puffed out his chest proudly. "That's what happens when you get yourselves an educated crime boss."

"Where was he educated?"

"Dunno," Nat said. "I reckon Jemma was his teacher or something. They've known each other longer than the rest of us."

Briar had noticed Archer's erudite vocabulary, but he could have picked that up from listening in on his marks. His accent was difficult to pin down. Sometimes he sounded as if he could be a prosperous merchant's son, and other times he sounded as if he'd grown up working a fishing vessel out of Chalk Port.

She leaned toward Nat. "How did you meet them?"

"Mud Market. I was looking to get into the criminal business, you see. It sure beats raising pigs out by the border."

"And you just asked around for gangs of thieves who might be hiring?"

"Not quite. Archer caught me trying to pick his pocket." Nat grinned at the memory. "I thought my blood was going to spill right there in the street, but then Archer says, 'You seem like an enterprising fellow. How would you like a job?' So I say, 'I don't know what enterprising means, but if you'll teach me a trick or two and promise not to slit my throat, I'm in.' Then Archer says, 'That's enterprising enough for me. You're hired.'"

"How old were you?"

"That was two years ago, so fourteen." Nat picked at a loose string on his patchwork coat. "Archer himself ain't much older than twenty, I reckon, but he tells folks he's twenty-four. I seen him when he was barely shaving, so I know the truth."

Briar poured herself another cup of tea, pondering the information. "Why is he in charge instead of Jemma or Lew?"

"I wondered the same thing in the beginning," Nat said. "You'll come to understand it soon enough. Jemma's got the smarts, but Archer's got 'em, too, and he's got a certain kind of vision, we like to say."

Briar was about to ask what Nat meant, but she realized she didn't have to. Wherever Archer had come from, he gave the impression he knew exactly where he was going. Whether the adventure or the money or the challenge was driving him, she didn't doubt he saw the way ahead clearly.

"And Lew?"

Nat shrugged. "I reckon Lew would rather work the land back in Twickenridge than take what others've earnt, but he'd never leave Jemma, and he's a good man in a fight."

"Do you fight often?"

"More than we ought to and less than we like," Archer said, appearing suddenly between them and making Briar jump.

She hadn't known he was so close. He looked very tall as he loomed above them.

"Nat, go have a word with Jemma. She has a list of things for you to pick up from the market. We're all going in separately so as not to draw undue attention."

Nat scrambled to his feet. "Sure thing, boss."

"And Nat?"

"Yeah?"

"Don't talk about my business unless I give you permission." Archer turned deliberately toward Briar so neither would miss his meaning. "Especially to strangers."

"Ain't she one of the crew now?"

"No, she is not," Archer said. "She said herself she has no intention of joining our merry band. It would do you good to remember that."

Nat's cheeks reddened. "Won't happen again, boss." He gave Briar an apologetic shrug before hurrying over to join Jemma, who was sorting through half a dozen small purses jingling with coins.

Archer squatted on his heels beside Briar as if nothing had happened. Nerves fluttered through her belly like moths in candlelight. She couldn't tell if he was angry about her efforts to dig into his past.

"You'll be going in with me to meet your paint merchant," Archer said.

"I thought we were splitting up to avoid attention."

"If something goes wrong, we can pick up all our supplies in other towns except for this snail paste of yours. You can't do the curse without this particular paint, right?"

"That's correct."

"Then I will accompany you to make sure we get it."

Briar frowned. "I can go by mys—"

"I don't trust you," Archer said.

"Of course not." Briar reached reflexively for the paint satchel that wasn't there. "You've certainly made no effort to hide it."

"That's right." Archer's eyebrows, so much darker than his

blond hair, drew together, and his voice took on a touch of menace. "Nat means well, but he is the least senior member of this gang. Ingratiating yourself with him won't save you if the rest of us decide you're a danger to us."

"I understand."

"Good. Now," he went on in a tone that would have been appropriate for discussing the weather or the price of fish, "can you think of any problems we might encounter in Mud Market? Specific people who would recognize you, or anything like that?"

Briar tapped her fingers on her tin cup, considering how much to tell him. "I've been there a few times, but the supplier we're going to see is the only person I've spoken to at length."

"Does he know your profession?"

"He sells paints. He knows enough."

"Trustworthy?"

Briar met his eyes. "I trust him more than I trust you."

Archer fell silent for a moment. Then he adjusted the quiver of arrows strapped to his back and said, "If you plan on trying to escape, I suggest you do it now. If you wait until we're in the market, when it could cause a scene, I'll have to kill you."

His tone remained light, but Briar suspected he meant it. He veiled threats in pleasantries just as Jemma did. Briar was more afraid of Jemma than of Archer, though.

"I don't plan to escape," she said evenly.

"Are you sure? You have a free pass if you take it now."

"You don't mean that."

"I do, actually. I don't want anyone on the team who's not committed to the mission." Archer's mouth quirked in a half smile. "And I don't want to be a murderer any more than you do."

Briar was surprised to find she believed him. She examined the tin cup, tracing the simple etching with her fingers, and considered taking him up on the offer to leave. She didn't want to go back to being worse off than when she'd first arrived in Barden County. Despite the threats and the layers of secrets, the pay for Archer's job was too good to walk away from now that she had lost everything.

Besides, she wanted to see if she could break those spells. "I will keep my word," Briar said at last. "You needn't fear betrayal from me."

"Good."

He gave her a full smile that might have even been genuine, and for a brief moment she forgot all about the threats. Her fingers twitched as if she were about to paint magic.

"Well, you'd best go see Jemma," Archer said, springing to his feet. "She has a baby for you."

Briar dropped her tin cup.

CHAPTER 6

Archer strolled toward Mud Market with Briar on his arm. He wore Lew's broad-brimmed hat pulled low enough to block the noonday sun and hide his eyes. The heat of summer still lingered, rendering his itchy, rough-spun clothes far too warm. He carried a plain work knife at his belt, having left his bow and quiver behind. He felt a bit naked without them, truth be told. A blade of grass between his teeth completed the disguise.

At his side, Briar had a bundle of clothes stuffed beneath her faded, powder-blue dress, making her look at least eight months pregnant. Her thick hair was pulled back in a tight bun, and she'd adopted a remarkably convincing waddle. They looked like a young couple heading into town for supplies before the arrival of their bouncing bundle of joy.

"I don't see why I have to be pregnant," Briar muttered. "I could walk faster without all this extra fabric."

"But you're doing so well." Archer patted her hand in what he imagined was a husbandly manner. "Besides, we shouldn't rush. Country folk take their time in Mud Market. We don't want to attract attention."

"What kind of attention are you worried about?"

"We have prices on our heads for our audacious deeds. You probably do, too, by now, but no one is looking for a young mother."

Briar glanced up at him through long eyelashes. "Have you done this before?"

"We tried, but the belly looks less convincing on Nat."

They fell silent as a pair of farmhands joined them on the dirt road into town, greeting them with cautious nods. Archer nodded back, drawing Briar a little closer. He found he didn't mind her warmth at his side, despite the heat of the day.

The northernmost tract of Mere Woods rose on their right and barley fields stretched to the left in a vast golden wave. The barley grew tall and lush, ripe for the harvest. Many farmers would send their workers to Mud Market for last-minute trades before the busy harvest season began, and the little town nestled between the woods and the fields was already bustling. Archer's last visit to Mud Market had been nearly a year ago, but some things didn't change.

"Which inn do you usually stay at when you're here?" Archer asked when the two farmhands passed out of earshot.

Briar hesitated. "The Bumblebird."

He barked a laugh. "Classy."

"I've been short on coin."

"Let's take a room at the Window Inn, then."

Briar stiffened, her grip tightening on his coat sleeve. "We can't do that."

"We're not going to stay the night." He patted her hand again, hoping she wasn't about to bolt. "You need to rest your swollen feet before we brave the Mud Market. It's the first thing a young couple like us would do after a hard walk, given your condition." Archer had no idea if that was true, but he had his own reasons for the stopover.

"I mean we can't go to the Window Inn." Briar lowered her

voice as they reached the stone plinth marking the town border, where a few local watchmen loitered, inspecting the new arrivals. "I cursed it last time I was here. Every fourth person who walks through the front door gets the runs."

Archer choked on his blade of grass. "That's a pretty nasty curse."

"All curses are nasty."

"Still, what did the Window Inn ever do to you?"

"Nothing. It was a job." She looked up at him, eyes fierce. "But the owner used to harass the serving girls whenever he checked up on the place. Now he stays away, and his business is dying."

"I wasn't judging you for it," Archer said, surprised by her vehemence. "Although you did tell me you've only talked to the paint seller here."

Briar's gaze darted to the side, as if checking for escape routes. He didn't think her wariness meant she was afraid, but she picked her battles carefully. "I'm entitled to a few secrets."

"Fair enough." Archer decided not to push it. They needed the day to go smoothly. Bringing Briar into town with him was already enough of a risk. "Hasn't the innkeeper noticed the pattern of illnesses?"

"Yes, but last I heard, they hadn't found the curse. I put it in an inconspicuous spot."

"Care to fill me in?"

The ghost of a smile crossed Briar's lips. "It's on the underside of a floorboard behind the bar. I put the barman to sleep with a small curse and pried up the board to paint the big one where no one would find it."

"Clever."

"Thank you." Briar lapsed into thoughtful silence for a few paces, then she said, "I don't talk about my work much."

"That's a shame. It sounds like you're good."

"There are no good curses." Her brow wrinkled. "That's the problem."

"You're skilled, then." Archer gave her a friendly nudge, but Briar's smile didn't return. He was beginning to understand what she meant about only working for a particular type of client. She wanted to be a *moral* curse painter. What a life that had to be. He wasn't sure it was even possible. The curse on the Window Inn's owner, for example, would have negative repercussions for the customers and the servings girls who may find themselves out of work before long. Briar had set herself a difficult task.

They walked farther into town, the dirt streets around them coming to life with scurrying farmers and eager craftsmen, hawkers and gawkers, and merchants of all types. Mud Market took its name from the sprawling covered market located beside the banks of a narrow fork of the Sweetwater River. The river marked the boundary between Barden and Larke territory, and some believed the fork's location made the town part of Larke's land too. Fortunately for Archer and others of his ilk, the ongoing disputes over jurisdiction kept the authorities occupied, making Mud Market an excellent place to flout the law.

The end-of-summer rush swelled the town's population by threefold. Many of the visitors were honest, hardworking farm folk, who stared wide-eyed at the crowds, intent on drinking in a year's worth of humanity before returning to their isolated fields. The myriad distractions presented by Mud Market made the rural visitors easy targets, though Archer preferred not to steal from those who had little to begin with. He didn't have a problem with stealing in general—that would be no attitude for a career thief—but he focused on wealthy people with soft hands and heavy purses. They made for more interesting targets, with their bodyguards and their strongboxes full of coin.

Abruptly, Archer recognized a corpulent merchant he'd once held up on the road outside of town. No fewer than six armed guards surrounded the fellow as he ambled toward them, heading away from the market proper. Archer quickly steered Briar down a side street.

"How did you put the barman at the Window Inn to sleep?" he asked as they cut through an alley beside a stable reeking of horse manure. "Did he let you paint his hand or something?"

"I used a scrap curse."

"Eh?"

"It's just what I call them," Briar said. "You can paint a curse on something, like a scrap of canvas or a rock, and touch it to your victim to get the magic to affect them. It's called the Law of Proximity."

Archer glanced behind them, but the corpulent merchant was no longer in sight. He drew Briar out of the alley and into the next street over. "I didn't know curse painting has laws."

"Three," Briar said. "The Law of Proximity is number two. It says that a curse applied to an object can affect any person who comes in direct contact with that object except the painter. There's also the Law of Wholes—a curse applied to an object affects that object in its entirety, regardless of whether the pieces are intact—and the Law of Resonance—a curse applied to an object of emotional significance can affect a person from a distance."

"Emotional significance?"

"That's right. Resonance is the strongest of the three laws. Touching someone with a random cursed object isn't as powerful as, say, painting a curse on their favorite hat, which can work from a distance."

Archer pulled Lew's broad-brimmed hat off his head. "So you could paint something on this that would affect Lew clear on the other side of town?"

"Correct." Briar touched the thin strip of red silk encircling the hat's crown. "The stronger the emotional connection—the resonance—between the object and the person, the greater the distance can be between them. If it were a shirt he'd only worn a few times and didn't care about, it probably wouldn't work unless I could actually see him."

Fascinated, Archer barely paid attention to the crowds as they ambled down a busy street lined with inns and taverns. He knew about the different types of art mages: curse painters, voice mages, and fortune scribes. They could do some of the same magic, like burning or moving things, but their abilities had limits. He'd never heard of the three laws, though, and he hadn't realized how much a curse painter could do from afar.

"So these scrap curses can work with any object and any person as long as they're touching?"

"Right."

"Can other people use them, or does the curse painter have to be the one to touch the scrap to the victim?"

Briar gave him a bemused look, as if she could tell exactly where his thoughts had turned. "Anyone can use them, though obviously you wouldn't want to touch the scrap with your bare skin or you'd wind up cursing yourself. But if I wanted to put you to sleep, and I didn't have anything of yours, I could leave a scrap curse where I was sure you'd pick it up."

"Huh." A slow grin spread across Archer's face at the thought of everything he could do with a stash of pre-painted curses.

Busy imagining all the fantastical possibilities, Archer accidentally jostled a broad-shouldered young man with a comically large mustache—a mustache he had seen Nat carefully applying to his face with paste that morning. The sight of one of his crew in disguise reminded Archer they had work to do.

He flipped Lew's hat back onto his head. "Let's take a room at the Dandelion. Unless we'll end up with vomiting fits?"

"That one should be safe," Briar said, "at least from me."

The Dandelion Inn was a ramshackle place tucked between two larger establishments, and it appeared to be suffering from the competition. Only a quarter of the tables in the common room were full, even at the lunch hour. The innkeeper handed a brass room key across her desk listlessly, as if she didn't care whether or not they returned it.

The room, located up a rickety staircase, wasn't much bigger than the hollowed-out oak back at their camp, and it smelled of moist wool and despair. As soon as they were inside, Archer tossed his hat on the lumpy bed and began to take off his clothes.

Briar stiffened. "What are you doing?"

"Hand over your baby," Archer said. "Jemma stuck a few things in there for me."

Briar narrowed her eyes, and again Archer couldn't tell if she was poised to fight or flee. She yanked the bundle of rags out from beneath her dress and tossed it to him across the cramped room. She turned away as he tugged his coarse woolen shirt off over his head.

Archer chuckled. "Didn't figure you for a prude, Miss Painter."

Briar snorted, keeping her back to him.

He pulled a new shirt over his head, this one made of fine—albeit wrinkled—silk. He used the rough farmer's shirt to scrub the mud off his boots and breeches. Finally, he splashed some water from the washbasin onto his hair, slicking it back until it shined. In all that time, Briar didn't once turn to look at him. Archer felt a little disappointed by that.

"I'll be back in an hour," he announced. "Don't open the door for anyone but me."

Briar spun around. "Wait! Where are you going?"

"I'm off to see a man about a dog. We'll head to the market as soon as I return."

"But—"

"Don't forget to rest your swollen feet, darling."

Archer closed the door before Briar could object further. He was gambling that she would actually listen and remain in the room. She couldn't accompany him to his meeting, and it would be a good test of her trustworthiness before he risked taking her on the job. He needed to know she wouldn't run off at the first opportunity. Besides, the whole team was in town in various guises. They would keep an eye out for her.

He slipped out through the common room without the innkeeper so much as looking up from her desk and set off, adopting the saunter of a man with too much money and not nearly enough sense. He needed to drop in on his old friend Kurt at his favorite tavern to see if he would help with a missing piece of the plan. It shouldn't take more than an hour.

CHAPTER 7

B riar marched back and forth across the tiny room, debating how much longer she should wait. Archer had been gone for nearly four hours. Afternoon light slanted sharply through the leaded windows, illuminating a patch of the threadbare bedspread. The market would close at sundown. If Archer didn't return soon, they would be stuck there overnight. Briar didn't like the idea of sharing that lumpy little bed with him, though she supposed it would be better than the floor.

The memory of the smooth plane of Archer's back popped into her head unbidden. She'd snuck a glance at him as he'd changed his shirt, though she didn't think he'd noticed.

Don't be ridiculous, she told herself severely. She tugged her hair out of the tight bun, letting it fall loose over her shoulders, and rubbed her aching scalp as if to scratch out the illicit image.

Archer had obviously been held up. Dare she venture out to secure the paint supplies on her own? Jemma had given her some money, and it would save them further delay, but she wasn't sure she could find her way back to the hollowed-out oak alone. The others had probably already finished their shopping and left town. If Archer had run into the local authorities, Briar could be the only thing standing between him and a slow swing on the gallows.

She would face that and worse if she got caught, though. Sheriff Flynn could even now be scouring Mud Market for her, if his search had brought him that far. She couldn't just wander around out there.

Although she had only known Archer for a few days, Briar felt rudderless without him. Archer had the vision, as Nat said, and since joining his scheme, she'd felt as if her life was actually going somewhere—though the direction was unexpected. She wanted to see where the path led.

"If he ever comes back," she muttered. "What is taking so long?"

The light was fading fast outside. Briar couldn't afford to wait any longer. She stuffed the remaining rags and Archer's muddy farmer shirt under her dress, attempting to make her belly the same size as before, and snuck out through the common room. The innkeeper was snoozing at her desk. Briar nicked the woman's inkwell as she passed. Curses made with coal ink like that would be rough, but it was better than nothing. She needed magic in her hands again.

The bustle of activity in Mud Market had changed from industrious to celebratory while Briar had waited at the Dandelion. Their shopping done for the day, the out-of-towners sought drinks and entertainment in the taverns surrounding the market proper. Spirits high and arms overflowing with packages, they laughed and called to each other as they tramped through the streets. Briar watched out for members of Archer's band, though she wasn't sure she would recognize their disguises.

Her own disguise drew more attention than she liked, with well-meaning people stopping to wish her good health and inquire when her child was due. Next time, she would try an eyepatch and a hat. With luck, Sheriff Flynn hadn't distributed Briar's description so far from Sparrow Village anyway.

The market wasn't hard to find. Once stretching from the town square to the muddy banks of the Sweetwater's southern fork, the market had grown over time, and the stalls sprawled all the way across the square and squeezed amongst the bordering houses. So many burlap awnings stretched between the stalls and the rooftops that they formed a single canopy blocking out sun and rain, encompassing nearly a third of the town.

The venders were already packing up their merchandise for the evening when Briar walked beneath the patchwork canopy. The stifling air within the market smelled of sweat, cut wood, and a multitude of spices. Anything could be purchased in Mud Market, from farm tools to textiles to metal works to herbs and edible delicacies. A few mages even set up shop peddling healing spells, fortunes, and minor curses. Most were unlicensed, and they had to be ready to disappear at a moment's notice in case of a raid.

The paint seller's wares were technically benign, and his stall was in the same place Briar had last seen it. She approached cautiously, relieved he hadn't yet gone home for the night. The other vendors were too focused on their work to pay her much heed.

Briar paused in a narrow aisle to allow a woman with an armful of pale linens to totter across her path. Still twenty paces from the paint stall, she was about to continue onward when a shock of blond hair and a familiar face caught her eye.

So that's where Archer has been all day.

Briar turned aside and headed down another cramped aisle toward the town square, located entirely within the sprawling market. Archer knelt at its center, his neck and arms clamped into wooden stocks. He still wore his fine silk shirt, but bits of rotten vegetables smeared his hair, and he had the makings of a rather impressive black eye. A town watchman sat on a stool beside the stocks, whittling a stick into splinters.

Briar hid behind a large stack of barrels smelling of brandy and watched Archer for a moment. A group of children with dirty feet darted up to spit at him then dashed away, cackling madly. Until then, Briar had wondered if Archer's absence had been a test to see what she would do when left to her own devices. The others could be watching her, ready to stab her in the gut if she tried to give away their plans, but Archer looked like he was really in trouble.

Another passerby spit at the shackled outlaw, and he gave a forlorn sigh. Briar couldn't help feeling sorry for him. She scanned the market for familiar faces once more then marched toward the center of the square.

"Well, this is undignified," Archer said as she approached.

"What happened to you?"

"I cheated someone at cards last time I was here," Archer said. "Turns out Mud Market folk hold grudges."

"Is that right?" Briar sensed a lie—or at least a half truth. She checked for signs of an ambush, but the watchman was still whittling away. He looked her over then returned to his stick, clearly not worried the young pregnant woman would either endanger or liberate his prisoner.

Archer lowered his voice. "Any chance you could curse this thing off me?"

"I'm sure I could."

"Will you?"

"That depends." Briar moved closer so the watchman couldn't overhear. "This seems like a good opportunity to ask for something. You'd probably give me whatever I want if I help."

"I get it." Archer sighed theatrically. "You want me to promise you the, uh, pleasures of my company if you free me."

Briar blinked. "That isn't even remotely what I meant."

"Are you sure? Because if you're interested ..."

Briar gaped at him. "Excuse me?"

"I am joking, of course," Archer said quickly, his cheeks going red. "Nat might tear me limb from limb. I wouldn't do that to the lad."

"Sure you wouldn't."

"I happen to be a gentleman."

Briar folded her arms and quirked an eyebrow, imitating Archer's typical expression. "A gentleman in the stocks in the middle of Mud Market. Never thought I'd see the day."

Despite her breezy tone, Briar felt wrong-footed. She was supposed to be the one with the power. What did he mean about not doing that to *Nat*? And why did the statement leave her with a vague feeling of disappointment?

Archer cleared his throat and jiggled his hands. "Are you going to let me out or not?" His wrists were raw and bleeding from the rough wooden stocks, and his neck looked almost as bad, even without the smudges of rotten tomato and carrot marring his skin.

Briar took pity on him. "I'll need some paints." She tapped a finger on her lips, considering the stocks and the whittling guard. The longer Archer stayed there, the higher the chances that one of them would be recognized. "And I'd better get my purple before the market closes. Don't move until I get back."

Archer bared his teeth, and she grinned sweetly at him before walking away.

The paint seller was a diminutive man called Gideon with sun-browned skin and dark, bristly hair. A wide grin split his face nearly in two when she waddled toward him, holding her belly.

"Miss Briar, what a treat this is! Come, sit. You must rest."

"I'm all right. I just need to—"

"Please, take this stool. I've been sitting all day."

Gideon ushered her onto the three-legged wooden stool behind his stall and proceeded to fuss over her while she tried to order the necessary paint supplies as quickly as possible. The stall consisted of a table covered in jars of pigment—some mixed with oil and some still in their dry forms—and larger containers stacked on the ground for those who purchased their pigments in bulk. Racks nailed to either side of the table held string-wrapped bundles of paintbrushes ranging in size and shape, from fat brushes for painting walls all the way down to little slivers of horsehair for inscribing minute details on porcelain cups.

"Do tell me all about your happy news," Gideon insisted, only half paying attention as Briar pointed out the colors she needed. "You must not have been showing last time you were here. I apologize for not congratulating you sooner! Babies are such a delight."

Briar was surprised at how happy Gideon was about her pregnant belly, and she had to invent a whole origin story for it as she selected her paints. She chose some that were premixed with linseed oil in case she didn't have time to make her own on the road. To her relief, he had the marine snail purple in stock.

"You and your new man must dine at my home," Gideon announced as he weighed the jar of costly purple paint. "My wife and I have three children, and my darling will surely have some good advice for you."

"That's very kind, but—"

"It's nothing! A young mother needs support. Your own parents aren't around, are they?"

"I ... no, they died years ago."

Gideon clapped a hand over his heart. "Then you must join us!"

Briar didn't want to offend him, but Archer was waiting on her, and she couldn't explain his current condition without inviting awkward questions. Besides, she didn't want to introduce him as her "new man." She pleaded swollen feet and illness and finally got Gideon to pack up the paints and brushes in a burlap bag.

"That's the last of it. Be careful with the purple, now," Gideon said as he handed her the heavy bundle. "It gets harder to find all the time."

"I'll only use it for special projects."

He nodded approvingly. "And watch out for yourself on the road. There's bandits and thieves about."

"I've heard."

Gideon kept a hand on the burlap bag, as if he didn't want to let her go. "Sometimes the authorities are as bad as the bandits."

Briar frowned. "What do you mean?"

"We Mud Marketers like to think of this as neutral territory, but both Barden and Larke's men think they're in charge lately. You don't want to be caught in the middle, especially with a baby on the way." He hesitated. "And you may want to consider taking a break from your profession for a while."

"Oh, I—"

"You don't need to confirm or deny anything, Miss Briar." His gaze flitted around the emptying market. "You should know Sheriff Flynn is expected in town tonight, though."

Briar's fingers curled around one of her new paintbrushes. "When?"

"He was supposed to be here before dark." Gideon glanced meaningfully at a gap in the market canopy, where the last hint of daylight was disappearing from the sky. "I should discuss it with my wife, but if you need somewhere to stay until your child is born, we can offer you refuge."

Briar stared at him in surprise. She'd never expected such kindness from a mere acquaintance. The Sparrow Village blacksmith's betrayal still stung, and she knew Archer and the others had only taken her in because they needed something from her.

Her heart swelled, a lump knotting in her throat. She hadn't thought she had a friend in the world, but Gideon was opening his home to her despite knowing about her illegal vocation. He might help her with more than just a place to stay if she asked. He could lend her paint supplies until she started earning money again, giving her a chance to start anew.

Briar looked toward the stocks, where Archer was waiting for her—and for the sheriff he didn't know was coming. Could she abandon him and their scheme now that she had another option?

No, she had struck a bargain, pure and simple. When the job was finished, she could walk away. She didn't want to be beholden to Gideon or anyone else. Besides, Archer needed her.

"That's very thoughtful of you, Gideon," she said at last, "but I need to start for home this evening." Briar gently tugged the burlap bag toward her and gave his pigment-stained hand a brief squeeze. "Thank you for the offer and the warning. I ... I really do appreciate it."

Gideon smiled kindly. "Take care of yourself, Miss Briar. I hope I'll see you here again."

She bade him farewell and hurried back toward the stocks, staggering under the weight of the burlap sack. Archer looked decidedly grumpy, his blond hair drooping, forlorn bits of silk poking through the stocks around his reddened wrists. Briar hoped Esteban could be persuaded to fix his bruises and the crick in his neck.

The thought of the others made her pick up her pace despite being laden down as she was with the paint supplies. It was growing darker, and the sheriff could arrive at any minute. Jemma and the crew would be worried too. Briar and Archer should have been back long before sundown.

She was almost to the square when three men marched into it ahead of her, cutting off her path to Archer. They wore the mustard-brown uniforms of Lord Barden's household retainers and carried heavy iron halberds. Briar veered off sharply, taking refuge behind a stack of barrels at the edge of the square.

The men headed straight for Archer.

"Look what we have here, lads."

"Well, if it isn't the prodigal thief himself."

"I reckon it is."

The whittling watchman stood up, but at a look from the leader of the gang, he made himself scarce, hurrying off toward the public privy. Briar poked her head out of her hiding place to observe the three men.

The leader swaggered over to Archer and leaned against the stocks. "Looks like he's come down in the world."

"Even farther than the last time we saw him," said his companion, an unkempt-looking man whose mustard-brown surcoat hung open, the lapels splattered with mud.

The leader gave a nasty smile. "I used to say this one was a social climber—"

"Climbing in the wrong direction," Archer interrupted. "Yes, we've all heard that one, Pratford."

The leader's grin widened, revealing tobacco-stained teeth. "You're going to be in trouble when his lordship gets here."

Archer paused for a beat. "Lord Barden's here?"

"Ain't you heard his daughter's been taken?" The one with the muddied uniform leaned on his halberd. "He's recruiting someone to save her."

"Is that right?"

Briar winced at the faux surprise in Archer's voice.

She spread the contents of her burlap bag on the ground, only half listening to the conversation. She broke the seal on a new jar and began painting an image on one of the barrels. The deepening darkness made it hard to see the colors. Her fingers tingled with magic, and sweat broke out on her forehead. She didn't have much time.

"I bet that just twists your gizzard, don't it?" asked the leader, Pratford, his voice turning poisonous.

"What does, boss?" asked the third man, who sounded much younger than the other two.

"This young fella had his eye on Lady Mae for his own self."

Briar paused halfway through a second curse.

"I heard something about that," the unkempt one said. "Might have had a shot, too, if he still had his papa's riches."

Pratford gave an unpleasant chortle. "I reckon his papa would share some of those riches if we delivered the prodigal son to him."

"I highly doubt that," Archer said.

"Ah, don't be so hard on yourself." The leader patted Archer's head, smearing the rotten vegetables. "If your papa don't want you, he might still pay for your head."

The unkempt man hefted his halberd. "Worth a try, ain't it?"

Briar finished the second painting with a quick flourish and stepped out from behind the stack of barrels. "I highly doubt *that.*"

The youngest man jerked upright in surprise, and the others turned as she walked toward them. She began a silent countdown. *Ten ... nine ...*

Pratford took a lazy step forward, no longer leaning on the stocks. "Who're you?"

Briar faced him dead on, her hands buried in the folds of her skirt. "I'm the reason you are going to walk away and forget you ever saw this man."

Pratford chuckled, and his companions relaxed their grips on their weapons. Sensing they weren't about to stab her, Briar strode directly to Archer and planted herself beside him, one arm holding her rag-filled belly, the other hidden in her skirt.

"Took you long enough," he muttered.

"I had to prepare a few things," she shot back, still counting down. *Six ... five ...*

"Would you look at that?" Pratford walked a few steps farther from the stocks to slap his unkempt friend on the shoulder. "A lady coming to rescue Archer, the big bad thief."

The other man laughed lasciviously. "She's a cute thing, ain't she?"

"And with child?" Pratford revealed his ugly, yellow-toothed grin. "Well, that's a scandal if I ever seen one. Does she know who your papa is?"

"Shut up," Archer hissed.

The men laughed. Briar wanted to know what else they had to say about Archer and his father, but she had already set the curses in motion.

Three ... two ...

The first explosion was small, just enough bang to make the men turn toward the pile of barrels.

"What was that?" gasped the young, scrawny one.

"It came from that barrel," Pratford said.

The unkempt man clutched his halberd. "I ain't never heard an empty barrel make a ruckus like that."

While they were talking, Briar hurriedly scrawled a curse with the loaded paintbrush she'd concealed in her skirt onto the iron lock holding the stocks closed. She smelled linseed oil and a whiff of smoke, then the metal gave a faint hiss and began to melt.

Pratford whirled at the sound. "Hey, what are you—"

The second explosion erupted from the bottom of the stack of barrels, that one with enough bang to send Barden's men stumbling backward. The barrels careened toward them, bouncing on the hard-packed dirt.

"She's some kinda mage!"

"She's a witch!"

"Grab her!"

"Are you mad? Don't touch her."

Briar ignored them, focusing on her painting. The curse finished eating through the lock, and the metal pieces fell to the ground with dull *clunks*. She hauled open the stocks and tried to help Archer stand. He got to his feet stiffly, brushing off her assistance.

She was about to berate him for being too stubborn to accept her aid when a third explosion took her by surprise. It wasn't one of hers.

CHAPTER 8

Archer didn't know for sure whether Briar would help him until the first barrel exploded and she tackled the iron lock with a paintbrush. He wouldn't have blamed her for using his predicament to escape. His team would free him from the stocks eventually, but he hadn't expected to feel so embarrassed to be seen like that. By her, specifically.

Archer was mulling that over as the second, larger explosion sent barrels tumbling across the square. He rubbed his wrists and wiped tomato juice out of his hair, trying to hide how sore he was. It wasn't as bad as the three days he'd spent in the stocks on a prior occasion, all things considered, and he didn't want to look any more pathetic in front of the curse painter than he already did.

Then the third explosion erupted across the market.

"Did you—"

"Wasn't me," Briar said.

Archer swore, wondering what else could go wrong.

"I heard the sheriff's coming to town," Briar said. "Could be his pet voice mage."

"Just what we need."

Shouts came from the direction of the third explosion along with the thud of boots and the rattle of halberds.

"We don't want to stick around to find out." Archer grabbed Briar's hand and began hobbling for cover.

"Wait, I need my bag."

"Leave it."

"We can't do the mission without those paints."

Archer released her hand, wincing at the delay. As quick as a squirrel, she darted back to where she'd left her supplies. Wide-eyed faces peeked out from beneath tables in the market, watching the commotion. The erstwhile watchman poked his head out of the privy then shut himself right back inside. Barden's retainers were still crouching as if they expected the barrels to leap up and pummel them.

Briar gathered her stuff hastily, but those few seconds cost them.

"There's the witch!" one of the men called, leaping to his feet. "Get her!"

"Hurry!" Archer shouted. "I'll carry that."

Briar dashed toward him with her sack of paint supplies. She looked ready for a fight, teeth bared and eyes blazing. Archer took the bag and slung it over his aching shoulder, grunting at the weight, then he and Briar flew toward the opposite side of the square and into the market.

Barden's lackeys gave chase, brandishing their heavy halberds and shouting obscenities. Archer and Briar raced up a narrow aisle, Archer overturning tables every few paces to slow their pursuers. Textiles and rare spices spilled in the dirt, their vibrant colors marking Archer's passing. Market vendors shouted oaths to rival those of their pursuers.

The townspeople were another story as they hastened in the opposite direction, toward whatever chaos had erupted across town. They barely noticed the pair running from the mustard-uniformed goons.

Archer led the chase out of the market and bolted down the main road, Barden's men close on his heels. The streets were crowded with shoppers and revelers, making it difficult to find a path through the throng. The heavy sack thudded on Archer's back with each stride.

"They're catching up," Briar called.

"This way!" They turned down a side street. More men in mustard-brown surcoats were gathering ahead of them. Archer pulled up sharply, skidding off balance. How many were there?

"Okay, not this way."

They turned again, ducking in and out of little alleyways, continuing their frantic flight through town. Archer's shirt stuck to his sweaty skin, and his chest heaved. Adrenaline washed away the soreness from the stocks. Briar kept pace with him despite the changing directions.

They careened down another side street, where halberds caught the light of a dozen torches.

"There's another group!" Briar shouted. "They're everywhere!"

Archer growled in frustration. They couldn't afford to be caught. They had so little time left to complete the mission.

A familiar sign caught his eye on a nearby building, an arrow piercing a wine goblet in the hand of a muscular woman. Laughter and music spilled out of the doorway.

"Cut through that tavern."

Briar sprinted toward the raucous tavern. She held the door open for Archer and the load on his back, then they charged through the crowded bar together. Farmers in from the countryside gaped at them, and merchants' guards glowered over their cups. Archer recognized a few of the guards from other jobs. *Great.* Now even more people would know he'd been in

Mud Market. He might as well have pinned his itinerary on every village noticeboard in the outer counties.

"Go left!" he yelled as Briar darted nimbly through the throng ahead.

His own progress was less graceful, and he accidentally knocked over a tavern wench as he barreled after Briar. The woman let out an indignant squawk.

"Sorry!" he shouted as the churn of carousers hid the woman from view.

Up ahead, Briar broke through the crowd and skidded to a halt at what appeared to be a blank wall. She turned to face him, her hair a wild halo around her face, her eyes as bright as twin moons.

She sure is pretty. The thought stopped Archer in his tracks. Why had he babbled like an idiot about the pleasures of his company earlier?

"You said go left," Briar said, snapping Archer's attention back to their plight.

"There's a panel underneath that yellow chair," he wheezed. "Give it a tug."

Briar scrambled beneath the chair, dropping her rag-cloth baby belly so she could move more easily. There was a click, and a hidden door in the wall popped open, revealing an opening no bigger than the chair. Briar dove through it without hesitation.

"Good," Archer said, following on her heels. "Turn right at the end of the ..."

His words died in his mouth as he stumbled out of the secret entrance and found two of Lord Barden's men waiting in the alley. One was Pratford, the leader of Archer's erstwhile harassers. The other was Mage Radner himself.

The voice mage seized Briar's frizzy hair before she could take two steps.

Pratford sneered at Archer, showing off his yellow teeth.

"Think you're the only thieving bastard who knows about that wall, eh?"

"He is still an amateur, for all his cheek," said Mage Radner calmly.

The mage had a fistful of Briar's hair. Archer didn't dare advance. Radner wasn't using his magic yet, but one wrong move … Radner's hand raised, pulling Briar's hair taut. She let out a whimper.

"Let her go." Archer stepped forward. "She has nothing to do with this."

"And I'm the king's twin brother," scoffed Pratford. He pointed the wicked crescent blade of his halberd at Archer, forcing him to stop. "Lord Barden will want to speak with both of you."

Archer caught Briar's eye, hoping she had another trick up her sleeve, but her eyes were fearful, rimmed with silver tears, and her hands were empty. Out of nowhere, he remembered sweeping her onto the back of his horse, her arms wrapping tight around his waist.

Pratford noticed where Archer was looking and swung his halberd to point at Briar instead. He grinned triumphantly, as if he'd discovered a weakness to exploit. Before Pratford could even voice the threat, Archer heaved the bundle of paints at his face, knocking him flat.

Then he tackled Mage Radner.

The mage was too surprised to utter more than a gasp as Archer crashed into him. They hit the ground hard, Briar crying out as she was pulled down by her hair. Archer punched her captor in his ugly, pinched face, forcing him to release his hold on the girl. Then he kept punching, blind rage scorching through him, lending his fists strength.

"Come on!" Briar shouted, grabbing his arm. "Archer, more are coming."

Archer realized the mage was unconscious beneath him

and his knuckles were covered in blood. He scrambled back, reeling from the sudden flare of rage.

He reached for the sack of paints he'd thrown, but Pratford grabbed it at the same moment with a wordless snarl. Archer tried to wrench the bundle out of his hands to no avail. They tugged the burlap between them, locking eyes like wolves fighting over carrion. Then came a ripping sound, the crunch of jars striking the ground.

Briar appeared at Archer's side and hurled a large rock at Pratford's face. He toppled backward, his grip on the bag of paints loosening, and he hit the ground, out cold.

"We have to go!" Briar shouted.

"The bag ripped." Archer struggled with the bundle, trying to keep more paints from tumbling out.

"Here, use this." Briar undid the clasp on Mage Radner's well-worn cloak and yanked it out from under his unconscious body. Archer avoided looking at Radner's pulverized face as he and Briar tied the cloak around the ripped bag of paints and brushes. It had been a long time since he'd lost control like that.

Boots pounded and halberds clattered at the mouth of the alley. A wave of mustard brown and steel surged toward them.

"Good enough." Archer hoisted the new bundle on his shoulder, and he and Briar bolted for the other end of the alley.

Their two attackers remained lying in the dirt behind them.

"What kind of curse did you use on that rock?" Archer asked as he and Briar cleared the alley and raced toward the town boundary.

"I didn't have time for a curse," Briar said. "I just threw it really hard."

The Mud Market churned like a kicked anthill, the sounds of scattered fighting echoing across the town. Archer and Briar managed to evade Barden's men as they hurtled through the darkening streets, passed the stone plinth at the town's border, and slipped into the countryside unseen. Archer would no doubt be implicated in the chaos anyway. It might do his reputation as a dreaded outlaw some good.

They didn't slow to catch their breaths until they reached the woods, and even when the trees enveloped them, they didn't dare stop. They walked with hands outstretched, feeling their way into the welcoming arms of the night-dark forest.

Archer couldn't believe the day had gone so poorly. He should never have left Briar at the Dandelion to go see Kurt. The churl had called the town watchman before Archer had even finished his pint, using Archer's personal history to buy himself a shot at the reward. *So much for honor among thieves.*

Archer had concocted elaborate epithets to describe his lousy excuse for a friend while he'd been locked in the stocks. The arrival of Lord Barden's cronies had been just another blow in the beating. Kurt had said something unexpected, though, and Archer hadn't been able to get it out of his head, even with all the excitement.

"I heard Drake and his team made it into the castle a week ago, and she wasn't there. Dunno where else Larke would keep her. Oh, look, it's the watchman. I wonder what he's doing here."

Archer had been too busy getting arrested and shoved into the stocks to ask more, but the news troubled him. If anyone could retrieve Lady Mae before he could, it was Horatio Drake's band of mercenaries. Archer had hoped to reach the castle first, but if Drake had already been into the tower and emerged empty-handed, was it possible they had all gotten something important wrong, namely the location of Lady Mae's prison? *She wasn't there*, Kurt had said. *Dunno where else Larke would keep her.*

Archer felt a horrible sinking sensation, like a castle-sized hole opening in the pit of his stomach. Kurt and Drake may not know any other place apart from Larke Castle where Mae could be, but Archer did. That location would be far more difficult to crack, maybe impossible.

He contemplated the new destination as he and Briar traveled deeper into the woods, becoming more and more certain Larke would consider it a better hiding place for the kidnapped girl than his primary castle. Archer had nearly made a terrible mistake.

The moon rose overhead, dappling the forest floor with light and making it easier to find their way. Pine needles crunched beneath their feet, and a pair of squirrels chattered in the trees.

"I think we lost them," Briar said after a while. Her steps were spritely, and she showed no sign of fatigue, perhaps still riding the adrenaline rush of escape, of being alive after such a close call.

"*They* lost *us*, you mean," Archer said. "You're fast."

"You were carrying all the heavy stuff."

"I wouldn't have offered if I'd known a few paint jars would be heavier than a sack of bricks."

"Liar."

Briar grinned up at him, and Archer blinked at the happy, almost relaxed expression. She was usually so cautious, a bird poised for flight. She seemed to realize she had let her guard down at the same moment he did, for her face snapped closed like a treasure chest.

Archer nudged her arm. "Thank you for rescuing me."

"We're even now."

"I guess we are."

Briar fell silent, and Archer found himself thinking of how he'd felt when that cretin had grabbed Briar by the hair. His scorching rage at her being hurt had surprised him. He'd thought he'd overcome that particular weakness. He had been an angry youth, more vim and ire than sense, but the precarious life of an outlaw had forced him to rein in his temper. That had changed when Briar was in trouble.

"Archer, those men said you ... never mind."

He glanced down at her. The last vestige of joy had slipped from her face and with it the sense of comradeship they'd enjoyed during their flight from Mud Market. The silence between them thickened like porridge.

He sighed. "Go ahead and ask." They might as well get it over with before they reached the others.

Briar kept her gaze lowered. "Those men mentioned your father."

"They did."

"He's a rich man."

"He is."

"And you've cut ties with him."

"I have."

"Why?"

Archer brushed a hand through his hair. He'd lost Lew's hat somewhere. "The short version of the story is I don't like the way he conducts his business."

"He's not Lord Barden, is he?"

Archer paused. "What makes you say that?"

"I was just wondering if this quest to save Lady Mae was more personal than you've been letting on. She's not secretly your sister, is she?"

Archer chose his words carefully. "She's not my sister."

"But you have history."

"We do."

Briar nodded, as if it were something she had suspected all along. "So Lord Barden isn't your father?"

"No, he is not."

Briar looked up at him, shadows falling from her long lashes. "You're not some secret prince, are you? I figured you came from money because you're clearly well educated, but—"

"I am neither prince nor duke nor long-lost king. I swear it on Sheriff's life." Archer adjusted the cloak-wrapped bundle weighing down his shoulder. "My father makes his money through trade. Not all fine, upstanding citizens are good men, though."

"That's something I understand," Briar said. She didn't ask for any more details, and he wondered how long it would take her to figure out the rest.

They continued on in silence. Archer thought it was relatively companionable. The escapade had shown him he could trust Briar not to abandon their mission, but the thought of Mae tempered his enthusiasm for that development. He couldn't waste any more time or take any more risks. His own life aside, Archer didn't know if Briar and the team could—or would—finish the job without him. At the end of the day, most of them were in it for the money, and they could get that other ways with the right initiative.

The horses were saddled and waiting when they reached the hollow oak tree, and the campfire smoldered, recently doused. Sheriff howled and bounded over to greet them with his sloppiest kisses.

Jemma marched after the dog, looking as if she couldn't decide whether to slap Archer or hug him. She often looked that way, come to think of it. "It's about time you got here! I was about to send in the cavalry."

"Have no fear, Jemma. I've been in tighter scrapes than this." Archer tried to give a bow and a flourish, but his back still ached from spending the afternoon in the stocks. He handed the bundle of paints over to Briar and settled for a stiff nod.

Jemma glanced at Briar, her expression frosty, as if she

suspected their tardiness was her fault. "Lew went back to look for you. Did you at least get everything?"

"Nearly," Archer said. "No luck with Kurt. Turns out I over-estimated our friendship." He rubbed his wrists. There would be time to tell the rest of the story later.

"I didn't think he'd join us." Jemma tucked a few strands of silver-and-blond hair behind her ear. "We will make do without him."

"At least you got the paints," Nat said. He sat on his heels beside Briar, holding a lantern for her as she opened the stolen mage's cloak and took inventory of her purchases. "I've never seen such bright colors."

"We'll have even more colors after I finish mixing the pigments," Briar said. "It shouldn't take too long to ... oh no."

She grabbed the burlap sack, which had a large rip from Archer and Pratford's tug-of-war, and turned the whole thing inside out. Sheriff trotted over to sniff at it, his tail drooping.

Archer moved closer. "Problem?"

"The purple," Briar said. "It must have fallen out during the fight."

Nat brightened. "There was a fight?"

"More of a skirmish, really," Archer said. "Are you sure it's gone?"

"Yes. The umber is missing as well, but I can forage for materials to make that along the way. That purple, though ..."

"We'll have to go back for it." Archer was starting to wish he had taken a nap at the inn when he'd had a chance. He kept moving one step forward and two steps back.

"The market is closed," Briar said. "Unless it's exactly where we dropped it ..."

"Can't you just mix blue and red paints?" Nat asked.

"Unfortunately, no. The spell-unravelling curse requires the exact substance."

"No matter." Archer offered Briar a hand to help her to her feet. "Shall we?"

She blinked in surprise at the gesture, but she accepted his hand and allowed him to pull her to her feet. Nat looked quickly between the two, a hint of suspicion flickering in his eyes.

Before Archer could think of something clever and casual to say, a sharp whistle interrupted him.

"That's Lew's warning," Jemma said.

"We've got company," Archer said, dropping Briar's hand. "Get ready to ride."

The others untied the horses while Jemma scattered pine needles to hide how recently the camp had been occupied. Briar packaged up the remaining paints in the voice mage's cloak and secured them to her saddle. They were all on their mounts by the time Lew galloped through the trees.

"There's been a tussle between Barden and Larke's men in the village," Lew said, the dark-brown wig he'd worn into town hanging askew. "Barden's men seem to think Archer was behind the flare-up."

Jemma turned in her saddle. "Archer."

"I was in the wrong place at the wrong time," Archer said. "But they've been itching to get into it for months. Barden hates that Larke's men have had the run of Mud Market for so long."

"Agreed," Lew said. "I'm not surprised he's reasserting his hold on the place after Lady Mae."

"You weren't supposed to be seen," Jemma said.

"It can't be helped now. At least I knocked out Radner."

Esteban looked up from where he'd been adjusting the ties on his saddlebags. "The voice mage?"

"Is he the one who always looks like he just sat on a porcupine?" Nat asked.

"One and the same," Archer said.

Jemma definitely looked like she wanted to slap him. "I thought you said it was just a skirmish."

"Do they know where we are?" Archer asked.

Lew nodded grimly. "Barden's men got wind that we're in the woods, and they're sending a party our way. We'd better leave the pack animals. We need to get across the Sweetwater to Larke territory as quickly as possible."

"But we didn't get the purple paint," Briar said. "I have to go back to look for it."

"It's too late now," Archer said. "We'll get it some other way."

"But—"

"None of us want to be caught by Lord Barden's men, least of all you. His cronies won't be satisfied with just burning down your cottage."

Briar set her jaw, her eyes burning like torches in the darkness. Archer didn't envy Mage Radner if he ever met *her* with a full supply of paints in hand.

"You hired me to do a job," she said. "I'm telling you it won't work without that paint."

Archer hesitated. After the news from Kurt, he was pretty sure she was going to need a whole new set of curses anyway. With luck, maybe they wouldn't require the purple at all. He appreciated that she was committed to the job, but they wouldn't make it in and out of Mud Market a second time that night.

"Your concerns have been noted," Archer said. He flung up a hand to keep her from arguing, and she gave him a murderous scowl.

"I hear them coming," Lew said.

"*Archer*," Jemma hissed.

"Well, what are you all standing around for?" Archer asked. "We need to get across that river!"

Archer vaulted onto his horse and whistled to Sheriff. The

dog gave a long howl and set off into the woods. Archer led his people in the opposite direction. As always, he said a prayer to the higher realms for his canine friend. Sheriff had a sharp mind in that wrinkly head of his, and he would lead Barden's men on a merry chase. Sometimes Archer wished he were as clever as his dog. He couldn't believe he'd been about to break into the wrong castle.

CHAPTER 9

Briar and the outlaws rode hard through the night, Lord Barden's men in hot pursuit. Branches lashed their faces, the darkness seeming to morph into enemies at every turn, but Briar wasn't as frightened as she'd been the last time she'd fled through the woods. She had paints again, and if she got caught, she would not be helpless.

Still, the loss of the purple pigment troubled her as they got farther from Mud Market. Archer didn't seem to understand how impossible it would be to just "get it some other way." Most curses didn't require that particular paint. Unravelling magic was a mysterious and little-understood practice—one that had especially fascinated Briar's father. He was always experimenting with marine-snail purple in his studio by the sea, but no supplier between here and Larke Castle was guaranteed to have the pigment on hand.

She'd tried to explain it to Archer, but he was too focused on barreling forward through the darkness. Briar clutched her reins in frustration, making her horse snort and toss its head. She wanted their quest to succeed. She had become fully invested the moment she'd helped Archer out of the stocks instead of accepting Gideon's charity. Besides, Mage Radner had seen her with Archer. It was too late for a clean break. The least he could do was listen.

Archer rode at the head of their party, the darkness revealing little more than the outline of his bow and quiver, once again strapped to his back, and his blond hair blowing in the wind. There was more to their job than Archer had told her—and more to Archer himself. She'd heard enough from Barden's men to guess he was a wealthy merchant's prodigal son who wanted to marry a baron's daughter. Archer must believe rescuing the fair maiden would win her hand—and return him to the affluent society from whence he'd come. Perhaps he was even in love with Lady Mae. What would he do if Briar's curses failed to save her?

"Personal crusades are always messy." A long-ago warning from her father seemed to float out of the forest. *"You can't let your clients' passions interfere with your work."* Most of her clients came to her for revenge, so avoiding their passions wasn't possible. She was far more involved in the mission than usual, though. Briar sincerely hoped she was wrong about Archer's devotion to Lady Mae. Otherwise, they might both come to regret the loss of that purple paint.

Just before midnight, their group left the woods and crossed into a stretch of rolling hills. Starlight flooded the sky, an endless expanse of dancing fireflies. The horses' hoofbeats echoed across the hills, making it difficult to tell if their pursuers were still behind them. Briar felt at one with her saddle, with the creaking leather and the smell of horse sweat. Her mount's mane whipped at her face, and the paint jars in her saddlebag rang with each stride.

They barely paused all night, only slowing to a walk when their horses couldn't run anymore. Archer or Jemma occasionally galloped ahead to scout their path, and Lew kept a close watch at the rear. All of them looked back often to see if the authorities were catching up.

The sky glowed pink by the time they crested another hill and found a broad, powerful river running through a shallow gorge below. The Sweetwater, which marked the boundary to Larke County, glimmered in the morning light. The land on the other side was pockmarked with rock formations, hinting at ample hiding places.

"Finally!" Nat exclaimed, slumping in his saddle, his patch-work clothes even more rumpled than usual. "I thought we'd never get here."

"Barden's minions would love an excuse to violate Larke's borders," Archer said, wiping sweat from his high forehead. "We're not safe yet."

"Nowhere is safe."

Briar thought she'd spoken quietly, but Archer looked over and met her eyes with steady intensity. She was the first to drop her gaze.

"Boss, we might need a detour." Lew trotted up the shallow gorge toward them. He had been scouting along the riverbank, which twisted out of sight to the west.

"Trouble?"

"The bridge is out downriver, and the water is too deep and swift to cross here."

Archer muttered a curse—the vulgar sort, not a magical one—and checked the road swooping across the hills behind them. It was empty. "What are our options?"

Lew waved to the east. "There's a crossing a few hours upstream. It'll take us out of our way."

"We've already lost too much time," Archer said.

Jemma and Lew began discussing possibilities for fording the river. Nat fiddled with his reins, anxiously scanning the countryside behind them. Archer's horse danced beneath him, suggesting his rider was more nervous than he looked.

Briar touched the bundle of paints attached to her saddle. She had a few tricks that could help, though she wasn't sure revealing them would be wise. She had committed to the job. She might as well go the whole way. She cleared her throat. "I can get us across the river."

Archer turned toward her, quirking an eyebrow. "How?"

"I know a curse that'll lift us clear over it."

"An ambulatory curse?" Esteban guided his scrawny mare closer on her other side. "Those are too volatile."

"I'm very good at them," Briar said. "Anyway, we've been in our saddles all night. They'll respond well."

"Someone want to enlighten me?" Archer asked.

"An ambulatory curse is what I used to throw you out of my cottage," Briar said. "I can paint them right on our saddles to lift us across the river."

"In my professional, *licensed* opinion," Esteban said. "That is a moronic idea."

"I've seen it work, though," Archer said. "Why not let her try?"

"Because we could all end up with broken necks, that's why," Esteban said.

"You have any better ideas?" Archer asked.

Esteban stared at him for a prickly moment. "You know anything I do will draw the authorities right to us."

"Well then, let Briar try," Archer said. "Can't hurt."

Esteban's mouth tightened into a knot, his narrow shoulders quivering, but he didn't continue the argument. As soon as Archer turned away to address Jemma, Esteban shot Briar a look of pure venomous hatred. She understood why. He had been with the team far longer than she had, and he was a more experienced mage. Archer should trust his opinion over hers. Yet he had sided with her. Why? She felt flattered and a little nervous about it, but she didn't have time to worry about Archer. They needed to be out of sight among the rock formations on the far side of the Sweetwater before Barden's men reached it.

They scrambled down to the riverbank at the bottom of the gorge, which smelled of mud and summer moss. Little insects hovered above the rapids, iridescent wings flashing in the early sunlight. The river was wide and wild, the opposite bank much farther away than it had seemed from the top of the ridge. Briar felt a hint of misgiving. She'd never covered that much distance with an ambulatory curse before.

"Stay in your saddles, please," she told the others as she prepared her paints. "The longer you've had contact with the item the more effective the curse will be."

"Do mine first," Archer said. "If someone's going to break their neck, it might as well be me."

Esteban snorted, folding his arms over his thin chest.

"Very well." Briar guided her horse alongside his bay stallion and handed him her reins. "Keep the horses still."

"Don't worry." He winked. "I've seen what happens when your work gets messed up."

Briar grimaced, pushing away the memory of the nails pinging out of Winton's house. She needed to concentrate.

She tucked a few small paint jars into her left hand, selected a fine-tipped brush, and leaned in close to Archer's leg to paint the curse on the pommel of his saddle with her right hand. It was awkward to work at such close quarters, and she had to lean on his thigh to keep from falling off her own horse.

Archer went utterly still, as if afraid to breathe with her pressed against him like that.

He's probably just praying I don't accidentally curse off his manhood. She tried not to think about the tension in his leg muscles, the warmth of his body near hers. Sweat broke out on her forehead, and her fingers tingled with magic.

A bird soaring over a river took shape on the saddle. Once, her hand slipped, but Archer didn't flinch, holding the horses steady. She felt a jump in his pulse when she adjusted the arm leaning on his thigh, though. Her own pulse was racing just as fast. She didn't dare meet his eyes.

After what felt like an eternity, she painted the final verdigris stroke and sat back.

Archer grinned nervously at her. "I hope I haven't just made a terrible mistake."

"Me too."

Before he could respond, there was a leathery creak, and his saddle lifted into the air, taking both horse and rider with it. The others gasped and pulled back, as if afraid the horse would careen out of control and crush them.

Hovering a few inches off the ground, Archer and his mount drifted slowly across the riverbank like a pair of very heavy ghosts. The horse's eyes rolled wildly, and its hooves churned as it was carried out over the water. Their weight had no bearing on the curse itself, but Briar feared the girth strap would break right off the saddle. She wished she could do something to reinforce it. Curses did damage by nature. Ambulatory curses were dangerous in their own right, but she could still make use of them. In order to make the strap stronger, though, she would have had to turn it to stone. The horse wouldn't appreciate having a saddle cemented to its back—not that it was particularly enjoying being carried through the air.

Nat covered his eyes with his pudgy hands, watching Archer's progress through his fingers. Jemma clutched Lew's sleeve as if to keep from launching herself at the river, and Lew's face took on a green tint. Briar avoided looking at Esteban.

Archer's horse got more nervous as they drifted across the rapids. The animal thrashed its hooves, the saddle groaning dangerously. Archer leaned close to the bay's neck to speak soothing words and stroke its heaving sides. The creature calmed a bit as they floated across the expanse.

After what felt like a year, the curse deposited both horse and rider on the opposite riverbank. The horse tried to bolt the instant its hooves touched the grass, but Archer reined it in with a steady hand. He waved at them across the river.

"All clear!"

Briar released a breath. Nat whimpered, deflating in his saddle. Lew's forehead glistened with sweat. Jemma and Esteban both stared at Briar with new eyes, calculating eyes.

She lifted her paintbrush. "Okay, who's next?"

Moving the rest of the team was less stressful since she knew the curse worked—less stressful for Briar anyway. They blindfolded the other horses to keep them from panicking on their way across the river. A few of the humans looked as though they wished they were blindfolded, too, but they allowed Briar to work her magic.

Painting the ambulatory curses was a lengthy process requiring over forty strokes for each saddle. If she'd simply thrown them across the river—the way ambulatory curses were normally used—it would have been much faster, but Briar had dampened and drawn out the effects of the curse through the use of painstaking detail in order to make the journey safe. She couldn't remember the last time she had painted so many complex curses in quick succession. Her eyes felt grainy, and her fingers were trembling by the time she sent the last outlaw —Nat—across the river, clutching tight to his horse's gray mane. Only one more to go.

Briar cursed her own saddle last—or at least she started to. Then she heard the telltale thunder of hooves on the road behind her. Their pursuers had caught up.

Archer saw Sheriff Flynn first. He charged onto the ridge above the river on the Barden side, leading a posse of mustard-uniformed men. He looked like an angry bull after spending all night in his saddle—red-faced, round bellied, and agitated. He raised his sword, bellowing wordlessly as more men galloped up behind him.

Briar was still directly in their path at the bottom of the slope.

Archer started forward without thinking, and Jemma seized his arm.

"We have to get out of sight," she hissed.

"We can't leave her," Archer said.

Jemma's grip tightened. "They must not learn what we're doing."

"Barden's men already saw me in the market."

"You could have been doing anything there, but if he sees all of us on this side of the river, word could get back to—"

"I know."

Archer had taken pains not to be seen with Jemma and Lew over the past few months. If anyone saw them on Larke land, in the company of a licensed mage and a curse painter no less, the game would be up. But they couldn't leave Briar after she had gotten them safely across the river. It wouldn't be right.

"Get the rest of the team behind those rocks. I'll catch up. Esteban, you stay and help Briar."

The mage coughed. "I will do no such thing."

"You have to hold them off while she crosses the river."

Esteban raised his arms, baring the ends of his tattoos. "Why would I further implicate myself for *her*?"

Archer seized Esteban by the collar and hauled him halfway out of his saddle. "I said hold them off."

Esteban scowled, his eyes going black and hooded. Archer knew the old man could blast him halfway to High Lure with a word, but he didn't back down. He'd had enough of Esteban's attitude. He tightened his grip on the man's collar.

"Fine, I'll do it." Esteban wrenched himself away from

Archer, rubbing his throat. He climbed off his scrawny mare and scrambled down to the water's edge.

Jemma gave Archer a hard look then motioned for the others to follow her deeper into Larke territory. Their argument wasn't over, but that was a problem for Archer's future self. First, he had to make sure Briar was safe.

A dozen riders had joined Sheriff Flynn at the top of the ridge on the Barden side of the river. They were far enough away that Archer hoped they hadn't seen most of the team. He yanked the blanket roll from behind his saddle and tossed it over his head to obscure his own identity. Then he dismounted, snatched up his bow, and slid down the shallow embankment toward his voice mage.

On the opposite riverbank, Briar was still painting her own saddle. The sheriff waved his sword and pointed it at her as if he were a wartime king. His riders whooped and charged down the hill in a thunderous torrent, heading straight for Briar.

Archer's boots slid in the mud. He was almost to Esteban. Just before Archer reached him, the voice mage opened his mouth and unleashed the highest note Archer had ever heard.

Wheels of fire spun out of Esteban's mouth and flew across the river, twirling fast, gathering strength with each spin. Flynn's riders scattered like pigeons, and the fiery wheels exploded on the slope.

The sheriff bellowed at his men, red-faced and raging. The riders reformed around him, still only halfway down the embankment. Flames licked the grass, sending smoke into the morning air.

Esteban's shoulders tensed. He sang another high note, harsher this time. More flaming spirals formed and spun across the river. The riders dodged them, keeping their heads a little better the second time. They were almost to the bottom of the hill.

Briar still bent over her saddle, fingers flying as she scribed her curse. The riders drew closer. Archer reached for an arrow, tangling with the blanket he'd tossed over his head.

Then Esteban shrieked, and a dozen arrows shot from his mouth. The conjured steel streaked across the water, flying faster and farther than anything Archer could shoot from his longbow.

The arrows hit an invisible wall. They hung suspended for an eyeblink then fell to the ground and vanished.

Barden's men had a mage too. Had Radner recovered from his beating already? It was hard to pick him out without his cloak. Archer scanned the riders for his sleek brown hair and sneering face.

Then a volley of fiery arrows sped back across the river toward him and Esteban. Archer ducked, but Esteban sang a series of low, deep notes, and the whole river rose up to quench the burning darts, the water curling like a silver snake in a single rippling mass.

Archer stared. That was *not* ordinary magic. The king had lost an immense talent when he'd offended Esteban badly enough to drive him away. Archer would have to take care not to do the same.

The river crashed down, once more filling the riverbed. As the water settled, Archer saw Briar and her horse still on the ground on the opposite bank. She had stopped painting, her hand poised over her pommel, a brush tipped with green in her grasp.

What is she waiting for? The sheriff and his men were almost upon her.

Briar's brush hovered above the curse as she waited for the right moment to paint the final stroke. The riders were drawing nearer. Any second a halberd could skewer her or a sword could separate her head from her shoulders, but she couldn't launch herself over the river when the two voice mages were shouting deadly spells through the air. They needed to stop long enough for her to cross. Esteban had to give her an opening.

Across the river, the gaunt old man was sweating as he traded blows with the other mage—Briar was pretty sure it was Radner. She recognized some of the spells Esteban was using. Battle spells, the kind only the most powerful mages learned in the service of the king himself. Esteban was more than he seemed.

The battle spell he used to turn the river into a silver snake was especially rare. It snatched a volley of arrows from the air as if protecting the walls of High Lure itself. As the water crashed back into its banks, Briar managed to catch Esteban's eye at last. He stared back at her, his face impassive.

He's not going to help me. The realization made her go cold. He would do enough to show Archer he'd tried, but then he was going to let the sheriff catch her, or kill her.

Briar fumbled for more paints, but she had no time to defend herself. The riders were surrounding her. She smelled the sweat of their horses, glimpsed the whites of their eyes. Radner was there, his face bruised and swollen. He opened his mouth.

Then, when Briar was certain all hope was lost, Esteban changed his tune. A great wailing cry issued from his throat, and a fist of smoke formed in the spray from the agitated river. The fist hardened like marble and punched into the sheriff's men, knocking them off balance. Radner yelped, struggling to stay astride his rearing horse.

Despite the incredible complexity of his song, Esteban managed to utter a note meant for Briar's ears alone. "Now," he sang.

Briar flicked the final bit of verdigris paint onto her saddle.

Her horse rose into the air, shuddering at the pressure around its belly. Briar added an extra flourish to increase the speed of the curse, risky as it was, and she and the horse soared across the river. Behind her, Esteban's misty fist pounded into the sheriff and his men again and again.

Briar's horse landed hard on the opposite side of the Sweetwater, jarring her teeth. For a moment, she couldn't move, paralyzed with relief. That had been way too close.

Archer and Esteban scrambled back up the bank to join her, the younger man assisting the older. A blanket slipped from Archer's shoulders, tangling in his quiver. His blond hair stood on end.

"You made it!" Archer shouted gleefully. "They can't catch us now!"

Briar thought they probably could, with Radner's help. She wanted to curse the man to dust for what he'd done to her cottage, but she tucked her paintbrush into her belt, resisting the urge. They had nothing to fear from Radner with such a powerful voice mage of their own. Briar nodded at Esteban, silently thanking him for not abandoning her after all. He ignored her completely and scrambled back onto his horse.

Then they were off, flying into the rocky landscape, leaving the river and their pursuers behind.

CHAPTER 10

They traveled as far from the river as possible in case Sheriff Flynn decided to risk entering Larke's territory to capture them. Unlike the forested vales of Barden County, Larke's northern land was open and sprawling, strewn with jagged rock formations and vast purple heaths. They could ride faster there than they had in the woods, but the night had been long and difficult, and the horses were spent. They took shelter in a cave well before the sun went down.

Briar was utterly exhausted. Painting so many intricate curses in a row had left her fingers numb and her back aching. The others noticed her stumbling footsteps, and Nat offered to take care of her horse so she could rest. She barely managed to scarf down a few bites of hard cheese and jerky without nodding off.

The cave smelled of bat feces and bone dust. Briar spread out her bedroll on the softest patch of rock she could find, wishing they could stay in an inn just once. Stealth was more important than ever since they'd entered Larke County, though they hadn't exactly been models of discretion so far. Archer seemed to leave nothing but chaos in his wake. Briar had that in common with him.

The others were still tramping around the cave as Briar lay down to sleep. Perhaps due to her weariness, it was the first night she didn't set up her bedroll as far from the others as she could get. She felt safe with them—at least for the moment. She hid some paint supplies in her blankets, though, a brush at her fingertips. She never wanted to be defenseless again.

Esteban squatted to build a fire on a flat stone a few paces from her. Pushing his sleeves above his tattooed elbows, he used flint and tinder rather than magic to light it. After announcing his presence at the river, he couldn't reveal which direction they were heading with so much as a whispered spark spell.

Briar watched him strike at the flint, wondering why he'd helped her back at the river. He didn't like her, and for a moment, she'd thought he would allow her to be captured. Had he changed his mind out of a sense of team solidarity? Perhaps he wanted to prevent her from telling Sheriff Flynn everything she knew about them.

She knew less than she'd thought. Esteban was no ordinary voice mage for starters. Battle spells were rare, especially among grumpy old hedge wizards in the outer counties. Esteban had worked for the king once. She was sure of it.

Esteban grumbled over the flint and tinder for a few minutes before the kindling ignited into a proper flame. He finished building the fire and, perhaps sensing Briar's eyes on him, approached her bedroll and knelt beside her, smelling of smoke and old parchment.

"You are more than you claim," he whispered. "You have not always been a seller of petty revenge. Who are you?"

"I'm Briar," she said evenly. "I don't see how my employment history is any of your business."

Esteban snorted. "Only a handful of mages can paint ambulatory curses as precise as the ones you created at the river, much less do it over and over again. Archer might not understand how impressive that feat was, but I do."

Briar's fingers twitched toward the paints in her blankets. "Is that supposed to be a compliment or a threat?"

"Consider it a warning. I will discover your secret."

"Does Archer know *your* secret?" Briar whispered back. "That you used to be a Crown Mage, possibly even *the* Crown Mage?"

Esteban's mouth tightened. "He knows. If you figured that out from a few battle spells, that tells me even more about you." He studied her in the feeble firelight. "You can't have practiced for long at your age, but your teachers must have been exceptional."

Briar tensed. Esteban would know her parents' reputation even if he wasn't connected enough to High Lure to recognize her. He'd apparently been wandering the outer counties for decades, but they were the deadliest curse painters in the kingdom. Whatever he suspected about her, it was unlikely he would connect her to Saoirse and Donovan Dryden themselves. Still, she had to deflect his suspicions.

"How do you know I'm not self-taught?"

Esteban sniffed. "Don't insult me."

Briar raised herself up on her elbows so he couldn't loom over her. "You've been your own man long enough to know there is power outside the Hall of Cloaks."

"Indeed." A shadow flickered across Esteban's gaunt face. "And I know a mage or two who has adopted that philosophy to the detriment of the kingdom. But a self-taught virtuoso wouldn't know about Crown Mages and the frictions in the Hall of Cloaks."

Briar ground her teeth, wishing she'd kept her mouth shut. The destructive urge roiled in her chest. Tired as she was, she was already planning out six different curses to use against Esteban. That would definitely give away her identity.

"Can I get some rest?" she asked, keeping her voice level with effort. "Or do you want to threaten to kill me if I betray the team? You'd need to get in line."

"Quite the opposite." Esteban hunched his thin shoulders, as if surprised and a bit irritated by what he was about to say. "If you have truly stepped away from the life I suspect you led before, this team might be the best place for you. Goodnight, Miss Briar."

He scuttled off toward the mouth of the cave, where Lew and Jemma were silhouetted against the starlight, lingering over their cold suppers. Briar watched him fold himself to the ground beside them, feeling unsettled. Was that Esteban's way of saying he approved of her after all? Or even that he understood where she had come from—and why she wanted to leave?

She needed to be careful. He could still betray her secrets to Archer and the others. They might not be so willing to welcome her to the team if they knew the full extent of what she'd done. As Archer had said, they were thieves, not murderers. She was beginning to feel comfortable with the gang, enjoying their camaraderie and their commitment to each other. She'd spent most of the past year alone, except for meetings with her clients. She hadn't realized how much she'd missed having company.

Briar pulled her blanket up to her chin and closed her eyes, but sleep eluded her. She couldn't help thinking about the life she'd left behind—not the one in the cottage, always too idyllic to last, but the one she had escaped. Tired and drained as she was, it was difficult to keep the memories at bay.

So much pain had flowed from her brushes. So much evil coated in pretty colors. The faces of the people she had harmed swirled around her, drenched in paint and blood. She had been seven years old the first time she'd cursed another human being. She'd barely understood what she was doing, but the sound of her victim's leg snapping and the scream that followed were all too clear. That snap had reverberated through her memories for a decade, the rhythm for all her regret-filled nightmares.

In their studio by the sea, her parents had taught her to think of the people she cursed as subjects not victims. Curse painting was a calling, a vocation. They were artists, talented at finding new and creative ways to add evil to the world. Her mother, Saoirse, was explosive, with a gift for incendiary curses and destruction. Her father Donovan's work was subtler, emphasizing illusions and nightmares and psychological terror. The pair had no equals—something they told her regularly—and they wanted Briar to be even better than they were.

But she didn't want to be better. She wanted to be *good*. Briar had asked why she couldn't learn kinder spells as a child, when she realized the beautiful paintings her parents taught her to make, the ones that made their eyes shine with pride, always seemed to result in other people's tears.

"I want to make something nice," she'd said to her parents once as she ground precious lapis lazuli to make ultramarine blue in their studio. "Like the voice mages who make roses for the queen's garden in winter."

"Your paintings are more beautiful than the queen's roses." Her father had looked out from behind a large canvas, his eyes as large and owlish as her own. He was a handsome man, as handsome as her mother was beautiful. "They are far more than *nice*."

"But they always do bad things," Briar said. "They hurt people and break things."

"They are exquisite," her mother said. She twisted back Briar's frizzy hair to keep it out of the paints and wrapped her

JORDAN RIVET

favorite emerald-green scarf around her temples. "And one day, you will make true art."

Briar blushed as her mother knotted the silk scarf with her paint-smudged hands. Her parents knew no higher compliment than to call something art, but she had seen art cause pain. She didn't understand how it could be so good and important when it did that. She wanted to heal and build and strengthen, not destroy. But no matter how hard she studied, how hard she tried, curses were the only tools her parents gave her.

It would be a while yet before Briar understood that art wasn't inherently good at all—and longer still before she realized her parents didn't care about good and evil. For them, it was about the creative act, the hot rush of producing unique works more beautiful and complex than any other artists could. If they had been anything but curse painters, they might not have traveled such a dark path. For them, pain and death were byproducts of their calling not the ends.

As she witnessed more snapping bones and tear-filled eyes, Briar had tried to assert her burgeoning sense of morality, though she lacked a model for it in the closed world of their studio. By age twelve, she was going out of her way to avoid hurting people with the curses her parents assigned her. After one such incident, the two of them cornered her on their flat rooftop, where she often retreated for a view of the sea.

"Did you warn Lord Randall's carriage driver?" her father demanded.

"That curse you had me paint on the carriage would have hurt him." Briar avoided her father's gaze. "I just told the driver not to sit on that tall seat for a few hours. The curse worked."

The fine carriage had exploded in a shower of splinters and ripped silk in the king's courtyard, her paint on the footboard, the driver nowhere in sight. Briar had enjoyed the blast all the more because no one had been hurt.

"You ruined a carefully laid plan," her mother said.

"The driver was supposed to get hurt? I thought you just wanted to break the carriage."

"And cause Lord Randall a minor inconvenience?" Her father raised an eyebrow. "Of course the driver was supposed to get hurt."

"You are old enough to know better by now," her mother said irritably.

At the time, Briar hadn't admitted that she knew her parents had intended the driver to die when the carriage collapsed, though she didn't understand the reason. The driver was kind, and his young wife had recently given birth to a baby boy. Briar had watched from the hayloft in the castle stables when the young couple had brought the baby to pass among their friends, all taking care to support his little pink head. Briar had wanted to hold him, too, but her fingers had been stained with paint. She couldn't touch the innocent little thing with hands that had caused such pain.

Even as she'd begun to resist her parents' instructions, she'd struggled to admit they were bad people. It had taken her far too long to leave them. The day she'd finally broken away, the result had been as bad as anything else they'd made her do. She could run from them, but she couldn't outrun her destructive power.

After fleeing to the outer counties, she'd tried to forge a new path by favoring weaker people over the powerful, even if they were only after revenge. She'd made some strides with her magic, such as figuring out how to make a dangerous ambulatory curse slow enough to safely transport people across a river, but she'd destroyed so much in the process. There had to be a way to live that would allow her to stay in a peaceful cottage smelling of oil paint and wood smoke and dry thatch, far away from snaps and screams and tears.

Briar rolled over on her bedroll, a paintbrush jabbing her

side. A few members of the team were still talking quietly by the cave entrance. Someone on the other side of the fire—she thought it was Nat—snored loudly, but the ripping snores couldn't drown out the memory of all the destruction her family had created together.

Even in the northernmost county in the kingdom, far away from High Lure, Briar couldn't escape her parents' art. She liked the camaraderie of the team and the positive nature of their mission, but they wanted destruction from her too. They'd gotten a taste of her power at the river, and she feared what else they would ask of her now.

CHAPTER 11

Archer watched Briar tossing and turning beside the fire. His gaze strayed to her often lately. He told himself it was because he had just seen her do something remarkable. Lifting them all to the other side of the river had been a magnificent deed. But she'd done remarkable things every day he'd known her, and it felt different somehow after their time in Mud Market.

She gave a little sigh, her lashes fluttering, and he wondered what was going on behind those eyes, beneath that frizzy hair.

"Are you listening to me?"

"Huh?"

Jemma rolled her eyes. "You were the one who called this meeting. Pay attention, won't you?"

"Sorry." Archer repositioned himself so he was facing Lew, Jemma, and Esteban, who had gathered at the cave entrance for a conference while Briar and Nat slept. "What were we talking about?"

"The fact that the whole county knows we're here, thanks to Esteban hollering his location to the four winds," Jemma said.

"King Cullum himself probably knows what we're up to by now."

"I was following orders," Esteban said sullenly.

"We didn't have a choice," Archer said.

"Actually, we did." Jemma looked over at Briar's blankets and lowered her voice. "I understand she's useful, but there's no point having a powerful curse painter if we make a scene every ten miles. You should have left her on the other side of the river."

"After what she did for us?" In addition to hoisting them across the river, Briar had saved Archer's life. He had wanted to test her trustworthiness, and as far as he was concerned, she'd passed with flying colors. "She could have walked away with her new paint supplies and left me to Barden's cronies even before the river."

"This is what she does for a living," Lew said delicately. "I doubt it would hurt her feelings if we let her go with payment for services rendered."

"Lew is right," Esteban said. "She's a hired contractor. She understands this is business, probably better than you."

Archer bristled at that. "You're just annoyed because her plan to cross the river worked when you didn't think it would."

"I am not annoyed," Esteban said with what Archer was quite certain was annoyance.

"There's no point in arguing," Jemma cut in. "After all that ruckus, we should assume the authorities on both sides of the river know what we are intending to do, curse painter or no curse painter. Larke will prepare accordingly."

"Let's not overstate the problem." Archer pulled an arrow from his quiver and used it to scratch an itch on his back. "They know where we are, but that doesn't mean they know we're trying to rescue—"

"You told Kurt yourself," Jemma said. "If he sold you out to the town watch, nothing will stop him from selling that information to others."

"I am counting on it."

"What?"

Archer figured this was as good a time as any to tell them the new plan, which he'd worked out as they rode through the night. After what Kurt had told him about Horatio Drake's failure at Larke Castle, he was certain the old plan had to go. And there was another part of the job he hadn't told them about yet.

"I'm counting on Kurt peddling the information I gave him like golden teeth. He'll send the authorities in the wrong direction."

"I get it," Lew said, combing his fingers through his red beard. "A bluff."

Jemma looked skeptical. "So, where does he think we're going?"

"Larke Castle."

Lew's grin faded.

"And where do *you* think we're going?"

Archer prepared to leap up and run for it if one of them decided to thrash him for what he was about to say. He ought to be able to escape Jemma, Lew, and Esteban by virtue of sheer youth and stamina.

"I know you're going to hate me for this, Jem," he said, "but I have reason to believe Larke has chosen a location other than his castle for Lady Mae's confinement."

"Her *what*?"

"Her confinement. Her lying-in. Her labor and delivery."

Jemma's face paled, looking ghostly in the moonlight. "You can't be serious."

"Serious as a taxman." Archer glanced at the huddled forms of Briar and Nat.

They were definitely still asleep, though Nat's snoring made it sound as though he had transformed into a bear. A bear with a sore throat, who was in the middle of being choked to death.

Archer turned back to the three older members of the team, the core group he trusted more than his own flesh and blood. "Lady Mae is going to have a baby," he said, "which means we have to rescue two people, who will hopefully still be attached by the time we get there. But after talking to Kurt, I no longer think they're in Larke Castle at all."

"You're going to be the death of me, Iva—Archer," Jemma said, massaging her temples with grimy hands.

Archer winced. That slip of the tongue wasn't like her.

"If you say you're the father, I shall have my darling, docile husband beat you within an inch of your life."

"I am not the father," Archer said, "but I have a vested interest in this child's survival. I couldn't risk Lord Barden finding out about it while we were on his side of the river."

"You didn't trust us?" Jemma asked.

"Weren't you threatening to have Lew beat me within an inch of my life a second ago?"

"But after everything we've done for you—"

"It's not about me," Archer said. "This is bigger than me. It's even bigger than Mae and her baby, who we will henceforth refer to as her 'complication.'" He glanced over at Briar again. "I think she's with us, but I don't want her to find out about the baby until we see how she responds to the change in targets. She'll have to prepare a whole new set of curses."

"And we'll have to come up with a whole new plan." Jemma rubbed her temples so hard it was a wonder she didn't break the skin. "Are you one hundred percent certain Mae is not in Larke Castle?"

"Yes," Archer said without hesitation. He was only about eighty-nine percent certain, but they didn't need to know that. Lord Larke wouldn't want anyone to discover Mae's condition. On reflection, the castle was far too busy to keep a secret like that. He should have realized it even before Kurt told him about Horatio Drake's disappointment. But the castle wasn't the only secure place Jasper Larke owned.

"Well, where is she, then?" Esteban grumbled.

"Yes, spit it out, lad," Lew said, taking his notebook from his vest pocket. "We have schemes to plan."

"I believe Mae and her bouncing bundle of complication are being held in Narrowmar Stronghold."

There was a moment of silence, during which Archer heard a faint, sleepy sigh from Briar. She had stopped tossing and turning, but it sounded as if her dreams were troubled. He knew a thing or two about that.

"Impossible," Esteban said hoarsely. "We barely had a chance with the castle. We will not remove anything from Narrowmar that Larke wants to keep there, living or dead."

"I have faith in us," Archer said. "I fully expect to get both of them out alive." His fist tightened on the arrow, bending the shaft. "I'm willing to die trying, though I understand if the rest of you don't feel that way."

"Oh, don't pretend you're the only brave and noble soul here," Lew said. He glanced at his wife, his face sober. "We all agreed to do whatever it takes."

Jemma sat utterly still. Archer held his breath. Jemma knew more about Narrowmar than most of them. She understood the risks the change in direction would involve. For a heart-squeezing moment, he was afraid she would say no, afraid she would say it was impossible. But she met her husband's eyes steadily, then she pulled her red shawl tighter around her shoulders and nodded to Archer.

He released a breath. Once Jemma gave her assent, the others would as well.

"Fine," Esteban muttered. "We'll figure out a way."

"Good," Archer said. "So, shall we talk about our new route? I'd like to sleep a wink before the sun rises."

Their new course would change everything. He was about to take a massive gamble, but at least the others finally knew how perilous Mae's condition was. He pictured her sunny smile, her quick laugh, her terrible taste in food—and men. She hurled herself headlong into every pursuit, sometimes to her peril. He wished she'd made some different choices, but she didn't deserve to bear her child in that spooky old stronghold, surrounded by her father's enemies. Archer wished *he'd* made some different choices too. Then maybe neither of them would be in this mess.

It felt good not to carry the secret alone anymore. Archer was one of the few people Mae had told about her pregnancy. He had visited her in Barden Vale six months before while preparing for an elaborate burglary that would have relieved her father of the many gifts and trophies he kept in his great hall. Archer had warned Mae not to share the happy news with anyone—even the child's father. The suggestion had offended her deeply. Archer's face still stung from the slap, which he might have deserved, except that he was absolutely right about the baby's father.

Mae must have told him. There could be no other explanation for why Lord Larke would break the king's truce and steal Lord Barden's daughter. Archer doubted Lord Barden knew about his grandchild. Otherwise, he would march on Larke Castle openly and bring the king's wrath down on both counties. He wouldn't waste time offering discreet ransoms and skirmishing in the Mud Market with Larke's goons. Archer couldn't wait to see the look on Barden's face when he was the one who collected the reward for Mae's rescue.

As if that's what this is about. Even he couldn't pretend the money was his primary motivation anymore, but the team deserved it after all their trouble.

Just hold on a little longer, Mae. We're coming.

THIS IS THE STORY OF A MISSION. It was an important mission, bigger than a damsel in distress and a spell-guarded fortress and a merry band of thieves. It was the kind of mission that could shake the earth if it succeeded—or if it failed. The outlaw called Archer alone knew how the kidnapping of the damsel would reverberate across forests and counties and make the world a demonstrably worse place. Saving her would surely be considered noble, but Archer didn't care about that any more than he cared about the reward.

For him, the mission was personal.

CHAPTER 12

Narrowmar Stronghold was tucked into the base of the Bandon Mountains a week's ride north of the Sweetwater River. Archer feared switching their destination would put them farther behind schedule, but Lew knew a route that would shave a day off the journey. They set off into a hardscrabble wilderness full of towering rock formations and wind-ravaged scrubs.

Everything between the Sweetwater and the Bandon Mountains belonged to the Larke barony. Archer knew the countryside well, but it had been years since he'd last crossed those lands. He hoped Lew's shortcut would make up for the time he had squandered in Mud Market. Travel would only get more difficult for Mae in her condition. They needed to get her out of Narrowmar with time to spare before her baby arrived.

They followed a treasure map of large rock formations and scattered settlements through the lower reaches of Larke County, keeping a careful watch out for Lord Larke's tax collecting parties and the burgundy uniforms of his household retainers. The last thing they needed was to cross paths with the lord himself before they reached the stronghold. Fortunately, the bare, windswept region remained quiet, and they encountered only shepherds and lonely peddlers on the packed-dirt roads.

They spent much of their time debating the best strategy to infiltrate Narrowmar. Jemma led the discussion, and the puzzle proved difficult even with her experience of the place. Esteban rode slumped over in his saddle, still recovering his strength after the encounter with Mage Radner, but he roused himself to offer the occasional suggestion. When the debates grew heated, Lew sometimes split off from the group to ride ahead or behind. He valued his solitude, and Archer was happy to indulge his loner tendencies in exchange for the use of his sharp scout's eyes. Nat was less bothered by the details of the plan. He spent most of his time pestering Briar with questions about her magic.

Briar herself acted more relaxed since she'd gotten paint supplies again, no longer on the verge of running for the hills or fighting like a cornered badger at the slightest threat. Whenever they stopped to make camp, she could be found grinding up pigment or boiling flax to make more linseed oil. She took out the horsehair brushes she'd bought in Mud Market to test her creations, producing little explosions and puffs of smoke and dust.

Archer was beginning to feel as if Briar had always been with them. He appreciated the way she examined the world with those wide, solemn eyes and the way she didn't shirk from difficult tasks, whether cursing them out of trouble or helping to build the campfire and care for the horses. After their caper in the Mud Market, he hoped she might consider a more permanent role with the team. Her skills were bleeding useful, and Nat would like having her around. Yes, it was just *Nat's* feelings Archer was thinking of. The lad was smitten.

He wished Nat wouldn't take up so much of Briar's attention, though. Archer sent him out on errands to give her a break—and took his place at her side as often as not. He liked the way her fingers moved when she unpacked her paints, the way she sat on her horse like she was about to take it over a jump.

He frequently found himself riding next to her as they got deeper into the desolate countryside, chatting about the weather, about curses, about the rock formations squashed together like crooked teeth.

"Think Sheriff will catch up?" she asked on their second afternoon in Larke County.

"Huh?"

"Your dog," Briar said. "I was worried about him when we crossed the river."

For a minute Archer couldn't think straight. "You were?"

Briar looked at him questioningly, as if she didn't understand why he was pleased to distraction. Sheriff would have been delighted to know she cared about him too.

"He'll find us." Archer shifted in his saddle, fingers brushing the curse she'd painted on the pommel. "He always does."

"It might be wiser for him to avoid Narrowmar."

Archer glanced over at her. "How much do you know about the place?"

Briar studied a rock formation that looked like a turtle with stubby stone legs. "Not much. It's supposed to be impenetrable."

"That's what they say."

"And the magical protections might be different than the ones we planned for at Larke Castle."

Archer shrugged, trying not to let on how worried he was about that exact problem. "It's a challenge. I know you like those. You could do what no other curse painter has done before."

"That's not always a good thing," Briar said. "You start

trying to surpass what's been done before, and pretty soon you're in danger of stepping over the line."

"I, for one, have always liked crossing lines," Archer said with a wink.

Briar looked at him steadily. "In my business, that can be deadly."

Archer shifted in his saddle, finding her wide brown eyes too intense for once. Briar seemed troubled by her work, at war with herself, even though she was more relaxed with paints in hand than without them.

"Are you still up for the job?" he asked.

"I said I would do it."

Her tone sounded distant and guarded once more. Archer wondered about her history. Her accent suggested she'd lived in High Lure before moving to Sparrow Village, and Jemma believed she'd killed people before. To his surprise, the more he got to know her, the more plausible that sounded. They were all keeping secrets on top of secrets next to more secrets.

He would do well to be cautious, and he should warn Nat not to get too attached.

By their third day in Larke County, the twisted rocks and gnarled scrub gave way to rolling sunlit fields scattered with farmhouses. The cultivated fields and sheep grazing in grassy pastures gave the valley an idyllic, pastoral feeling. Villages were dotted here and there, each composed of little more than a strip of houses, a market, and a blacksmith.

They replenished their supplies when needed, no more than two of them going into the villages at a time. Archer himself stayed out of sight. He had history in those lands—and he wasn't particularly proud of the things he'd done there. The cool north wind blowing through his hair carried memories he'd long since left behind. Each day they became harder to ignore. He found himself tugging up the collar of his indigo coat anytime they passed farmers on the road, just in case they recognized him.

By contrast, Briar's guarded manner relaxed bit by bit as they got farther north. She spoke more freely, and Archer even caught her smiling sometimes. She indulged Nat's endless questions and listened graciously when Lew read snippets of poetry from the notebook he kept in his vest pocket. She became increasingly involved in the discussions about how to tackle the job ahead, asking about Narrowmar's layout, history, and possible defenses. She'd even come to an uneasy truce with Esteban, though Archer didn't understand why. Perhaps her work back by the Sweetwater had impressed the voice mage as much as it had impressed Archer.

Four days after they crossed into Larke County, Briar rode up beside Archer as the afternoon light turned gold and hazy.

"I've been working on something for you." Her saddle creaked as she leaned toward him. "There's one set for everyone, but I can make more if needed."

She held out a small burlap bag made from the sack they'd ruined while trying to get the paint supplies out of Mud Market. Small objects clicked together inside as he accepted it.

"What are they?" Archer asked.

"Curse stones."

He nearly dropped the little bag on the ground.

"They won't work unless you touch the stone directly." Her tone became noticeably drier. "That's why they're in the bag."

"Right."

"These are sturdier versions of those scrap curses I told you about. The stones are all different, so make sure you grab the right one. Use a glove or the side of the bag to touch them."

Archer opened the bag carefully and peered inside, where he found three stones of different colors, tiny images painted on them with a fine brush. He imagined they hummed with magic, though that could have just been the wind.

"What do they do?"

"The blue one puts someone to sleep," Briar said. "They'll go under as soon as you touch them, but you have to rest the stone on their skin once they're down."

"What happens if it loses contact with their skin?"

"They'll wake up instantly."

"So be ready to run?"

"Exactly. The gray stone with the white design unlocks any door, providing it doesn't have a spell on it. I've only ever done those on canvas, which tends to wear out quickly." Briar's voice took on an eager tone, a hint of genuine pride in her work. "I'm hoping painting it on stone will mean you can unlock several doors before the curse wears out. We might need them inside the stronghold."

"Brilliant. And the black one?" The darkest stone had flecks of yellow and brown swirled into the black paint.

Briar hesitated, her eyes darkening despite the sunlight.

"That'll cut like a knife," she said. "And the wound will keep bleeding unless a mage heals it."

"Whoa, Briar, don't you make any nice curses?"

A pained expression flashed across Briar's face, almost too quickly to catch, and her eagerness vanished. "I wasn't sure if I should include that one, but after those men almost killed us, I thought ... Just don't use it unless you absolutely have to. Please."

"I won't." Archer felt bad for making light of Briar's contribution. She had asked not to kill anyone, but a cut that required mage healing would be a death sentence in many cases. Giving one to each of them had cost her, and the significance wasn't lost on him. "Thank you for this."

Briar blushed, tugging a strand of hair across her cheek. "It's nothing."

Archer knew it wasn't nothing. Esteban and Lew were wrong. It wasn't just another job to Briar. She might not know it herself yet, but somewhere along the way—perhaps in Mud Market or after the Sweetwater crossing—she had started to consider herself part of the team too.

Briar rode off to give the others their bags of curse stones. Nat listened so carefully to her instructions, he let his horse wander off and chew on the long grass at the roadside. Briar had to follow him into the weeds to finish her explanation. Nat held the bag of curse stones with such reverence that Archer nearly took it just so he would pay attention to his surroundings.

"I can handle this, Archer," Nat said fervently. "Blue for sleep. Gray for locks. Black for death. Easy."

Briar grimaced at the reference to death, but she didn't correct him. She moved on to present a bag of stones to Esteban, who accepted them with sullen politeness. He appeared to be trying to be more cordial to the curse painter, but cordiality for Esteban was a large stride away from civil for everyone else.

"Our curse painter is certainly full of surprises," Jemma muttered, falling in beside Archer. She held the bag of curses as if it were a dead rat.

"Even you can see how useful these will be."

"I'm not complaining," Jemma said. "But I don't think we've seen our last surprise from Miss Briar. I told you she's dangerous."

Archer didn't argue, but whatever dangerous past Briar had left behind, it had nothing to do with their mission. She might be at war with herself over how she wanted to use her abilities, but she would get the job done. He felt increasingly confident that hiring her had been the right move, no matter what she was hiding.

CHAPTER 13

Briar was determined to crack the puzzle of Narrowmar Stronghold. Set directly into a natural fissure in the mountains, it made an even more interesting challenge than Larke Castle. She mulled over how to tackle the fortress as they veered to the northeast through sprawling farmland. Ruins scattered across the surrounding countryside suggested the area had once been far more populated, its inhabitants owing fealty to the lords of Narrowmar. In ancient days, it had housed the kings of a lost nation.

Briar didn't mind the change in destination. Narrowmar was as far from High Lure as one could get without leaving the kingdom. No one out there would recognize the young woman formerly known as Elayna Rose Dryden.

But by their fifth day in Larke County, they still hadn't figured out how they were going to break into the stronghold. Archer seemed confident they would find a way in, even though Narrowmar had never fallen in its centuries-long history. Jemma had been there before, and she'd drawn them rough maps of its interior and surroundings, but she had precious little information about its magical defenses. Briar didn't have the purple paint to unravel magical protections, anyway. They would need a more creative solution.

She worked with her paints by firelight, the magic surging in her fingers, colors dancing before her eyes. No matter how much she claimed she wanted a quiet life, practicing serious magic still thrilled her. She couldn't quit entirely, even though that would have been one way to live the good life that had eluded her. Saving the others with her ambulatory curses had been both exhilarating and deeply satisfying, giving her just a hint of what her curse magic could become. She wanted to capture that feeling again, but the problem of Narrowmar confounded her.

Only Esteban could help, although he didn't create any magic himself lest it give away their position. A fragile rapport had developed between them since the Sweetwater. They occasionally talked about their respective art forms, choosing their words with care. On the fifth evening, when they had camped by a spring at the edge of a wheat field, Briar asked Esteban how he'd known which spells protected Larke Castle.

"Archer sent me to investigate while he was taking care of another task."

"What task?"

"I don't share other people's secrets." Esteban gave a dry cough. "I'm extending the same courtesy to you."

"Fair enough."

They were sitting near the campfire, Esteban polishing the silver tooling on his boots. He had a fastidious streak, and his fine clothes were always pristine. Archer and Nat practiced archery nearby, the thud of metal striking a tree stump providing the background rhythm for their conversation. Lew sat by the bubbling spring with a notebook on his knee and a quill between his teeth. Jemma sorted through their food supplies over by the horses.

Briar twirled a paintbrush between her fingers, considering

the old mage. "Do you think we'll find all the same spells at Narrowmar?"

"Doubtful," Esteban said. "Narrowmar has only one entrance, a great stone door in the mountainside. Those spells were more appropriate for a building with many access points and a less stable structure."

"Do you think the same mage secured it at least?"

"That I don't know. Larke wants people to think the young lady is in his castle. It would raise suspicion if he sent his most trusted voice mage—his name is Croyden—off to his remote stronghold. Croyden has served him for two decades and rarely leaves his side."

"Do you know him well?"

"Croyden?" Esteban's gaunt face twitched. "We've run into each other on several occasions. He's a self-important fopdoodle who thinks—no matter. Larke could have hired another for the task of guarding Narrowmar."

Briar sighed, dabbing her paintbrush in a slick of malachite green. "The fortress is secure enough without magic."

Esteban picked at a speck of ash on his sleeve. "If Larke thinks that's the case, it will likely make your job easier."

"How so?"

"There are only so many protective spells you can put on one door."

Briar went still. *But what if we don't use the door?*

The rough outline of a plan floated suddenly before her, a wisp of inspiration. She closed her eyes, trying to grab hold of it before it slipped away. Her idea was ambitious, especially since she would need to work very fast to keep from getting caught.

"I think I have something," she murmured.

Esteban sat silently for a moment, seeming to sense her need for concentration. When she didn't share her thoughts, he shuffled away, his fine boots scraping the dirt.

Briar sat with her eyes closed, considering the shape of the necessary paintings, the potential obstacles. Her typical stable of curses might not be enough. Her parents had always liked to experiment, and they believed they hadn't yet reached the limits of what curse magic could do. She might need to invent a new technique to avoid some of the more obvious problems—problems that would likely stop a lesser curse painter from even considering her approach. No matter what, it would require more power than she had ever used for a single task. She would be at risk of exhausting herself before the job was done, but it just might work.

Her fingers tingling with anticipation, Briar opened a jar of brown ochre, selected a flat stone from the spring, and began a new curse.

⚜

"You look like you could use a break."

Briar looked up to find Archer squatting on his heels beside her. She rubbed her eyes, surprised at how dark it had become. She must have lost track of time. She hadn't heard Archer's arrows hitting the target in a while. She had been painting rock after rock, practicing destructive curses that would eat holes into stone. When the inspiration had seized her, she hadn't dared pause in case the idea slipped away.

"Working too hard is bad for your health, you know," Archer said.

Briar rolled her shoulders, attempting to loosen the tension that had built up without her noticing. The fire burned low, and the others were already snoozing in their bedrolls.

"I didn't want to lose momentum," she said. "I'll go to sleep in a minute."

"You could sleep," Archer said, "or you could join me on a quick errand."

"Now?"

"I have an old debt to pay. Wouldn't mind a little company." He held out a hand.

Briar hesitated. She wanted to take his hand, but lead white and umber paint streaked her palms, and her fingernails were stained with blue smalt from the sleep stones she'd made earlier.

"I promise I won't bite," Archer said when she didn't move.

"Well, why didn't you say so sooner?" Briar wiped her hands on a rag, feeling oddly flustered, and scrambled to her feet without taking Archer's hand.

He shrugged and nodded toward the darkness beyond the spring. "This way, if you please."

Jemma had the watch, and she was sitting cross-legged on the other side of the spring with her shawl wrapped tightly around her. Her eyes narrowed as Archer and Briar strolled past. Archer gave her a toothy grin and offered no explanation.

"Where are we going?" Briar asked as they left the camp behind and walked along the edge of a vast wheat field.

"You'll see." Archer winked. "I'd hate to ruin the suspense."

He swung his arms casually as he strolled through the night, seeming to know exactly where he was going. Briar kept a hand on the bag of curse stones she'd slipped into her pocket. Archer acted at ease with her, as if he truly trusted her, but she couldn't strip away the wariness of a lifetime so easily.

The fresh-cut aroma of harvest season tickled her nose and made her skin itch. The farmers had been scything across their lands, piling straw in stacks and bringing the wheat in for threshing. The crispness of early autumn filled the air, and the stars burned bright overhead. It would be their last night in the open countryside before they reached the forest pooling at the bottom of the Bandon Mountains and disappeared once more into the trees.

"What were you working on so intently back there?" Archer asked after a while.

A smile tugged at Briar's lips. "I have an idea for how to get into Narrowmar—something I didn't even consider at first because of the dangers involved. I don't know if it'll work yet, but if it does, we should be able to build a solid plan around it."

"I knew you'd come up with something." Archer glanced down at her. "There doesn't seem to be much you can't do with your curses."

"Well, I need a few more trials," Briar said. "I don't want to promise anything I can't deliver."

"You're very particular about your work."

"Isn't that why you hired me?"

"I suppose it is." Archer nudged her playfully with his elbow. "I ought to send Willem Winton a gift for bringing us together. I hear he likes ornate armor."

Briar snorted. She wasn't sure what to make of Archer's behavior toward her lately. He had threatened her and told her explicitly she wasn't part of the team, yet he also flirted with her and seemed to genuinely appreciate her skills. His admiration rattled her more than the threats.

"So, what's this debt you need to pay?" she asked. "And why tonight, when we're trying to avoid notice?"

Archer sobered, and she couldn't read his expression in the darkness.

"I blame you for this, actually. Your insistence on only cursing people who deserve it got me thinking about some of the less-than-noble jobs I've pulled off. One in particular stuck with me."

They reached the far corner of the wheat field and turned down a path strewn with chaff. A hint of music drifted through the night. It was faint at first, distant, but soon it swelled into a tapping, stomping rhythm. The sounds of laughter and conversation spilled toward them.

Briar slowed. "Maybe we shouldn't—"

"No one will see us. Don't worry so much."

Briar followed Archer apprehensively toward the noise. They had avoided people as much as possible since entering Larke County, and she wasn't sure why he would walk toward them now.

A little farmhouse was nestled between the wheat field and a dark-green expanse of alfalfa. Beside the house rose a large barn. Torchlight flooded out of its wide-open doors, dulling the stars. People milled between the house and the barn, dressed in humble clothing of rough wool and scuffed leather.

Briar caught Archer's sleeve. "We can't—"

"Shh, over here." Archer slipped through the darkness alongside the barnyard to where a wagon lay just outside the spill of light. He hid behind it, positioning himself so he could watch the barnyard.

Briar crouched beside him, certain they would be spotted at any moment, but the farmers were having too much fun to pay attention to the strangers skulking in the shadows. They chatted and laughed and tapped their feet to the music. Many wore bright knit scarves or ribbons in their hair. Inside the barn, a table was spread with the remnants of a large meal.

A thin, dark-haired man stood by the barn door playing the fiddle. A young girl with similar features sat beside him, keeping time on a calfskin drum. Father and daughter struck up a livelier tune, and the others began to dance, twirling across a packed-dirt area that likely doubled as a threshing floor.

"They do this at different farms most nights throughout the harvest season," Archer whispered in Briar's ear. "They like to have a little fun after the threshing."

The farmers danced faster, kicking up dust and chaff, filling the barnyard with motion. Briar spotted a few family resemblances—hair of a particularly red shade, a unique knobby nose—and she guessed four or five local families plus their hired hands were gathered for the celebration.

"It's our lucky night," Archer said. "This'll keep them busy."

"What exactly are we doing here?"

"I stole from the family who works this farm a few years back." Archer's voice lowered, becoming serious. "I was desperate, and I probably would have starved if I hadn't. Still, I prefer to steal from people who have coin to spare. Since we're in the neighborhood ..."

He drew a fat purse out of his pocket and tossed it in the air, catching it with a metallic clink.

"You're paying them back." Briar was starting to realize she knew very little about thieves—and this thief in particular. The purse looked heavy. The family had probably never owned that much coin. "With interest."

"It's your fault really," Archer said. "I guess you could say I was inspired."

Briar blushed, tucking a strand of hair behind her ear. She was hardly the type of person to inspire good deeds in others.

"Why do you need me, though? You want me to paint a distraction?"

"I don't need you," Archer said. "I mean—I just wanted your company." He cleared his throat, turning so she couldn't see his expression. "Follow me."

They left the shelter of the wagon and crept toward the farmhouse, music and laughter filling the night behind them. Archer moved stealthily, his boots barely making a sound in the grass. He climbed the front porch in two long strides and bent to lay the purse on the stoop.

Suddenly the farmhouse door swung open, nearly hitting Archer in the face. Briar's hand went to the curse stones in her pocket. A small boy stood in the doorway holding a cat slung dejectedly over one arm. The boy looked about five years old. He stared at Archer, who stood frozen like a child with his hand in a sweet jar.

"Who are you?"

"Uh, hello," Archer said. "I'm, uh, a traveler."

"You want some food?"

"No, thank you," Archer said. "I was just—"

"Mama!" the boy shouted into the house. "We got more hungry people out here!"

"We don't—"

Before Archer could retreat from the porch, a woman appeared at the door behind the little boy. She was young and pretty, with wispy brown hair and bright-green eyes.

"Can I help you folks?"

"We're just passing through, ma'am." Archer held up the coin purse, his accent becoming noticeably rougher. "I was hopin' to buy a spot of food for the road."

"Nonsense," the woman said. "We have plenty to spare, at least for tonight. Come on out back."

"We don't want to impose," Briar said quickly. "We need to return to our camp before—"

"Don't be silly," the woman said. "Half the valley is here anyway." She caught sight of the way her little son was holding the cat and gave an exasperated sigh. "Put her down, Abie, and go ask Grampa to fix up two more plates."

The little boy relinquished his hold on the cat—who immediately bolted for the safety of the fields—and ran around the side of the house toward the barn.

"Where are you all headed?" the young mother asked as she followed more slowly with Archer and Briar.

"New Chester," Archer said at once.

"Oh, I haven't been that far north in years," the woman said. "I grew up west of here, over t'ward Shortfall Lake."

Archer's steps faltered. "We really shouldn't stay," he said. "Looks like you folks are busy here."

"Not many villages in these parts," the woman said. "We eat what we can grow or catch, mostly. If you don't have enough food, you won't buy it for a day yet."

"We don't want to interrupt your celebration," Briar said, sensing that the woman's origins made Archer nervous. Shortfall Lake was right beside Larke Castle. They reached the torchlit barnyard, where the dancing had become more exuberant.

"It's just a harvest dance." The woman grinned. "We don't need much excuse for a dance and a good meal round here. The more the merrier."

A few people looked up curiously as the woman led the two strangers into their midst, including the dark-haired fiddler, who missed a few notes when he spotted them weaving through the dancers. The little drummer girl gave an exasperated cry, and he set to his fiddle once more.

"My husband," the woman said, nodding at the fiddler. "He's careful of strangers, but I reckon you folks aren't here to steal if you come waving coin."

"You've been robbed before," Archer said. It wasn't a question.

"Aye. We don't have it as bad as places closer to the highways." She looked them up and down then, as if realizing it was a little strange for travelers to come so far from the main roads.

"I didn't catch your name," Briar said before the woman could ask what they were doing out there.

"Juliet," the woman said.

They entered the barn, where platters of food covered a long pinewood table. Briar's mouth watered at the sight—chicken legs, fat brown sausages, bowls full of berries, the nubby end of a loaf of brown bread. A few sturdy ponies chomped away at their evening meals, their flanks still wet from a long day in the fields. A farmhand was snoozing on a pile of straw nearby, an empty mug in hand.

At the table, a spry old man was piling food onto a plate as the little boy held it steady.

"You've met my Abie," Juliet said, "and this is my father."

"Evening, folks." The old man glanced up from the plate. "Will it be chicken or sausage or both?"

"Both," Archer said at the same time Briar said, "Chicken, please."

"I'll give you a bit of everything," he said. "Don't drop that now, Abie."

Only after he'd filled the second plate did the old man pause to study them. He watched them juggle their plates and wooden spoons, his gray-eyed gaze lingering on Archer's long belt knife and Briar's paint-stained hands.

"You're travelers?"

"Just passing through, sir," Archer said. "I'm Fletcher, and this is Rose."

Briar stiffened at the sound of her real middle name. Just a coincidence. Rose was a common enough name.

"They call me Grampa," said the old man. "I reckon you can, too, so long as you like my cooking."

"Much obliged."

While they ate, Archer chatted amiably with the older man and the young mother. Briar was impressed with the way Archer's accent seemed to mirror theirs, as if he hadn't grown up all that far from their farm. The lilt was markedly different from the way he'd spoken to those men back in Mud Market and the way he ordinarily talked to the team.

He didn't speak without purpose, though. He slipped in questions about how often they saw the sheriff of that particular county and when they'd last seen Lord Larke, who was supposed to be out collecting taxes.

Grampa spit in the dirt. "His men have already been this year, though I reckon they'll be back when they hear how good the wheat harvest is. Wouldn't be the first time they've taken an extra cut."

Archer wiped his mouth and set aside his plate. "I hear

Larke's taxes are higher than those of the other outer-county barons."

"He claims it's for the king," Juliet said. "We know he pads his own coffers."

"Can't you appeal to King Cullum if he's gouging you?" Briar asked.

"And get our fields burned for our troubles?" Juliet shook her head. "Complaining only makes it worse."

Briar ground her teeth, thinking suddenly of a wildflower wreath in a faraway smithy. It wasn't fair that poorer people had no recourse when the country lords and their friends took advantage. She understood why Archer wanted to pay them back for the coins he'd stolen. She wished she had something to offer too.

"Have you ever met Lord Larke?" Archer asked.

"Years ago, when he toured the county with his eldest son," Grampa said. "He'll be just as bad as his father, by all accounts."

"Tomas," Archer said, his dark eyebrows lowering. "Lord Larke's son is called Tomas, right?"

"Aye. Larke is still as hale as ever, though. I reckon it'll be a while yet before we have to deal with his heir."

"Mama, come outside!" someone called from the barn door. The little drummer girl appeared, clutching wooden drumsticks. "We're going to play your favorite song."

"I wouldn't miss it, darling." Juliet smiled at them. "Excuse me."

Archer and Briar finished their meal and moved to help Grampa clean up the plates.

He waved them away. "Go on and enjoy yourselves for a bit, folks. I'll pack up some leftovers for your journey."

Archer tried to press his coin purse into the man's hands. "For your troubles."

Grampa frowned. "Unless this is full of brass, it's too much."

"Please take it," Archer said. "Just don't tell the taxman."

"We don't take charity, Mister Fletcher."

"And I don't give it," Archer said, closing Grampa's gnarled hands firmly around the purse. "I have to pay for our meal. *I* don't know what meat costs in these parts."

The older man studied Archer with narrowed eyes, something solemn and unspoken passing between them.

"For the grandkids," Archer prompted.

At last Grampa nodded. "For the grandkids."

Archer turned suddenly to Briar. "Fancy a dance, Rose?"

She was too surprised to object as he grabbed her hand and pulled her out into the barnyard. He seemed lighter on his feet, as if that purse had weighed on him more than the coins it contained, and his smile was wide and bright.

Juliet twirled with Abie in the middle of the threshing floor while her husband and daughter played the lively tune. Sweat dampened their collars, and pink stained their cheeks. The other farmers either clapped their hands or danced in an unruly circle around them, no longer paying attention to the two travelers.

"I think I know this one," Archer said. Then he hooked his arm around Briar's waist without warning and spun her into the fray.

She could barely follow the steps. Archer's boots beat an uneven rhythm in the dirt, joyous as a summer rainstorm. His dancing was exuberant and wholly unskilled. Briar had never encountered anyone who danced so terribly with such confidence.

"I don't think this is right," she gasped, clinging to his arms to keep from flying right off her feet.

"When has that ever stopped me? Now spin!"

Briar spun, her hair flying around her face, half blinding her. She nearly careened into another couple, but Archer pulled her in close at the last second, catching her against his chest. He held her, his heartbeat thundering in time with hers, and she smelled the clean sweat on his shirt, a hint of wheat and honey. Then he spun her out again.

Soon, Briar was breathless from trying to keep up. By the time the song ended, she was laughing.

"Now there's a sound I wasn't sure I'd ever hear," Archer said as they escaped to the side of the dance floor, chests heaving and faces flushed.

The farmers were already calling out requests for the next song.

"It's your dancing," she said, unable to suppress her giggles.

"What's wrong with it?"

"Nothing, it's just ... vigorous."

"That's a nice way of saying bleedin' awful." Archer grinned. "I know my strengths and weaknesses, Rose."

Briar's smile faded. "What made you pick that name?"

"Sweetbriar roses used to grow in my mother's garden, may she rest." His mouth turned up in a half smile. "I still remember the smell, like sweet apples, even though the roses died soon after she did."

"They were my mother's favorite flower too," Briar said.

"Yeah? What was she like?"

Archer looked down at her expectantly, as if they could just chat about their mothers like it was the most ordinary thing in the world. But Briar hadn't had an ordinary mother.

When she didn't speak, he reached out as if to touch her arm. "I'm sorry. You don't have to—"

"She was intense." Briar looked up and found his gaze steady on her face. There was something more than curiosity there, and her stomach fluttered. "Not the sort of woman you would expect to have a favorite flower, actually. We lived in the city, where we couldn't grow them, but she would seek out the sweetbriar roses anytime we visited the countryside or a clien —a *friend* with a garden."

The words came in a rush, and Briar found herself wanting

to say more. She wanted to tell him exactly how intense her mother had been. She wanted to describe the roar of the sea a few streets from her childhood home. She wanted to talk about the cool spray on her face when she snuck to the beach, the way the sand mixed with her paints and muddied the colors, but she held back. Archer might be an outlaw, but he had a goodness about him, too, almost an innocence. He wouldn't understand what Briar had been in that city by the sea.

Somewhere along the way, what Archer thought had started to matter to her. She'd insisted she only wanted to do the one job to make enough coin to start her new life, but something made her want to linger. Being with Archer was like being dropped from a great height and painting a powerful curse and rolling up in a warm blanket all at once.

She still didn't know what had happened between him and Lady Mae—or what their relationship was—but she had to wonder if he felt what she had when they'd danced.

In the barnyard, the little girl set aside her drums, and the fiddler switched to a slower, sweeter tune. The farmers began to pair up, swaying through the firelight with gentler steps.

Archer stepped closer to Briar. He didn't speak, his face a question Briar wasn't sure she was ready to answer. Her breath hitched as if she were standing at the edge of a precipice, deciding whether or not to leap.

The slow song curled around them, as tantalizing as the aroma of sweetbriar roses.

She swallowed, her throat dry. "Another dance?"

For the space of a smile, Archer looked as if dancing with her was the only thing he wanted in the entire world. He leaned toward her, hand extending. Then a shadow crossed his face, and he shook his head. His hand dropped into a fist at his side. "We've already stayed too long. We should get back before Jemma worries."

"Oh. Sure." Briar straightened her skirt, trying to pretend the sudden reversal didn't sting. "Lead the way."

Archer hesitated, as if he wanted to say something else after all, then he turned resolutely into the darkness.

They slipped away from the farm without taking any more of the family's food and walked single file along the edge of the field.

Briar studied Archer's back as she followed him to camp, neither of them speaking. A breeze whispered through ripe wheat and stirred his unruly hair. She didn't want to read too much into a single dance, but she had seen the way he sometimes looked at her when he thought she wasn't watching. And she hadn't imagined the way he'd been leaning toward her, the way he had stolen the breath from her chest.

Briar knew that if he asked her to stay with the team then and there—to stay with him—she would say yes. But whatever Archer felt for her, he chose not to act on it when he had ample opportunity. That told her enough.

Still, as they walked silently back to camp, the memory of the bright barnyard lingered, the families spinning across the earth after a good day's work. After fleeing her parents' home, Briar had struggled to create a picture of the life she wanted instead of the one they'd modelled for her. She had loved the smell of wood smoke, oil paint, and dry thatch in her cottage. Now, she was adding to the image—a well-spread table, laughing people, fiddles and drums. The life she wished for was becoming clearer, taking on shape and hue. When the job at Narrowmar was complete, she would be free to seek it.

CHAPTER 14

Archer could have stayed in that barnyard all night. Briar's eyes had lit up as she danced, and it was all he could do not to put his hands in her wild hair and run a thumb over her smiling lips. She was normally so guarded, but she'd given him a glimpse behind her tall, tangled walls.

He had nearly kissed her when she'd suggested another dance, but he wasn't certain she would welcome it, and when she didn't speak to him the whole way back to camp, he was glad he'd held back. Well, almost glad.

In any case, Archer judged the evening well worth a light scolding. They returned to camp much later than intended and found Jemma pacing beside the spring, as agitated as a wolf who'd wandered into poison ivy.

"You could have been murdered," Jemma said the moment Briar rolled up in her blankets by the fire, leaving them to talk privately.

"I knew the farmers were good people." Archer sat on a mossy boulder, pulled an arrow from his quiver, and began trimming the fletching with his belt knife. "Otherwise, I wouldn't have bothered paying them back in the first place."

"I'm not talking about the farmers." Jemma jerked her head toward the fire. "Why did you bring *her*?"

"I figured Briar could use a break."

"Archer."

"We went for a walk. It's not a big deal."

"I warned you about her."

"She deserves a chance," Archer said. "And she says she has an idea for a curse that'll help us crack Narrowmar. I think she's finally starting to trust me."

"But what about Mae?"

"What about her?"

"*Archer.*"

"Briar has nothing to do with Mae." His shoulders hunched involuntarily, and he didn't quite meet Jemma's eyes.

She had to be contemplating what would happen to Mae after they rescued her—and the part Archer himself would play in that. But right then, with Briar's laughter pealing like a bell in his memory, he didn't much care.

"Traveling with a woman probably made me look less threatening to the farmers. They gave me food and information instead of running me off their property."

Jemma raised an eyebrow. "Information?"

"Larke was seen heading southwest." Archer gestured with the arrow. "We can finish the job without him turning up unannounced."

Jemma was quiet for a moment. "I suppose that is good news." She cast a meaningful look at Briar's sleeping form. "But I still don't like this."

"There's no 'this' not to like." Archer stretched his arms over his head and yawned. "Why don't you get some rest, Jem? I'll finish your watch."

"Don't you dismiss me. I agreed to follow your lead, but—"

"You did," Archer cut in. "And unless you're planning to

overthrow me as the leader of this band, I'm holding you to that agreement. I know what I'm doing."

Jemma bristled, and for a few tense heartbeats, she looked like she really would challenge him. Instead, she dropped a curtsy fit for a king and marched off to her bedroll. Archer winced. He didn't like pulling rank, but the closer they got to Narrowmar, the more important it was to remain united. Besides, he *had* gotten useful information, no matter what Jemma thought of his little expedition to see the farmers, and he wouldn't trade that dance with Briar for anything.

The next morning over breakfast, Briar told them her new idea for breaking into Narrowmar. Jemma studied her with pursed lips for a long time then opened up the rough map she'd sketched of Narrowmar to begin puzzling out a strategy.

By the time the others had tucked their breakfasts into their bellies and saddled their horses, Jemma had a fully-fledged plan. It was ambitious, and Archer, for one, hadn't even known the curses Briar had proposed were possible. The plan could go wrong in a hundred different ways. That was just part of the fun.

Their journey to Bandon Forest took all morning and part of the afternoon. Archer couldn't seem to catch Briar's eye as they rode. Was she avoiding his gaze deliberately? They hadn't discussed last night's jaunt, and Archer began to question whether she even felt the pull between them. Maybe she *wasn't* spending the entire day thinking about that swift, jubilant dance and the way they'd looked at each other in the breathless moments after.

Still, he couldn't stop glancing over at her despite how studiously she ignored him. Maybe she was looking at him whenever he turned away, stealing glances as furtive as his.

They'd barely spoken a word to one another by the time they reached the forest, the final obstacle between them and Narrowmar. Bandon Forest was older than Mere Woods, treed with sparse, venerable pine. The light filtering through the branches had a misty quality, and it was quieter, too, as if fewer animals crept through the underbrush and fewer birds livened the canopy.

As they went deeper in the hushed, thoughtful forest, Archer and Briar gradually moved nearer to each other in the column of riders. Briar kept her face turned to the road, but she tugged on the reins when her horse tried to charge ahead of Archer's, casually matching his pace. He eased closer until their knees were almost touching, drawn toward her like a fish on a lure. He hummed snatches of the song they'd danced to the night before, and a blush rose in her cheeks. He would get her to smile at him yet.

Lew tried to speak to Archer, but Archer was too busy admiring the way the wind stirred Briar's wild hair and wondering what it would feel like to run his fingers through it to track the conversation. Lew snorted and rode off before whatever he was saying could register. Nat kept frowning at Archer and Briar, worrying at the mismatched buttons on his shirt, and even Esteban eyed the pair with a glum sort of curiosity.

Once Jemma shouldered her mare between them, as if to remind Archer of her disapproval. Archer trusted Jemma with his life, and in a distant way, he knew he should heed her warnings, but Briar's pull was too strong. He was tumbling toward her with a recklessness that didn't even bother him, truth be told. He could only wonder if she was falling too.

Between Briar's not-quite-glances and Jemma's glowers, the atmosphere was rather fraught, and Archer felt himself winding as tight as a bowstring as the day wore on. If he could just have a few minutes alone with Briar—

He started in surprise when frantic hoofbeats announced Lew's return from another scouting expedition. Archer had an arrow halfway out of his quiver before he realized he was reaching for it.

Lew came in fast and pulled his horse up sharply, red beard flying. His face was pale. "There's a town ahead."

"We should be coming up on New Chester," Jemma said.

"Aye," Lew said. "But something's strange about it."

"What kind of strange?" Archer asked.

"There's no people there," Lew said. "No wood smoke rising from the chimneys, no lights in the windows, but the houses aren't burned or anything like that."

Archer grimaced and caught Jemma's eye. A mutual friend of theirs had moved to New Chester to open a country inn. Archer had hoped to visit for a discreet fact-finding conversation and a good night's sleep in a real bed. New Chester was the last town before Narrowmar.

"Maybe we should go around," Esteban said.

"We need to find out what's been happening at the stronghold," Jemma said.

"It doesn't look like anyone's there to tell us." Lew rubbed the back of his neck. "It was spooky."

Nat shifted in his saddle. "I don't like this."

Archer had to agree. Lew didn't rile easily, but he kept glancing behind him at the shifting afternoon shadows. Archer tapped his fingers on his knee, weighing how much they needed to speak to their innkeeper friend before approaching Narrowmar. Tomorrow they would reach the shallow, wooded ravine that led to the entrance of the mountain stronghold. There would be no turning back then.

Briar spurred her horse forward to address Lew. "You said all the houses are intact but the people are gone?"

"That's right," Lew said.

"How about animals?"

"Didn't see any of them either."

"Or hear them?"

Lew shook his head, and Briar frowned, twisting her reins pensively.

"You think it's some kind of curse?" Archer asked.

"Possibly. I'd need a closer look to know for sure."

"You could drop dead as soon as you crossed the town boundary," Jemma said. "We can't risk it."

Briar blinked, as if surprised Jemma cared whether she lived or died. Archer supposed things were rather frosty between them. He wondered if Jemma had ever threatened to beat Briar within an inch of her life. It was something she did frequently—and she usually meant it.

"Did you see any bodies?" Briar asked Lew.

"None."

"I think I'll be okay." Briar turned to Archer, meeting his eyes fully for the first time all day. "It won't take me long. I can meet you back here."

"I'll go with you." Archer had been waiting for an excuse to be alone with her. He had half a mind to finish what they'd started last night.

"That's not necessary," she said, not sounding as if she meant it.

Archer shrugged as casually as he could manage. "You need someone to watch your back while you're sleuthing."

She smiled, and for an instant, they were dancing across a torchlit barnyard, a fiddler playing in the background. "I suppose company would be nice."

Nat pushed to the front of the group. "I'll go!"

"No," Archer said.

"Maybe he should go, Archer," Jemma said. "We still need to work out some details for the plan."

"I don't mind, honest," Nat said.

"I have a few things I wish to discuss with you as well," Esteban said. "If you stay behind, we can—"

"I said no." Archer didn't care if he was being irrational. He wanted nothing more than to sneak away with Briar again—and something in her smile told him she felt the same way. He faced the others, avoiding Jemma's flat-eyed stare. "The rest of you make camp. The horses could use an early night."

"Whatever you say, Archer." Nat dismounted with a gloomy lurch. "Not sure I'll sleep well if all the people in the next town have dropped dead, though."

"I told you there weren't any bodies," Lew said.

"If it is what I think, it won't spread here," Briar said. "We'd better go in on foot, though."

The others scoured their immediate vicinity for a good clearing in which to stay the night while Briar and Archer readied their various weapons and paint supplies for the expedition. He finished preparing first and paused to watch her transfer brushes and jars to a canvas satchel Nat had found for her somewhere. She glanced up to meet his gaze, her deep-brown eyes holding a mixture of mischief and intensity. Why had he ever thought she wasn't interested? He felt giddy, like a boy sneaking away for his first kiss behind the stables. He could hardly wait to be out of sight of the rest of the team.

Esteban edged over to the pair, tugging his scrawny mare behind him. "Would you like me to accompany you in case this is a mage's work?" The offer sounded reluctant but genuine.

"We've already passed the point where it's safe to use your powers," Archer said. "Anyone watching will know where we're going if they detect you near New Chester."

"Very well." Esteban turned to Briar, his thin shoulders hunching. "Take care of yourself in the village."

"I will," Briar said. "And thank you."

Esteban's mouth twitched in a crusty attempt at a smile

before he wandered off. *Remarkable.* It seemed old Esteban had finally warmed to Briar. If only Jemma could do the same.

Their preparations complete, Archer and Briar set off into the trees on foot. The slanting green rays of evening light gave the forest an eerie quality, all the stranger with so few birds about. Archer didn't hear a single chirp or spot so much as a flurry of feathers as they walked through the woods. The air smelled odd, too, almost dead, and it seemed to grow heavier the farther they walked. The forest hadn't felt that way the last time he was there. He didn't like it.

The peculiar atmosphere doused Archer's hopes of a romantic rendezvous like a bucket of ice water. He stayed close to Briar, half to protect her and half for the comfort of her presence. Whatever was wrong in those woods didn't feel like something he could shoot with an arrow or punch in the nose. Briar seemed equally aware of the change in the air. She had a paintbrush in one hand and a jar of red paint half-open in the other.

So much for stealing away for a kiss.

"What's your theory about what Lew saw?" Archer asked to break the uncanny silence. "Could it really be a curse?"

"It's possible to curse an entire village with a powerful enough painting," Briar said. "It uses the Law of Wholes, if you do it right. Some mages use multiple images to anchor the curse when they're working on a large space, so we'll want to check the boundaries too."

"Why would someone want to hurt the whole village?"

"I was hoping you could tell me," Briar said. "What do you know about New Chester?"

"I've been there a few times," Archer said slowly. "There isn't a whole lot to it. A few farms in a clearing, an inn, a tannery. Most people make their living hunting and trapping in the woods. Their primary export is animal pelts."

"There doesn't seem to be much game around."

"I noticed that too."

The woods ended abruptly, the trees giving way to a grassy clearing. The village sat in the center, composed of a few rows of lumpy thatched houses and a large inn, also with a thatched roof. The tannery on the opposite side of the village was missing its usual smoky haze and pungent odor. It didn't smell much like the New Chester Archer remembered.

"That looks like a livestock paddock, doesn't it?" Briar pointed to a fenced pasture near them. "No animals there either."

"I don't like this."

"I can sense something in the air, or maybe a lack of something." Briar inhaled deeply. "It's getting stronger the closer we get to the buildings."

A queasy feeling swirled through Archer's stomach. "Maybe we should just forget it," he said. "There's no one left to give us the information, and we—"

"Wait!" Briar grabbed his arm to stop him. "Hear that?"

"What—"

"Shh! Someone's talking."

Archer held his breath, listening. Briar was concentrating too hard to notice she still held his arm, but a thrill went through him at her touch all the same. She felt warm and strong and—*focus, Archer.*

Gradually he became aware of a low murmur, as if someone were having an animated conversation at the bottom of a well.

"I think they're just on the other side," Briar whispered.

"Other side of what?"

She didn't answer, still scanning the clearing intently. Then she took a tentative step forward, as if testing the temperature of a swimming hole. She gasped and pulled back.

"What is it?"

"A cloaking curse. Come on. This will feel a little strange." Her hand slipped down to clasp his.

Archer marveled at the way their hands fit perfectly

together. She tugged him forward one more step. He shivered at a sudden coldness. It was like pushing through a cloud or the spray from a waterfall. Then, just as abruptly, they were on the other side of it. The town of New Chester was still there, now bustling with people and chatter and birdsong. It looked just as it had on Archer's last visit. A cow lowed nearby, serenading the setting sun.

The animated conversation rang loud and clear. A young boy was arguing with his mother over his failure to milk the cow properly. The cow stood beside them, shifting its weight and swatting flies with its tail. The woman, boy, and cow paid no attention to Archer and Briar as they walked past, still holding hands.

"They were just hidden?" Archer asked quietly. "But why?"

"I'm not sure yet," Briar said. "I don't think this curse uses boundary paintings. Let's try to find the anchor."

They strode between the nearest houses and entered the village proper. New Chester looked just as Archer remembered, all thatched-roof houses and cozy leaded-glass windows, but something felt off. It still didn't smell right. The people went about their early-evening business, coming in from hunting or hurrying home from the market, but they didn't look at Archer or Briar at all. He rolled his shoulders uneasily. It was a small enough town that two strangers ought to have attracted a few curious glances.

"They can't see us," Briar said, as if reading his thoughts. "We're cloaked to them by the same curse that cloaked them from outside."

"Why can we see them now?"

"The curse painter must have targeted the villagers specifically when they placed the spell. We'll know more as soon as we find it."

Archer suppressed a shiver and scanned the surrounding

houses, which were built of weathered pinewood with carvings on the shutters and doors to add variety. "So, we're looking for a painting? Will it be at the dead center?"

"Possibly. It's more likely we'll find it on an important building or meeting place, somewhere that affects the whole village on a daily basis."

"The tannery?"

"That or the most popular tavern."

"I see where you're going with this." Archer nodded at the slice of the main street visible between the next row of houses. "The common room of the inn is everyone's favorite watering hole here." He tightened his grip on her hand, pleased she still hadn't pulled away. "Shall we?"

The inn, called the Sleepy Fox, was the only two-story structure in New Chester. Archer had spent a number of evenings enjoying a pint there—compliments of his friend the innkeeper. The building had a thatched roof, half a dozen guest rooms, and a spacious common room, which doubled as the village tavern. Someone was lighting candles in the windows when they reached it, the last dregs of daylight fading from the sky.

As Archer and Briar paused to study the Sleepy Fox, a man with a bushy beard stomped up the road and nearly knocked into them. His unseeing gaze passed right over them as he entered the inn. A murmur of voices drifted out the door around him.

"Sounds busy," Briar said.

"The villagers love this place," Archer said. "It's always full."

"Then this is probably where the curse is," Briar said. "We're looking for a large and intricate painting for it to have this much power."

"Understood."

They circled the outside of the building together, looking

for anything unusual. Splitting up to search would have been more efficient, but something about the way the people looked straight through them made them want to stay close to each other. Archer checked the highest planes of the building carefully, remembering how Briar had hidden her curse under the eaves of Winton's house. Nothing marked the chipped whitewash as far as he could tell, though it was growing darker by the minute.

"I didn't see anything," Archer said when they reached the front again. "Do we need to climb onto the roof? Maybe find an accommodating maple tree?"

Briar gave him a faint smile. "Curses don't take well to thatch."

"Inside, then?"

"Yes, but try not to touch anyone. I'm not sure whether or not they'll feel it."

They waited on the stoop until a red-faced woman burst out the front door and stomped down the short flight of steps. Archer released Briar's hand to catch the door as it swung shut. He was a little surprised to feel the rough grain against his palm. New Chester felt like a ghost town, and it wouldn't have shocked him if his hand had passed right through the wood.

The tavern was busy, the sturdy wooden tables filled with local trappers who'd paused for a pint of ale on their way home. One man had brought the day's catch inside with him—a rather stringy hare—and the innkeeper was shouting at him about the blood dripping on her polished floor. She was a beautiful woman with finer clothes and a more elegant posture than one would expect in a place like New Chester.

"That's my contact, Miss Oleander," Archer whispered to Briar. Her hair tickled his mouth as he leaned close to her ear, and he found himself momentarily distracted by the smell of roses and linseed oil.

"How do you know her?"

"She used to work for my fa—friend." He had almost said father. He had to be more careful. He was in danger of losing his wits completely around this girl. "We'd better look for that curse, eh?"

"Already found it." Briar pointed across the common room at a massive painting hanging above the stone fireplace.

"Huh. I didn't expect it to be out in the open like that."

Briar hardly seemed to be listening. All the color had drained from her face, and her voice was a little unsteady. "Let's look closer."

They edged around Miss Oleander, who was still shouting at the trapper, and crossed the common room, taking care not to bump into anyone. Fortunately, the seats in front of the fireplace were empty, allowing them to examine the strange painting without alarming any of the patrons.

Bordered by a carved wooden frame, the painting depicted the village in impressive detail, from the smoky tannery to the surrounding pastures to the charming pinewood houses. It was like looking through a window from a distance except that the painting showed New Chester in the wintertime with a fine layer of snow coating everything.

Archer leaned closer to study the tiny white brushstrokes. "So all someone had to do was hang that up there and poof! All the people in the village are invisible?"

"They didn't hang it," Briar said. "It's painted directly onto the wall of the inn, making it part of the building. That would satisfy the Law of Wholes. The frame is hiding the edges."

"I see." The slats of finely carved wood framing the picture were nailed directly to the wall. Archer reached out to touch one of the nails.

"Don't!" Briar snatched his hand away. "There might be defensive spells. Experienced curse painters will go to great lengths to keep their work safe, especially if they intend it to last a long time."

"But why would they do this?" Archer looked back at Miss Oleander, who still hadn't so much as glanced their way. It was sobering to see his old friend caught by whatever strange force made him and Briar invisible to the villagers. "Are they trying to protect information by making it so the villagers can't talk to anyone? Any visitors would know something strange is going on."

"It could be a punishment." Briar studied the painting intently, tapping her finger on her bottom lip. "Maybe the villagers committed some offense, and now they're trapped here, unable to interact with the outside world."

"So they can't leave?"

"Most likely," Briar said. "And no one comes to this village anymore, as far as they know. They could spend years wondering why the world forgot all about them and have no way to ask for help. They could be driven mad worrying that it's just them, wondering why no one's coming to save them, despairing because things never change. Look."

She nodded toward the men sitting at their cups. Their expressions were bleak, as if they were trapped in an unhappy life—and they had no idea how to fix it. Many had multiple empty tankards beside them, working their way through far more ale than the hour warranted. Though the inn was full, the murmur of voices had a strained quality, not at all like the happy buzz Archer remembered from his last visit. He shuddered. He was starting to get the idea.

"Can we help them?"

Briar hesitated. "We'd have to break the curse."

"Would destroying the painting do it?"

"Yes, but like I said, there are probably protections." She twisted the strap of her canvas satchel nervously. "We could call the curse's creator here, but that's exactly the kind of attention we want to avoid. We should get out of here."

Archer grimaced. His innkeeper friend had stopped

shouting at the trapper, who hadn't bothered to move the hare carcass despite her harangue. Miss Oleander gave up and trudged back toward the bar, her steps heavy, as if she wasn't sure why she bothered anymore. Archer had known her as a lively woman who would never shout at someone or walk all slumped over like that. The curse had taken a toll, all the more insidious because it was subtle.

Archer clenched his fists, a familiar old anger beginning to seethe. "We can't leave them like this."

"There's nothing we can do," Briar said, her voice heavy with regret.

"I can light that damn thing on fire."

He moved to pluck a burning log from the fireplace, but Briar seized his arm.

"Wait. You don't know what you're dealing with."

"Some curse painter might be upset with me for messing up their precious picture? Bring it on." He tried to shrug her off, reckless anger burning in his blood, getting hotter with every glance at the melancholy villagers and his entrapped friend. They didn't deserve that life.

"Archer, listen to me," Briar said urgently, still holding onto his arm. "I ... I think I know who created this curse. Trust me when I say you do not want to touch their work."

Archer braced himself as she tried to pull him away from the curse painting. "Who are they, then?"

Briar bit her lip. "I can't tell you."

"Then, I guess they'll just have to introduce themselves." He twisted out of her grasp and grabbed a branch from the fire, sending sparks flying.

"Stop!"

Archer ignored her. More signs of bleakness came into focus around him—unkempt bodies, mud left to dry where it fell, despairing stares, all those empty tankards and drink-slackened faces. No one deserved such a nightmarish curse. "I'm not leaving these people to slowly go mad."

"You're going to ruin everything," Briar said.

Archer advanced on the painting with the burning branch.

"I said stop!" Briar reached for him again.

Archer saw something in her hand, a flash of blue, then the world went black.

CHAPTER 15

D arkness had fallen by the time Briar managed to drag Archer out of the village. He was more solidly built than his long limbs suggested, and she soon regretted not using an ambulatory curse. She'd been worried that getting out her paints so close to that elaborate curse would trigger its defenses.

It was difficult to keep the blue curse stone in contact with Archer's skin while hauling him along the rough ground by his boots, and she eventually forced it into his mouth, hoping he wouldn't swallow it. She could make him vomit out the stone, but she would already have enough explaining to do when he woke. She saw no need to make it worse.

The night was tranquil beyond the boundaries of the cloaking curse. Briar dropped Archer's feet at the tree line and knelt beside him. His blond hair glowed in the moonlight, and his sleep looked peaceful—though artificially induced. She watched him for a moment, his chest rising and falling in his indigo coat.

Briar hadn't wanted to believe it when she'd seen the painting of the snowy village in the inn. Only a few mages could create a curse strong enough to affect an entire town, so she'd had her suspicions, but the sight of that signature style had still been a shock. Instantly, she had been transported back to a studio near the sea, an owl-eyed man concentrating on a canvas bedecked in whites and blues, lead white for invisibility, azurite for anxiety, ultramarine for illusions, carbon black to bind it all.

A psychological curse, her father's specialty. Donovan Dryden had left his mark on New Chester. She had thought she could escape him so far from High Lure, but he had come to the outer counties in the flesh to paint that image. Maybe he was still there. Fear squeezed at her innards, making her nauseous.

Briar had panicked when Archer moved to destroy the painting. All would be lost if they drew her father's attention. She'd had no choice but to curse Archer to sleep. She had likely killed whatever had begun to develop between them in the process. Feelings of attraction aside, their trust in each other had been a fragile thing, like the first shoots in a spring garden. She had crushed it into the dirt in a matter of seconds.

Maybe it was for the best. She couldn't escape what she was no matter how far she ran. Archer would never understand.

With a sigh, she fished the blue-smalt stone out of his mouth to awaken him. His eyes snapped open at once. He looked up at her leaning over him, her hair falling around their faces. A smile tugged at his lips, and a sort of painful breathlessness clutched at her chest. Then Archer's smile faded, and she knew he was remembering where they'd been as he closed his eyes.

He sat up, reaching for his belt knife. "You cursed me."

"I can explain," she said quickly, scrambling backward.

"You'd better do more than that."

"I had no choice. If you had touched that painting—"

She squeaked as Archer seized her wrist and pulled her toward him. His knife caught the moonlight.

"Who are you?" he demanded. "Did Larke hire you to curse the town with that vile—"

"No! I was trying to stop you from attracting—"

"One of your friends?" Archer asked roughly. "Someone who wouldn't want their wicked little joke messed up?"

"They're not my friends. They're—"

"Then, what?"

"I'm trying to tell you, if you'd let me finish a sentence," Briar snapped.

Archer opened his mouth then closed it again. He lowered his knife a hair but kept hold of her wrist, watching her through narrowed eyes.

"I recognized the style of that curse," Briar said. "It belongs to a very dangerous curse painter from High Lure. He doesn't normally work in the outer counties."

Her voice sounded too loud, and she was keenly aware of the forest looming at her back. The silent shadow of New Chester wasn't much better. Anyone could be watching.

"I'm not sure how long that curse has been there," she went on, "but if the painter is still in the area, we do not want him to find us. I can only think of one place around here important enough to need a curse painter of that caliber."

"Narrowmar."

"Exactly." Sensing Archer wasn't about to stab her, Briar tugged her wrist out of his grip and rubbed it gingerly. "If that particular curse painter is protecting Narrowmar for Lord Larke, our job is going to be even more difficult than we thought. If he knows we're coming, it will be completely impossible."

"I see."

Briar winced at the flat tone. Archer's face had closed up

like a crocus in the dark and held no hint of the warmth he had shown her since Mud Market.

"I'm sorry I cursed you," Briar said, "but do you understand why I couldn't let you touch that painting?"

"I do." Archer stood, his movements brusque, professional. He didn't hold out a hand to help her up, as he had so many times before.

She got to her feet unaided, ready to run if he tried to grab her again. He simply looked at her, as if waiting for something.

Briar shifted her feet nervously. "Should we go find the others?"

"Not yet. I'm afraid I can't let your little secrets and insubordinations slide anymore."

Briar's eyes narrowed, her fingers inching toward her paint satchel. "Insubordinations?"

"I hired you for a job. It's my own fault for not checking your references thoroughly enough, but the team and I can't afford the liability anymore."

He was referring to her and the team as separate entities again—and it stung. She'd been right. The trust between them had been obliterated in a single moment.

She flattened her voice to match his, trying to hide the hurt. "What are you saying?"

Archer put his knife back in his belt and folded his arms over his chest. "I think it's time you told me exactly who are and how you're connected to this mystery painter."

Briar's shoulders slumped. After what she had just seen in the village, the signature style of the painting and its effects, she wouldn't be able to keep her identity hidden for much longer. Archer deserved to hear the truth from her. And so, with the darkness descending on the world, held back only by starlight and the glow of the enchanted village, Briar told her story.

THIS IS THE STORY OF A BLESSING. It was a little blessing, the kind that kept its parents up at night with squalling cries and tiny fists wrapped around paint-smudged fingers. It was the kind of blessing that inspired a fierce, stomach-churning desire to protect even in the haughtiest of fathers and the most ruthless of mothers.

The blessing's parents were in the business of adding large chunks of evil to the world, but that one time, at least, they made something good.

CHAPTER 16

"My parents taught me to paint," Briar began. "We spent hours in the studio in our house from the moment I could hold a paintbrush in my chubby little fists. I went from simple stick figures to rough landscapes to pictures that actually looked like their subjects in record time. My parents are both wonderful artists, and I was their best project. They taught me their theories about curse magic, too, but most of the time they just liked putting brushes in my hands and seeing what I could do."

She remembered laughter from the early days, the sea breeze flowing through the open windows, the pride in her parents' eyes. Once, she'd painted the sun and moon on her cheeks, hoping to make them smile. Both of them had dived toward her, fearful that she'd put enough magic into the images on her skin to hurt herself. They had scrubbed her face until her cheeks turned bright pink, warning her never ever to curse her own body. They loved her, Briar knew. That was part of what had made it so hard to realize what they were.

Archer was watching her, a safe distance between them. "That doesn't sound so bad."

"That's what I thought at first, but my curses only ever hurt people." She looked him in the eye. "I was eleven the first time I killed someone."

Archer winced, though he didn't pull any farther away. "Who was it?"

"A nobleman, Lord Darien." Briar knotted her hands around the strap of her paint satchel as if it were a mooring line. "He insulted Queen Valerie at her birthday feast, so King Cullum hired my parents to see that he met with an accident. I cursed a bridge as Lord Darien was crossing with his wife. My parents planned it so the incident would make another lord— one of their other clients—a hero. Lord Darien couldn't swim, and my parents' client jumped in to save the wife from drowning."

"That sounds complicated," Archer said.

"The more intricate the task, the more interested my parents were in the job. It worked too. Everyone talked more about the dramatic rescue than the deceased husband, and no one suggested foul play." Briar grimaced, remembering the cracking timber, the flailing nobleman, the greedy pull of the current. "My parents were proud of how quickly I brought down the bridge and eliminated my subject. They saw everything as a challenge—and they'd taught me well."

Briar was ashamed at how much she'd needed her parents' approval, how much she'd valued every word of praise. Even after she'd realized she didn't like hurting people, she'd continued trying to impress them with her skill.

"Isn't that kind of curse painting illegal?" Archer asked.

"Not if your clients are rich enough," Briar said bitterly. "That's who hired us—nobles, royals, wealthy men who wanted to get wealthier. The king himself allowed us to remain unlicensed so we wouldn't be accountable to the Hall of Cloaks."

Archer's brow furrowed. "Did your parents work for the king often?"

"Often enough. This is all strictly secret. No one wants to think their rulers use such dirty tactics. Most of the catastrophic disasters of the past twenty-five years were created by one couple, a respectable pair of artists who lived near the sea in High Lure—where they trained their daughter to follow in their footsteps."

A breeze picked up, carrying the strange dead scent of New Chester.

Briar nodded toward the cursed town. "My father did that. He specializes in paintings that affect people's minds. Illusions. Nightmares. My mother would have helped him plan it. She has a great mind for invention, for pushing the boundaries of what was previously thought possible, but she excels at destruction."

Briar remembered the feeling of her mother wrapping the emerald-green scarf around her hair, which was as lush and frizzy as her mother's. They shared their passion for destruction too. She felt an itch between her shoulder blades, as if her mother was about to reach out from the village and touch the back of her neck.

"Maybe we should walk," she said. "The others will be waiting."

Archer gestured to the tree line with something short of his usual flourish. "After you."

The moon glared down at them like a malevolent eye as they walked back into the woods. Pine needles crunched under their feet, the darkness wrapping closer around them.

"Why did they make *you* kill people?" Archer asked when the pitch-dark forest sheltered them once more. "Couldn't they have handled that part?"

Briar's mouth twisted. "I am a very good painter. My potential excited my parents, and it pushed them to plan worse curses, trying to stretch what my magic could do even as I objected more frequently. They became so bold that King

Cullum grew uncomfortable associating with them. They had no shortage of clients, though, and the king couldn't stop them."

Archer shook his head. "I should have heard about this."

"Why?"

"Because I—never mind." He rolled his shoulders. "That's a story for another time."

Briar frowned. Archer wasn't sharing his full story either. She wondered if he, like Esteban, had history at King Cullum's court.

They reached a break in the trees where moonlight filtered down on a patch of bare earth, and they stopped in unspoken agreement. It was a conversation they needed to finish before rejoining the others. The pine trees rustled eerily, the area still devoid of birdsong and animal noises.

"Eventually, King Cullum ordered my parents to get licensing tattoos. They refused outright. He tried to send the Hall of Cloaks after them, to finally keep them in check, but they protected themselves."

"With curses?"

"Curses, subterfuge, blackmail—they used it all to safeguard their home and business. Even when they were still working for king and kingdom, their magic was steeped in destruction. They crossed too many lines and became something evil, something separate from the people who used to celebrate my stick figures and take me to paint by the sea."

Briar wrapped her arms around herself, and Archer raised a hand, as if reaching out to comfort her. He trusted too easily.

"I add evil to the world, just like they do," she said sharply, stopping him in his tracks. "I try to use my power to balance out worse evils. That's the closest I can get to goodness, but the scales are already tipped too far after everything I've done."

"You left them, didn't you?" Archer asked. "You made a

choice to take another path. That ought to count for something."

Briar sighed. "Maybe if I had simply walked away, but that's not how it happened. My parents were the most powerful people in High Lure behind closed doors, all but myths. Even the voice mages at the Hall of Cloaks feared them. I knew they would find me if I ran away. I had to do something to convince them to leave me alone."

She brushed her frizzy hair back from her face, remembering the hours she'd spent sitting cross-legged on the rooftop, planning out her departure. She'd thought she was so clever. She'd been seventeen, proud of her abilities, certain she understood right and wrong better than her parents.

"I decided to send a message warning my parents to let me go, or I would reveal every curse they had ever created, even those that went well beyond the restrictions the king set for them. They took advantage of the freedom he gave them when it suited them—and I knew all the details."

"I'm starting to understand why you were hiding in Sparrow Village," Archer said. "I take it you didn't write this warning on parchment?"

Briar shook her head. "A show of strength is the only thing they would understand."

"You didn't try to kill them, did you?"

"No," Briar said. "I broke their defenses. I destroyed every painting protecting our house just to show them I could. They were supposed to come home to that and understand what I was capable of, but ..." Briar trailed off, remembering that horrible day when her youthful arrogance and self-righteousness had shattered.

"Did you accidentally knock the house down?" Archer asked gently.

"I wish I'd done something that simple." Briar picked dried pine needles off her skirt, letting them drop to the black earth.

"The night I broke the defensive curses, mages from the Hall of Cloaks attacked our house. They must have put a spell on it that would notify them if the defenses ever failed. I had no idea, and before I could do anything about it, an all-out assault had begun. My parents got home almost at the same time as the mages attacked."

"I might have heard about that," Archer said. "About a year ago, was it? The team and I were robbing a goldsmith's shop in High Lure when a huge commotion was blamed on unlicensed hedge wizards. The tumult made it easier to get away with our pockets full of gold."

"Glad it helped someone," Briar said dryly.

"So you brought the mages down on your family. Then what?"

Briar clutched the strap of her paint satchel, unable to meet his eyes. "I just ... ran. The last time I saw my parents, they were huddled beneath the windows, daubing curses all over the floor while the cries of voice mages filled the air. My message was lost in the chaos."

Archer gave a low whistle. "So they think you summoned the mages on purpose?"

She looked up. "I only wanted to be free—and to teach them a lesson. They must think I betrayed them."

Archer studied her, and she detected sympathy in his expression. "What did you do next?"

"I ran as far and as fast as I could." Briar gave a brittle laugh. "I wandered the far counties for a while, got turned in to various authorities when I tried to solicit clients, but managed to keep out of my parents' reach. Eventually I ended up in Sparrow Village." She glanced back in the direction of New Chester, the shadowy pine trees hiding it from view. "My parents will catch up to me one day. I can try to explain what happened, but I don't think it'll matter. My departure alone was a betrayal—and they are not forgiving."

Archer was quiet for a moment, as if absorbing the implications of her story. "So the most dangerous mages in the kingdom have a personal grudge against you?" he asked at last. "And you had that hanging over your head when I found you in that rundown little cottage?"

"I loved that cottage," Briar said softly. "I really did want a chance at a peaceful life. I tried to use my little bits of evil to help people who've been wronged, but I mostly ended up carrying out petty revenge or making things worse." She rubbed her toe through the pine needles at her feet. "Being good is more complicated than I expected."

Archer made a strange sound in his throat, and she looked up, taking in the moonlight shining on his blond hair and his grave expression. She wished for a curse that would help her read his mind. Now he knew the full danger he'd put his team in by hiring her. She wouldn't blame him for sending her away. Still, it was a relief to speak openly about it. It had been lonely trying to figure out how to live differently from the way she'd been raised.

"I guess it's naïve to worry so much about good and evil," Briar said when he didn't speak. "My parents would say that stuff is for stories."

"I think it's noble." Archer shoved his hands in his pockets. "And brave to make a new life for yourself, even if you botched it a bit."

"Do you really mean that?"

"Every word." He cleared his throat gruffly. "Your soul matters, Briar."

Briar's chest suddenly felt too tight. She examined the pine needles strewn across the ground between them, unable to articulate how much those simple words of understanding meant to her, that acknowledgement that she was struggling for something worthwhile, even in a gray and complicated world. She'd never dared hope someone could know what she had done and still think well of her. Her parents had always kept her apart from other people, believing friends and fellow painters were a distraction at best, considering others beneath them. Briar had watched children playing on the beach wistfully, jealous of their joined hands and easy laughter.

She snuck a glance at Archer and caught him staring at her lips. She blinked. It was probably just her imagination, an effect of the pool of moonlight and the intimacy of shared secrets. Still, she wondered what his lips would feel like against hers.

This is not *the time for that,* she told herself firmly. "Now you know my story." Briar offered a tentative smile. "Is it similar to what happened when you left your father's business?"

"My past has fewer magical explosions," Archer said. "I left the luxurious life of a rich man's son for the freedom of the forest and the open road. It was all rather daring and romantic, but I turned to a life of crime, not good deeds."

"What do you call this rescue mission?"

"We're collecting a ransom."

Briar raised an eyebrow. "Archer, I may not be as sharp as my mother, but I know there's more to it than that. I told you my story. Isn't it your turn?"

Archer sighed, his shoulders slumping. Before he could say anything, shouts rose from deeper in the woods.

"Archer, Briar, where are you? Come quickly! We're under attack!"

CHAPTER 17

B riar and Archer tore through the woods at full speed. Briar fumbled for her paints, though she had no idea what she would do if her parents had found them. Probably stare stupidly while they cursed the whole team into oblivion. Feeling unsteady at the thought, she followed Archer over the fallen logs and bramble patches lurking in the darkness.

Shouts reverberated through the trees, mixed with the sounds of flesh and steel colliding. Campfire light flickered ahead, guiding them onward. Briar's heart pounded like thunder. She wasn't even close to being ready to face her parents.

Then she and Archer burst into the clearing to find the team engaged not in defending themselves against curses or voice magic but in a good old-fashioned brawl. A patrol of soldiers wearing Lord Larke's burgundy had surprised the party of thieves at their supper. They fought amidst the sparks and ashes of the blazing campfire, both groups struggling to rally together, the whole clearing a riot of stamping boots and flashing blades.

Lew pummeled an attacker—who'd lost his weapon—with heavy fists. Jemma stood behind him, feet planted, swinging a cudgel at anyone who tried to come at her husband from behind. Esteban fought with a blade for once, a silver cutlass with a wicked curve that matched his silver-worked boots. His thin lips were clamped shut, as if to prevent himself from using any magic. Nat fought at his side, barely managing to hold his own against the older and stronger enemies.

Briar and Archer entered the clearing near Nat and Esteban, knives already drawn. The fighters were too entangled for Archer to risk using his bow. He gave a wild battle yell and hurled himself directly into the fray. He fought better than he danced, and an enemy fell to his blade within seconds of their arrival.

The soldiers turned to meet Archer's assault, giving Nat time to finish off one of his assailants. The others renewed their efforts, and the clash of steel against steel rang through the night, punctuated by grunts and screams.

Briar hung back from the tumult, seeking an opening where her curses would help the most, but the tide turned quickly after Archer arrived. His movements were swift—if not smooth —and their enemies weren't prepared for the fury with which he defended the team.

"Take one alive," Archer called as he skewered a man trying to stab Esteban. "We need information."

"I got it!" Nat shouted.

He drew back his arm and threw something blue at one of the attackers, using his sleeve to protect his hand. The man dropped into a pile of leaves with an almighty snore then immediately got back up again. Nat yelped and ran to retrieve the curse stone from among the dead foliage.

"It has to keep touching him!" Briar called.

"Right. I forgot." Nat snatched up the curse stone with his bare hand then immediately dropped to the ground, clearly forgetting it would have exactly the same effect on him.

His opponent gaped at the lad who'd fallen asleep in the

middle of the battle, and Esteban leaped forward to engage him before he could hurt Nat.

Another attacker lunged at Briar and attempted to pin her arms to her sides. She smelled campfire ash and a meaty odor on his breath. Before she could twist around to touch him with her own curse stone, he stiffened and slid to the ground, nearly dragging her down with him. Archer's knife was sticking out of his back.

"Are you all right?" Archer bent to retrieve the blade and wipe it on the dead man's coat.

"Never better," Briar breathed.

Archer winked at her and turned, putting his back to hers, his long knife at the ready. She held up a curse stone in each hand. They stood back to back, prepared to meet the next assault together.

No one was left to fight. Their enemies were laid out on the ground, either unconscious and bleeding or as dead as the leaves littering the forest floor. The team was victorious.

Briar's shoulders sagged in relief, her heartbeat nearly drowning out the crackling of the campfire.

"Nothing like a good brawl to get the juices flowing." Archer sheathed his knife and turned to the others. "Any idea what they were after?"

"We can ask this one," Jemma said. She and Lew had managed to take a man alive using another of Briar's stones. They tied up the sleeping soldier, tucking the curse stone into the bonds around his wrists to keep him docile, and dragged him over to the fire for questioning.

"It's almost too easy with those curses of yours," Lew said, going over to pluck the sleep stone out of Nat's hammy fist to rouse him. Nat sat up, looking bewildered after his midbattle nap. "A man could get complacent."

Esteban sniffed primly. "I think it was rather difficult enough."

Briar surveyed the fallen attackers. There were five of them, all wearing the burgundy uniforms of Lord Larke's retainers and armed with standard-issue short swords. "Where did these men come from?"

"New Chester?" Jemma asked.

"Probably not." Archer explained what they had seen in the village, leaving out the part about Briar's parents.

The others looked slightly ill at the description of the curse.

"So that painting is why I couldn't see them?" Lew asked when Archer finished. "And they can't see anyone who comes into the village?"

"Nope."

"And they can't leave it?"

"Doubtful."

Lew shuddered and moved a little closer to his wife.

"If they're not part of the New Chester watch, these fellows must be from Narrowmar," Jemma said.

"What are they doing all the way down here?" Nat asked.

"Let's find out." Archer donned a pair of gloves and knelt beside the prisoner still sleeping by the campfire and pushed back his burgundy sleeve so he could remove the curse stone wedged against the man's wrist. Just before it came loose, Jemma put a hand on Archer's shoulder.

"Perhaps you shouldn't be the one to talk to him," she said. "This close to—"

"Good point," Archer said. "Esteban, would you do the honors?"

Briar frowned as Archer and Jemma moved out of the prisoner's line of sight. They were afraid of being recognized close to New Chester? Or was it Narrowmar itself that worried them?

Esteban crouched over the prisoner like a scrawny vulture. He removed the curse stone with a black silk handkerchief and held it gingerly away from him, as if it were goat feces. "Wake up."

The prisoner's eyes popped open. Disoriented, he blinked at the mage glowering down at him. Blemishes pitted his face, and he couldn't be much older than Nat. He jerked his wrists a few times, but his bonds held.

"Who is your liege lord?" Esteban asked.

The young man jutted out his spotty chin. "I don't have to answer your questions, villain."

Esteban sighed and mumbled something that sounded like "one of those." He seized the prisoner's coat. "These are Lord Larke's colors. Unless you're an imposter—"

"I serve Lord Larke, as do all loyal freemen in this county." The young man looked affronted at the imposter suggestion.

"You're a long way from Larke Castle," Lew said calmly.

The prisoner started at the sight of Lew's hulking form at Esteban's side. "His lordship's dominion stretches—"

"We know where the county borders are," Esteban said impatiently. "If you're this far out in the woods, you must be based at Narrowmar, correct?"

The prisoner paled, the spots standing out on his chin. "I'm not going to tell a bunch of thieves anything."

"What makes you think we're thieves?" Esteban leaned closer, and the prisoner pulled back as far he could with the campfire behind him. The firelight cast lurid shadows across Esteban's gaunt face. "Did you know we'd be out here?"

"I don't even know who you are." A youthful squeak snuck into his voice. "I swear."

"Then why attack us?" Lew asked. "We were minding our own business. Last I heard, even Lord Larke doesn't order his men to murder private citizens for no reason."

The prisoner looked around nervously. Lew loomed beside Esteban, his arms folded over his chest in an intimidating fashion. Nat mimicked him, with slightly less successful results. But the blood on their clothes made them all look ghoulish.

Then the prisoner's gaze fell on the bodies of his comrades. "You're obviously criminals," he said. "We—"

"Attacked us without provocation, forcing us to defend ourselves." Esteban gave him a shake. "How did you know we would be here?"

"I ... I didn't. You were just ... that is, we thought ..."

"You thought you'd kill us in the woods and steal our horses perhaps?" Esteban rasped. "I wonder what Lord Larke would have to say about that. You'll be responsible, of course, as the only survivor."

"It wasn't ... I didn't ..." The prisoner broke out in a sweat, looking genuinely scared.

Briar didn't blame him. Esteban looked ready to cut the prisoner's throat out of pure irritation. She'd never seen the team look so dangerous.

When Esteban muttered, "I am bored of this circular conversation," the prisoner cracked like a pigeon egg.

"Everyone knows who you are," he blurted out. "There's a wanted poster in every village from here to the Northrun River with your faces on it. They're offering a reward and everything!"

"Really?" Nat relaxed his intimidating pose. "What's the reward?"

Lew rolled his eyes. "Would it be worth temporarily selling out the lad here?"

"They want us alive, right?" Nat asked, giving Lew a wounded look. "We're no good to them dead."

"You're no good to anyone." Lew cuffed Nat on the back of the head. "Don't get your hopes up. I've seen plenty of wanted posters in my day. They probably have one drawing to represent all the young farm lads who've ever turned to thievery." He combed a hand through his red beard. "The more distinguished among us, on the other hand—"

"You're both on the poster," the prisoner said to Lew, some of the color returning to his face. "And your woman and the voice mage." His eyes darted to Esteban, whose mouth twisted sourly at the news.

"What about me?" Briar asked.

The prisoner leaned sideways to get a better look at her. "No, you're not on there."

Archer's face was unreadable in the quivering shadows. He signaled something to Lew, who nodded and squatted down beside Esteban and the prisoner. "So the young lad, myself and my lady wife, and the mage are all called thieves on these posters?"

"That's right."

"But not the girl?"

"No."

"And no one else?"

"No one."

Briar looked at Archer again. If the authorities had such detailed knowledge of the gang, why weren't they asking for information about its leader? He didn't quite meet her eyes.

"Were these posters commissioned by Lord Larke?" Lew asked the prisoner.

The young man nodded. "He's the one offering a bounty for your capture, and he doesn't mind if you're dead."

"How did you know we would be here?"

"We really were on patrol." Since he had started talking anyway, the prisoner didn't hold back. "We're supposed to keep folks from wandering into New Chester, but when we saw you, we reckoned we'd try for the bounty too. We didn't account for the sorcery." The prisoner's gaze flitted from Esteban's face to the blue curse stone lying in the dirt beside him.

"Can you tell us what happened in New Chester?" Briar asked.

The young man shifted uneasily and glanced at the shadowy trees. "The villagers angered Lord Larke something fierce. His lordship's son was staying in the village inn a few months back, and they caused him some trouble. Something to do with a woman."

Esteban loosened his grip on the prisoner. "At last we are getting somewhere."

Lew frowned, his beard twitching. "Larke's son was giving a woman trouble?"

"I only know what I heard. She didn't want to leave the inn with the young lord, and the villagers tried to step in. His lordship got mighty upset, and he cooked up that nasty enchantment somehow."

"What happened to the woman?"

The prisoner shrugged. "Left with the young lord, I guess."

Archer signaled that he needed a minute. Esteban picked up the curse stone with a grimace and pressed it to the prisoner's skin again. The prisoner flopped sideways and began snoring.

"Lady Mae," Lew said as soon as the young man was unconscious. "The young lord must have brought her through New Chester on the way to Narrowmar. She revealed she was being kidnapped, and the villagers intervened."

"He cursed the entire village for that?" Nat asked. "For standing up for a scared girl?"

"I've seen worse curses laid for less," Briar said softly. The more she learned about Lord Larke and his son, the less she cared for them. They seemed like exactly the sort of people who would hire her parents to take revenge on a bunch of poor villagers.

Jemma hadn't spoken during the interrogation. She was studying Archer intently, as if his face held the answer to an old riddle. She wrapped her red shawl tighter around her shoulders. "Larke's son," she said at last. "He's the one?"

Archer paused for a beat. "Yes."

"The one what?" Nat asked.

"It all makes sense now," Jemma said.

"What does?" Nat asked. "What did I miss?" He looked at Briar, but she was just as confused as he was.

Archer and Jemma seemed to be communicating through eye contact alone. They looked a lot alike, Briar realized, standing on either side of the fire, the light illuminating their golden hair.

"They have to know sooner or later," Jemma said after a long pause.

"All right." Archer sighed and turned to the others. "This is a secret, so don't go shouting about it in your cups."

"More secrets?" Briar asked.

He met her eyes. "Secrets upon secrets next to more secrets."

"Whatever *that* means," Nat said impatiently. "You going to tell us or not?"

"Lady Mae is with child," Archer said.

"With what child?" Nat asked.

Lew rolled his eyes. "It means pregnant, dimwit."

"With a baby?"

"With Larke's son's baby," Archer said. "The father's name is Tomas. He is twenty-five years of age, and he has spent every one of those years being a raging scrotum face."

Briar wrapped her hands around the strap of her paint satchel, surprised but not entirely shocked that Mae's situation was more complicated than she'd been told. So she was carrying the grandson of her father's bitterest enemy. That *was* a dangerous secret.

"Tomas Larke is too old for Lady Mae, ain't he?" Nat asked. "She's practically a child herself."

"She's barely eighteen," Archer said. "And yes, that's part of why he's a raging scrotum face." His eyebrows drew down, mouth twisting as if he tasted something sour. "She was smitten with Tomas when they first met. She threw herself headfirst into their secret romance, believing it would last forever. To him, it was only ever a conquest."

"How do you know all this?" Nat asked.

"It's complicated," Archer said, catching Briar's eye again.

She was developing a theory about Archer's real identity and the unrequited affection he must feel for the girl they were going to so much trouble to rescue. Archer was risking his life to help Lady Mae out of a difficult situation another man had caused. It made Briar admire him more, but a sense of melancholy tinged her admiration. Archer's mission had only ever been about Lady Mae. Briar was an assistant, an accessory, a hired paintbrush.

"The important thing," Archer continued, "is that Tomas Larke discarded Lady Mae before she realized the baby was on the way. It would have been better for her to keep it a secret, but the elder Lord Larke must have learned his grandchild was to be born to the daughter of his worst enemy. He sent Tomas to Barden Vale to steal her away before her own father could find out."

"Are you sure Lady Mae didn't go willingly?" Briar asked. "If they had this secret love affair, maybe she wanted to be with the young Larke."

Archer ran a hand through his hair. Blood from the fight stained his cuff. "I wondered the same thing, but what happened in New Chester confirms she's being held against her wishes. Even if she left her father's house willingly, by the time they made it this far, she wanted to go home. She asked for help at the inn—and we've seen the result."

"I want to make sure you all understand what this means," Jemma said. A breeze sent the sparks from the fire swirling around her, ruffling her silver-and-gold hair. "We're not just taking back a prisoner of this petty rivalry Barden and Larke call a war. We're not just earning a reward or saving a kidnapped girl. We are stealing a man's heir out from under him."

"Potential heir," Archer said. "I suspect Jasper Larke is waiting to see if the child is a boy. If it is, they'll announce that the young lovers eloped, and the child will be declared legitimate. Mae's son will inherit both Larke and Barden counties—and Jasper Larke will bring him up to be all Larke."

"And if it's a girl?" Esteban asked.

Archer grimaced. "Unlike in the Barden family, there are other Larke males who'd inherit ahead of Tomas's daughter. Lord Larke might force Tomas and Mae to try again for a boy in that case, or he might want to brush this embarrassing incident under the rug and marry his son into a more suitable family. He might even kill the child."

"And what will happen to Lady Mae?" Nat asked.

"Her life is in danger either way," Archer said. "Larke could kill her to ensure that the child inherits all the Barden lands. Tomas has no lingering affection for her, and he'll be all too happy to have her out of the way. I doubt Tomas cares about the baby, but Jasper Larke wants an heir. Maybe he thinks if he has another chance to raise a boy, he can prevent him from becoming an amoral philanderer."

"And a raging scrotum face," Nat said.

"Yes, no one wants that," Archer said. "But no matter how the child turns out, it'll give Larke an opportunity to take over all of Barden County when his rival dies and subject it to the same draconian taxes and cruel treatment as the rest of Larke County. They don't deserve that."

Briar remembered the farmers who'd shared their food with her and Archer—Grampa and Juliet and little Abie. They'd been squeezed so hard by the Larkes. But even if Archer didn't want Jasper Larke's dominion to spread, it still didn't entirely explain why he knew so much about Tomas and Mae and Lord Larke himself. She remembered something Grampa had said as he'd fixed them a plate of food in the barn. He'd called Tomas the *eldest* son. Her theory about Archer's identity began to solidify.

An owl hooted in the trees, bringing her back to the campfire and the outlaws and the sleeping prisoner dressed in Larke burgundy.

"This is all very enlightening," Esteban said, "but it doesn't get us any closer to achieving our goal of extracting the lady from Narrowmar."

"True," Archer said. "But now you all know what we're dealing with and why it's so important that we get there before the baby is born. Also, the lady herself might not be able to leap from rooftop to rooftop during the escape."

"Lord Larke will stop at nothing to prevent her from being taken," Jemma said. "He believes that baby belongs to him, regardless of the mother's wishes."

"And he knows we're coming." Lew gave the woods a dark glance. "We don't operate in this county enough to justify a wanted poster in every town."

"About that," Briar said. "Why isn't your face on the poster, Archer?"

Archer shrugged. "Yours isn't either."

"I haven't been with you for long, but if Larke knows your team is here, he must be aware you are too."

"Perhaps," Archer said lightly.

Briar clearly wasn't the only member of the team who didn't know how Archer had gotten tangled up with Larke and Barden and their offspring. Nat squinted contemplatively into the middle distance, picking at a loose thread on his patchwork coat. Lew was scanning the woods as if expecting another attack. Esteban looked as if he were regretting signing up for their mission. Briar was beginning to think there weren't nearly enough of them to pull off the job, even with her cleverest curses.

Archer rubbed his hands together briskly and nodded at the prisoner. "That's enough storytelling for one night. Shall we wake this fellow up and see if he knows anything about our target?"

Esteban removed the curse stone from the prisoner's skin, and the young man came to again, blinking at his captors as if unaware he'd been unconscious for the past few minutes.

"What's going on?" he asked blearily.

"You were going to tell us about Narrowmar," Esteban said.

"Oh." The prisoner took a deep breath. "That's a real story." He looked around at them, perhaps assessing his chances of ever walking away from their campsite alive. They weren't good. "If I tell you everything, will you let me join your gang? I reckon being an outlaw would be better than going back after that."

Esteban snorted. "Why don't you impress us with something useful, and we'll consider your application?"

"All right." The prisoner sat up straighter, looking less afraid already. "Narrowmar. Where do I start?"

The answer turned out to be nowhere. As he began to speak, his eyes suddenly bulged, and his face darkened. A horrible gurgling sound came from his throat. He reached for his neck, spasming like a grotesque puppet. Esteban jerked back in surprise.

"What's happening?" Nat asked.

"He's cursed." Briar dropped to her knees at his side, searching his clothing for any sign of the offending painting. The boy reached for her with his bound hands, his eyes wide and rolling. "Hold still," she ordered him. "I'm trying to help."

She pulled back his collar and caught a glimpse of lead-tin yellow and bone black. The colors of illness and death formed a picture of a locked box—a curse to protect Narrowmar's secrets. Briar tried to unbutton the prisoner's coat, but the curse was too quick. He stiffened, and a final choking sound escaped his swollen lips. Then his eyes glazed over, and he fell straight backward onto the campfire.

The others leapt forward to grab him, shouting, and sparks filled the air. Briar dropped back, reaching reflexively for her satchel.

Archer drew his bow, training the arrow on the darkness. "Is there a curse painter out there?"

"I don't think so," Briar said. The smell of meat and burned fabric made her nauseous. "That curse prevents betrayal. If I had some purple I might have unraveled it in time." She couldn't look at the young soldier she'd been too slow to save.

Lew tried to revive the fellow, pumping his chest and listening for his breath, but it was no use. He sat back, shaking his head. A few sparks from the disturbed fire caught in his beard. "Poor lad. He was going to help us."

"Why did they do that to one of their own men?" Nat asked nervously.

"Larke views his men as expendable. He always has." Archer sounded angry, as angry as he'd been when they'd discovered the curse on New Chester. His knuckles whitened on his bow as he surveyed the darkness. The other members of the Larke patrol formed lumpy shapes in the firelight. At least they'd fallen in honest combat.

Briar glanced at the would-be outlaw and shuddered. No one deserved to perish like that. Worse, the curse that had taken his life had almost certainly been painted by her parents. She had hoped New Chester had been a one-time commission. Apparently, she was wrong. Cold dread crept through her body.

Archer released the tension on his bowstring and lowered the weapon. "We're moving camp."

Lew got to his feet. "I'll fetch the horses."

"We can't go to Narrowmar now," Briar said. "Whoever is guarding the place might know we're here after this." She had thought their mission stood a chance of succeeding when her parents didn't know they were coming, but if any of the patrol had escaped ...

"We are *not* giving up," Archer said.

Briar faced him, trying not to say too much in front of the others. "I told you it would be impossible if *anyone* knows we're here."

"It doesn't matter."

"Archer—"

He cut her off harshly. "I am going into that fortress whether you come with me or not. You claimed you were up for the challenge. You claimed you wanted to help the weak. If you're going to leave that pregnant girl at the hands of *anyone* who tries to hurt her, then you're not who I thought you were."

Briar's mouth tightened, and the old destructive urge rose up to batter against the seawall of his anger. He might be upset and desperate, but that didn't give him the right to fling what she'd told him back in her face. Her fingers twitched, wishing for a paintbrush. Her father had warned her that personal crusades were messy. *"You can't let your clients' passions interfere with your work."*

"And who are you, *Archer*?" she shot back. "Or are you going to keep denying that this quest is personal?"

Archer stared at her, chest heaving as if he was trying to master his anger. None of the others so much as breathed.

"I'm nobody," he said. "At least not anymore. Regardless of my personal history with the Larkes, I am not going to let them and their allies win. If you're going to leave, do it now."

He marched over to the horses and began saddling the bay. His tall shape looked even larger in the shadows cast by the scattered coals, almost menacing. Tension showed in the lines of his body and the jerky movements of his hands.

The urge to run roiled in Briar's chest. She'd spent the past year trying to avoid her parents' notice, hiding in the outer counties, changing her name. Leaving would be the logical thing to do, but it was spineless too. She had taken the coward's way out when she left High Lure. Breaking her parents' magical defenses and slinking out of the city wasn't the way to show them her strength. *And you thought you were so talented.*

Briar had thought she could live a better and more ethical life away from them, but she'd failed at that too. Instead of using curse magic for good, she'd added evil to the world, bit by tiny bit. She didn't know how to turn it into anything else.

Then Archer looked up from his saddlebags, his eyes finding hers. There was a challenge in them but also a hint of compassion, of understanding, of a desire to fix something in the world despite what he'd become.

She remembered what he'd said to her in the moonlight. *"Your soul matters."* She might have failed in her bid for goodness, but she was trying. She was struggling against her parents' legacy every day. That mattered. And even though they frightened her, maybe it was time to stand up and fight her parents directly. Thwarting them and their clients' schemes might be the only good she had to offer the world.

"I'm still in," she said at last. "No matter who is guarding Narrowmar."

"Good." Archer gave a grim nod, as if he could read her thoughts in the blaze of her eyes. "What do you say we go peel that place open like an orange?"

CHAPTER 18

As Archer marshalled his companions in the woods near New Chester, the captain of the Narrowmar garrison marched down the stronghold's central corridor. His boots thudded on the stone floor, and his sword swung at his hip, the leather sheath creaking with each step. Now in his seventies, the captain had had command of the stronghold for thirty-eight years, each quieter and dustier than the last. His bones ached often, and he'd begun to wonder if it was time to resign his post.

No one had attempted an assault on the fortress in his life-time. Narrowmar was so remote that it no longer made a viable target in wartime. In ancient days, it had been the heart and fist of another realm, but the centers of power had moved on, leaving a relic in the form of an impenetrable keep.

The stronghold was no traditional fort with turrets and towers and moats filled with sludge. Narrowmar was a natural wonder, a series of caves and tunnels cut deep into a mountainside. A spring burbled from its roots, and a great stone door guarded its only entrance. The formation was so perfectly suited for defense that some said the gods of the higher realms had built it to hold their darkest secrets. Whoever had won it from the gods must have been powerful, but these days, the fortress passed from father to son like a locked box.

The House of Larke had controlled the keep for generations but saw little need to maintain a large garrison. They'd built a grand castle near a major trade route and resented paying soldiers to sit in safety at the remote stronghold. The Larkes had stopped assigning recruits to Narrowmar nearly twenty years ago. The rooms had fallen into disrepair, and the vaulted ceilings sagged with the weight of years. Eventually, the remaining soldiers had moved into a single section of the underground barracks, giving the rest over to dust and spiders.

The old captain ran a hand through his thinning white hair, remembering the young wife who'd kept him company there for a time. Her laughter had filled the underground passageways, and the captain had been certain they were destined to stay forever, the unofficial lord and lady of the ancient hall. They would fill their domain with children, who would inherit the stewardship of the keep like the scions of ancient kings.

But the captain's young wife hadn't cared for Narrowmar as he did. She wasn't content to live beneath the mountain. One day she had gone out to pick wildflowers and met a young soldier from the king's army. He'd offered her a life where their children could live in the sunshine, not rule over corridors of dust. Within a fortnight of their meeting, she had gone. And the captain had settled deeper into the fortress, clinging like grime to its ancient stones.

Other soldiers accepted the same fate, living out their days in a deployment devoid of bloodshed and action. The captain oversaw those men faithfully, putting them through rigorous daily exercises. A handful could hold Narrowmar against whole armies, and the old soldiers stood ready. The captain had never held the great stone door against an enemy, foreign or domestic, but Narrowmar was his dominion, and he kept it well.

Then one day, Jasper Larke, the faraway liege lord of the forgotten fortress, had ordered a company of reinforcements to Narrowmar to prepare for the arrival of one Lady Mae Barden. It was the second time Narrowmar had hosted such a guest.

The old captain hardly knew what to do with the lively young men who suddenly occupied his barracks, filling the underground passages with clamor and warmth. When the daily exercises weren't enough to sap their youthful energy, he set them to cleaning up the fortress, sweeping dust from its corridors and repairing the ancient adornments—the statues and fountains and elaborate stone pillars, artifacts of a forgotten age. He began to feel that the old place still needed him after all.

Then came a summer evening when a well-dressed couple —he with luminous eyes and a haughty aspect, she with frizzy hair and fire in her gaze—arrived on horseback and informed him they were taking over the stronghold's defenses. The couple carried orders direct from the hand of Lord Larke himself, yet they spoke like people from High Lure, more suited to the luxuries of the king's city than the peace of the outer counties.

Unlike the young soldiers, the two strangers were not armed with bluster and fresh-forged steel. They carried boxes full of pigments, horsehair paintbrushes, and linseed oil. They set up their supplies in Lord Larke's chamber off the fortress's main corridor, and they set to painting.

The old captain knew little of mages and less of art, so he paid them no heed—until he saw their curses at work. It happened during the lunch hour. One of the newer soldiers was caught stealing decrepit sculptures from a little-used banquet hall to sell in the antique market back home. The captain would have docked his pay and been done with it, but the curse painters insisted on having him dragged before them in chains in the middle of the soldiers' mess hall.

The captain would have stopped them if he'd known what they had planned. He told himself so often.

The woman had taken the lead, standing over the young soldier, wild hair cascading around her shoulders like a queen's mantle. "Narrowmar is one of the finest examples of the ancient stone arts left in the kingdom of Lure," she said, her voice ringing as loud and clear as a struck anvil. "Such destruction cannot be tolerated."

"It was just a bit of a statue." The soldier looked embarrassed at being caught, but he wasn't wise enough to be afraid.

"That statue has graced these halls for hundreds of years," the woman said. "This fortress is wasted on Lord Larke, but he has asked us to protect it. That includes every cornice, every moldy tapestry, every marble bust, no matter how ugly. We will not allow a treasure such as this to be plundered."

"No one uses this pit," the soldier said. "And the decorations—"

"*Art*," the woman cut in, "does not need to be *used*."

"Yes," her husband said, his voice giving the impression of a cookpot bubbling inside him. "And it should not be commodified by a lowlife soldier with no inkling of Narrowmar's significance."

The old captain bristled at that. He might not be highborn, but he resented his men being called lowlifes by strangers from the city.

The woman bent closer to the soldier. "You will be punished for your lack of reverence."

"Now look here, sir, madam," the captain cut in. "We have a protocol to address—"

The woman raised a slim, paint-spattered hand, proffering the letter from Lord Larke granting her authority. "We shall handle any disciplinary actions from now on."

The captain scowled. "As the commanding—"

"What do you say, darling?" the woman asked her husband. "The incendiary?"

He inclined his head. "I think that's the right choice, given the damages done."

She smiled. "It's one of my favorites." She flicked her fingers at the old captain as if he were the lowliest servant. "I need an item of clothing from the culprit, preferably one he wears often."

The captain didn't move. He was *not* accustomed to taking orders in his own fortress. Then the woman turned to face him, and he recoiled. Her eyes were worse than cruel, seeming to contain every dark desire that had spilled forth from the captain's soul in his worst moments—the silent profanities he had slung at his wife as she left him, the verbal ones he had shouted to the mountain after she was gone. He saw the same darkness and anger concentrated in the curse painter's eyes—and he was afraid.

"A jacket or hat will do," she whispered.

The captain turned stiffly. "Your cap, soldier."

The young statue thief handed over his woolen cap, more confused than nervous. The woman plucked it from his hand without making eye contact with either the soldier or the captain. Her husband nodded, his large eyes mirroring her intensity. They moved as a unit, sharing a single purpose.

The woman knelt on the floor to paint an image of a cauldron hung over a blazing fire on the hat. The captain didn't claim to know much about art, but it was prettily done. He nearly offered her a compliment.

Then the soldier who had stolen the statue began to wail. The captain wouldn't soon forget that sound. It keened in his nightmares for weeks afterward, even though he heard worse cries later. That was the first, the moment he should have stopped it all, but he hadn't. He feared the curse painters, as anyone who looked into their eyes would, and he let them do as they pleased.

He picked up his pace, though his feet felt heavy and his bones ached worse than ever. Maybe stopping that first punishment wouldn't have done any good. Maybe the curse painters would have turned their fell magic on him, but that was the moment when he should have tried. Everything that had happened after was his responsibility.

It was that thought that tumbled around and around the old captain's mind as he marched down the corridor and listened to the pregnant girl screaming.

THIS IS A STORY ABOUT VILLAINS—and those who choose whether or not to stand against them.

CHAPTER 19

Archer and the team reached the shallow ravine leading to Narrowmar at midday. Clouds tempered the brightness of the noon sun, and the autumn air had a crisp edge so close to the mountains. Archer had allowed a brief rest in the small hours of the morning, needing the team sharp for what was to come.

His anger had distilled throughout the long night, ever since their prisoner had confirmed that Mae had asked for help in New Chester. No matter what she'd been thinking when she left her father's house, she'd known by then that she wasn't safe with Tomas Larke.

Archer's hands shook at the thought of Tomas, with his stupid face—just handsome enough to tempt an impressionable girl—and his utter selfishness. Archer should never have introduced them. He was the one who'd gotten Mae mixed up with the Larkes, handing Jasper Larke a weapon in his never-ending battle with Lord Barden. Archer had cursed her as surely as if he'd held a paintbrush. He reined in his anger, purifying it into a singular focus. He had to undo the damage he'd inflicted. Rescuing Mae was the first step.

The team halted a safe distance from the mountain strong-hold, where they could prepare without risking discovery. They took shelter behind a large, misshapen stone, the lower half of a gigantic statue. Only the knees and booted feet remained, covered with lichen and a scattering of fallen leaves.

While the others hobbled the horses by the broken statue, Archer beckoned for Briar to scout ahead with him on foot. The captain of the Narrowmar garrison might know they were in the area by then. The old man had been stationed there for as long as Archer could remember, and he'd guarded it well. They had to be careful.

The ravine leading to the tall spur of the mountain and the fortress entrance had a narrow, rocky road down its center. They approached along the upper ridge so they could watch the road without being seen, picking their way through twisted trees and thorny brambles, wincing at the snap of every branch underfoot. Taller and healthier trees—mostly wych elms—lined the ridge nearer to the mountain, providing enough cover for Archer and Briar to get close to the ravine and the fabled stronghold unseen.

They crawled to the edge of the ridge on their bellies to survey their target. The stronghold was built into a narrow fissure, a mere crack in the rock guarded by a large stone door. One could look at the entrance and think it hid nothing more than a stable or a shepherd's hovel, but within the mountain lay a vast womb that had never been breached in its three-hundred-year history.

Archer was determined to break that record.

"That's the only entrance," he whispered, pointing out the large door, which was the same shade of pale gray as the moun-tainside.

Briar gave a low whistle. "It wouldn't be easy to get through that even without the enchantments."

"It's worse once you're inside," Archer said. "There's a

central corridor with tunnels and doorways leading off it. Soldiers could be waiting to jump out at you at every step."

As he spoke, the door opened a crack, and six men marched out, wearing burgundy uniforms and carrying pikes. They crossed the bare rocky area in front of the door and proceeded up the road, passing just beneath Archer's position on the ravine.

"I think it's safe to say Larke sent reinforcements to the garrison," Archer said. "Seen enough?"

Briar didn't answer, busy scrutinizing the stone door. Archer was deeply relieved she hadn't abandoned them when she'd discovered her parents were tangled up with the Larkes. Jemma's plan would be impossible without her. It might be impossible anyway, but he wasn't prepared to accept that.

Archer studied Briar covertly out of the corner of his eye. She had done darker things than he had ever dreamed of, and he couldn't discount the dangers she presented to his mission and personal safety. But she had also stepped away and tried to live a better life despite terrifying obstacles. He couldn't help admiring her. He wished he could lift some of the weight she carried.

The wind shifted, and a hint of Briar's linseed oil and rose scent reached him, reminding him of their dance on the threshing floor and the way she'd laughed. He had a sudden urge to cup her face in his hands and bring it closer to his.

He shook his head. *Dangerous mission, remember? Powerful enemies and mortal peril and betrayal and—*

"I've seen enough." Briar looked up at him then blinked as if surprised at the look on his face. "Are you okay—"

"That patrol could look up here anytime," he said gruffly. "We'd best be getting back to the others."

They picked their way back through the twisted trees, taking even more care to be quiet, and rejoined the rest of the group by the ruined statue. Esteban was crouched on the giant stone feet like an old crow, massaging his throat. Jemma was examining a wound Nat had received during the fight by the campfire. Lew was scribbling furiously in his notebook.

"You'll be unsurprised to hear that Narrowmar looks as unassailable as ever," Archer reported.

"So, what's the play, boss?" Nat asked. "We impersonating Larke's men? Sneaking in with the ale? I reckon they go through a few barrels a day."

"Nothing so elaborate," Archer said. "I can guarantee every method of attack has been tried before—except this one." He grinned, leaning jauntily on the statue's cracked left boot. "We're going to make our own entrance." He nodded at Briar. "Or more specifically, she's going to make us an entrance."

Nat's eyes widened. "What, by cutting through the mountain?"

"Cursing through the mountain," Archer said. "With a little luck, we're never going to get near that stone door again."

Lew departed to keep an eye on the road from the safety of a tree branch while the others prepared for the operation. They fed the horses—keeping them saddled in case they needed to leave in a hurry—sharpened their weapons, and reviewed the plan Jemma had devised after Briar revealed she could curse a tunnel straight through the mountain. They would wait until just before the dinner hour to make their move, when the soldiers were looking to their suppers after a long, uneventful day guarding an unassailable door. Archer hoped to be far away by the time the stars came out.

Nat looked increasingly nervous as the shadows began to slant from the broken statue. The lad's clothes were more disheveled than usual, and he kept pulling on his ear and looking at Briar, who was too preoccupied to offer any reassurances. Her lips were moving, as if she were reciting her curse order—or perhaps a prayer—over and over again.

Archer strolled over to Nat and thumped him on his

rounded shoulder. "You all right, mate?"

"You reckon it'll make noise when she blasts a hole through the rock?"

"Almost certainly," Archer said. "That's why we brought a mage with a very fine voice."

Nat frowned. "I thought Esteban wasn't going to use his magic."

"Everyone has a role to play," Archer said. "Esteban is going to attempt to sing his way into one side of the mountain, covert-like, and while the defenders are busy catching him, our curse painter will burrow through the other side with a different sort of magic."

Archer had convinced Esteban it would be good for his reputation to get the credit for breaking Mae out of Narrowmar. His license tattoos would place him at the scene, even if he failed to breach the fortress. His voice, for all its power, didn't have the sheer destructive force of a painted curse. He couldn't punch a hole through a mountain.

Nat didn't look convinced. "Won't *he* need to be rescued then?"

"I have faith in Esteban's ability to evade capture," Archer said. "Besides, Esteban has been seen often in Barden County. Anyone who recognizes him will think this is an assault from Mae's father, which is the primary threat they've been expecting all along. They'll be too busy defending the fortress against him to see the real attack coming."

"If you say so." Nat wiped away the sweat beading on his forehead. "Remind me what I'm supposed to do again."

"You will watch out for Briar while she works and help get Mae out through the tunnel—carry her if necessary. You're the brawn, remember? You need to be extra careful with her in her condition."

"What about you?"

"I'm going to help Esteban with the diversion." Archer

counted the arrows in his quiver, making sure the fletching was straight on each one. "Between us, we're going to cause a ruckus to wake the lower realms."

They had only decided that part earlier that morning. Archer had originally planned to go into the tunnel with Briar to find Mae himself, but after their brawl with the patrol by New Chester, they had to assume Narrowmar's defenders knew his crew was in the area. One of the soldiers could have escaped amidst the confusion around the fire. If Archer wasn't with Esteban, they would know the voice mage was only a diversion. There was an outsized chance Archer would be captured, but that was a risk he was willing to take.

Nat still looked worried. "What about Lew?"

"He will be acting all diverting with me and Esteban. Don't worry, Nat. He'll be fine."

"If you say so."

Nat ambled over to Briar, who was rearranging the contents of her paint satchel with meticulous hands. "Are you really powerful enough to make a tunnel all the way into that mountain?"

"Let's hope so," Briar said.

"How do you know we won't punch right through to a room full of soldiers?"

"That's where I come in," Jemma said. She was tying stiff leather bracers onto her arms, knife hilts poking out above each wrist. Her cudgel swung at her belt, and her red shawl was knotted across her chest. "I lived inside that mountain in another life. I know it well."

"I thought it was Larke Castle you knew," Nat said.

Jemma's mouth tightened, pulling at her spidery wrinkles. "I've spent time in both places."

"And Archer?" Briar looked up from her paints. "You've also been inside Narrowmar before, right?"

Archer slung his quiver over his shoulder. "In another life, as Jemma says."

Nat looked between the two of them. "Am I the only one who doesn't have a secret history?"

"You're making your secret history as we speak," Archer said. "The reward for rescuing Mae will make you rich. You can set up as a gentleman somewhere and keep the story of how you came by your riches to yourself as long as you want."

"Huh," Nat said. "I'd never thought of that."

He wandered off to make sure the horses were securely tethered in the shadow of the broken statue. They would make their final approach soon. Archer was ready to get on with it. They had crossed river and forest and field for their mission, and the longer they waited, the more he thought of all the ways it could go wrong. They still didn't know what surprises the curse painters had prepared for them, but they were counting on the magical defenses being centered around the ravine road and the great stone door.

Archer walked over to where Briar was digging in her saddlebags and muttering under her breath about malachite, azurite, and ochre.

"Are you ready?"

"I think so." She pulled a jar of black paint from the bottom of a saddlebag and tucked it into her bulging canvas satchel. Her movements were jerky, betraying her nerves. "The mountain is bigger than I expected. I hope I have enough paint."

"I have faith in your powers of destruction."

She sighed. "I guess I'll take that as a compliment."

"Please do." Archer paused, gathering his thoughts. "I know you aren't always fond of your power. I'm sorry I dragged you away from your cottage and made you use it."

"That life was doomed anyway," Briar said briskly, still fiddling with her satchel. "Besides, you need me."

"I do. Maybe more than you think."

Briar looked up to meet his gaze. Archer remembered when

he first saw her peering out of that maple tree by Winton's house, owlish and devastating. He brushed a frizzy curl back from her forehead, his hand lingering on her cheek. She watched him with a careful stillness. He couldn't tell if she was about to lean toward him or pull away. He wasn't entirely sure what he was about to do either.

He wanted to kiss her. Of course he did. He'd wanted to kiss her every minute since she'd first fallen out of that tree and into his life, but his work wasn't done. Kissing Briar would complicate everything that had to happen after they completed their mission. He accepted that. It wouldn't be fair.

Still, his hand lingered on her face. She blinked, her eyelashes fluttering against his skin. Her sweetbriar lips parted. His pulse accelerated, beating like a drum. It may not be fair, but he was going to do it anyway.

Just as Archer was about to throw away every last scrap of caution and lean in, something large thudded into the back of his legs. He pitched forward, nearly knocking Briar down. They grabbed each other instinctively to keep their balance.

The large thing that had rammed into him had a big wrinkly head and sun-dappled gray fur. He leapt up on his back legs and began slobbering all over Archer's face.

"Sheriff! It's about time you showed up. You almost missed all the fun."

The dog continued to enthusiastically—and wetly—greet his master. Then he dropped back to all fours and regarded Briar with bright black eyes. She looked at him uncertainly, as if afraid she'd offended him by spiriting his master across the river without him. Before she could say anything, Sheriff leapt on top of her and proceeded to greet her as vigorously as he had greeted Archer himself.

"Okay, okay, she missed you too," Archer said, patting his old friend on his meaty shoulders and avoiding Briar's eyes so he wouldn't be drawn in again. It was better that way. "We have work to do. You reckon you can keep an eye on the horses for us?"

Sheriff whined his acquiescence.

"Good. Then I think it's time we follow up all this talk with a bit of action."

No sooner had he said it than trumpets blared through the woods loud enough to shake the leaves from their branches. Lew dashed up moments later, breathing heavily. He had twigs in his red hair, and bits of bark clung to his beard.

"A whole caravan of riders," Lew said, "coming up the canyon road."

Archer was already reaching for his bow. "More reinforcements?"

"Could be," Lew said. "They're still far off. Most are soldiers, but there's a fancy carriage too."

"Show me."

Lew led the way, and soon Archer was back on the ridge, though farther from the wych elms and the stone door than before. Two dozen armed and liveried fighting men were riding up the road, surrounding a carriage bearing a familiar sigil, one Archer had looked at with mixed feelings for most of his life. A man sat inside the carriage, his profile visible through the open window.

Rage bubbled up in Archer's gut, a familiar torrent of emotion that had gotten him in a great deal of trouble the last time he'd seen that man. That man was the reason Archer was there, the reason Mae and her child were in danger. He was why Archer's life wasn't truly his own, why he couldn't kiss Briar without feeling guilty, why he had committed himself to their mission and everything that had to happen afterward.

"Today is going to be more exciting than we thought," Archer said, fighting to keep his voice calm. "It looks like Lord Larke himself is here."

Lord Jasper Larke, Archer's father.

CHAPTER 20

" C hange of plans."

Briar looked up to see Archer marching back to where she waited with the others by the broken statue. His jaw was clenched, his dark eyebrows drawn low. The breezy bravado he'd displayed moments ago had disappeared.

"Lord Larke is coming up the canyon road with two dozen retainers. He'll reach Narrowmar in twenty minutes."

"He'll want to see Mae at once," Jemma said. "We were counting on her being alone."

Archer nodded grimly. "We can't wait until he leaves. He could stay until after the baby is born and take it with him when he goes."

"So we're too late?" Nat asked.

"Not yet," Archer said. "But we can't wait until suppertime like we planned. Esteban?"

"Yes?"

"What do you say we attack the caravan right now, before Lord Larke has a chance to reach the front gates?"

"Archer," Jemma began.

"It'll get their eyes on us, same as we planned."

Esteban studied Archer intently. "Just to be clear, instead of pretending to sing my way through the side of the mountain, you now want me to attack two dozen armed men out in the open?"

"That's exactly what I want."

A dark intensity burned in Archer's eyes. Something had changed in him at the sight of Lord Larke. It made Briar nervous, but it drew her in too. She recognized that intensity, that rage. It sang in time with the destruction crackling in her fingertips.

"We're too close to the stronghold," Lew said. "It would be suicide to attack outright."

"I'm not expecting to win," Archer said. "But Esteban can handle whatever Narrowmar spits out. Quickly. We have to ambush them right now, or it'll be too late."

"It's already too late," Jemma said. "Ambushes take planning. We can't just run down to the road and start—"

"Mae doesn't have any time left," Archer interrupted.

"We have to be smart about this, Archer," Lew said, raising his hands as if approaching a rabid animal. "Even with Esteban's skill—"

"We swore to do this no matter what it takes," Archer said. "Jemma, Nat, and Briar can get Mae to safety. Take her into the wilds if you have to. Just don't let her fall back into Larke's hands. Lew and Esteban, you're with me."

Jemma's face was white, her lips as bloodless as a corpse's. "Archer—"

"This isn't a discussion," Archer snapped.

The others looked stunned by his vehemence, but they moved, hands tightening on weapons, jaws setting with determination. Their easygoing leader was gone. Briar sensed the pull, the vision, that had made them follow him. Archer was no longer a thief working a job. He was a man on a life-or-death mission, and he would see it done no matter what.

Jemma was the only one who still hadn't moved. "Archer, if you die attacking his stupid carriage—"

"Then so be it. I won't let him get away with this, Jem."

They faced each other for a moment, and it was as if a shining tether connected them, a link Briar didn't understand. After a long, taut silence, Jemma nodded.

Suddenly, Archer whirled to face Briar, that dark fire still burning in his eyes.

"You have to succeed," he said hoarsely.

Briar swallowed. "I will."

"Good." He nodded sharply. "Good." Then he took two quick strides forward and swept her into his arms.

The rest of the team and the woods and the world faded away as Archer kissed her. It was a whirlwind and a churning river and a collapsing house and a blazing fire. She wrapped her arms around his neck and dug her fingers into his shock of blond hair. There was urgency to his mouth on hers, his arms lifting her right off her feet. When he set her down, Briar clutched the sleeves of his indigo coat to keep from stumbling, too hazy to think straight.

"It's about time," Lew muttered. "Now, can we get on with our suicide mission, please?"

"Let's do this." Archer stepped back from Briar and slung his bow across his shoulders at a jaunty angle. "Summon all the luck you have to spare, friends. It's time we got this rescue underway."

"For the reward and the challenge and the open road!" Nat said.

"For Lady Mae," Archer said, "and for everyone else Lord Larke thinks he owns."

Briar regained her senses enough to dig into her saddlebags and grab one last thing she had been working on.

"Take these." She handed out bundles of carefully wrapped stones. "They'll make little explosions if you throw them against something and make your enemies think there are more of you. Be careful." She reached Archer last and closed his fist around the sack of curses, trying to communicate a riot of emotion through the pressure of her hands. She didn't know what had prompted him to kiss her after he'd held back for so long, but she would make sure it wasn't the last time. "And don't die."

She released him and turned to Jemma and Nat. "Shall we begin?"

They left Sheriff to guard the horses, and Jemma led the way through the trees to the eastern side of the mountain, where Briar would carve a tunnel into Lady Mae's prison. As she and Nat followed Jemma up the slope, Briar strained to hear what was happening behind them, listening for Esteban to make his move.

The air smelled of pinesap, moss, and sun-warmed earth. The afternoon sun had dipped behind the peak, and the shadowy forest offered plenty of cover, making it a simple matter to hide from patrols. The stronghold's defenders would focus on the ravine and the entrance, especially with Lord Larke's carriage approaching.

Briar explained the risks they were about to undertake as they picked their way up the steep incline. "I don't know the interior composition of this mountain. There could be soft places where the rocks might collapse on top of us. Smaller curses would give us a better chance of getting through safely, but they'll take longer. I might need to try some bigger curses."

"Can you reinforce the ceiling?" Jemma asked.

"I've added something to the design for that," Briar said. "It's my own invention. When miners employ curse painters to make their tunnels, they brace them with wooden beams. It takes time and manpower and makes noise. There's no way we could carve that sort of tunnel into this fortress without getting caught, especially with such a small team."

"And your invention will help?"

Briar hesitated. "That's the idea. I'll displace the stone as carefully as possible, but my modifications might not work. If you want to stay outside until I'm through with the riskiest part, I completely understand."

"You'll need me to navigate once we're in the stronghold," Jemma said, "but I think Nat should stay outside to guard the tunnel."

"I agree," Briar said. "We can't have anyone coming in after us."

"Wait a minute." Nat stopped short, looking at Briar for the first time since Archer kissed her. "Don't leave me out."

"You won't miss anything," Briar said.

Color rose in Nat's cheeks, making him look very young. "We're supposed to be in this together," he mumbled.

Briar sighed. She'd hoped the mission would take his mind off his thwarted crush. "You can stand guard while I'm making the tunnel, and we'll call you in when it's time to breach the inner wall. Please? We need a lookout."

"Fine." Nat's wide shoulders slumped. "You better not have any interesting fights without me."

"We'll do our best."

They soon reached a place where a short cliff jutted out from the mountain. Juniper trees gathered at its base and clung to the slopes above, framing it with their twisted branches.

"This is the spot." Jemma set down her unlit lantern and laid a hand on the east-facing stone. The pale-gray rockface was as flat and inviting as an empty canvas. "If we go straight in from this point, we'll end up in a banquet hall that's no longer used. It's the closest we'll get to where I think they're keeping Mae."

"Okay then." Briar removed her satchel from her shoulder and spread her paint jars in front of the rock wall. This was it, the reason she'd been recruited for the team, even though she hadn't known her true enemy then. She felt a tingle in her fingertips, a hot rush of creation and destruction. "Brace yourselves. This could get messy."

CHAPTER 21

Archer watched the caravan from the branch of a wych elm at the top of the canyon. The fine carriage and its two dozen burgundy-clad guards were only a hundred paces from the stone door. Archer had always known they would be vastly outnumbered, and he'd hoped to avoid an all-out assault, but now that it came down to it, he felt a grim satisfaction that he would be facing his father directly.

Well, not quite directly. He fully intended to stay hidden in the tree for as long as possible, but it was a fight nonetheless.

Some of his rage cooled as he waited in the wych elm. Jasper Larke was a despicable excuse for a man, but Archer had broken free of him. He'd refused to live on Larke's terms any longer, and today, he would make sure Mae and her child and all the lands it would inherit didn't have to either.

He pulled on a pair of supple leather gloves and nocked an arrow, thumbing the fletching he had cut himself. He had spent long hours practicing with this bow despite—or perhaps because of—his father's insistence that he focus on the sword, like his older brother. Larke claimed the bow was for common soldiers, but the weapon felt right in Archer's hands.

Esteban perched in another tree farther along the ridge like a grumpy vulture. He gulped water from a skin and hummed softly, limbering up his voice. Lew had circled around to the other side of the canyon behind the caravan, his hands gloved and his pockets full of Briar's exploding curses. Archer and Lew had both stuffed knots of fabric into their ears to dampen the effects of Esteban's magical sound. They couldn't turn back.

Clinging to the tree branch with his legs, Archer let go of his bow with one hand and took a curse stone out of his pocket —this one bright red. He rolled it between his leather-clad fingers, wishing Briar fair luck on her mission. If he fell today, he trusted her to finish the job.

Time to give her that diversion.

He lobbed the stone out of the tree, and it ignited with a flash and a muted bang about twenty feet away. In answer, several small explosions flashed on the opposite ridge. Lew was ready too.

The men on the road below turned, looking for the source of the bangs, reaching for their short swords. Archer raised his bow. More explosions popped along the ridge, the flashes of light giving the impression that many men gathered in the trees. The soldiers searched for their hidden enemies, preparing to charge. Before they could do that, Esteban began to sing.

The song was beautiful and terrible even through the fabric plugging Archer's ears. He'd heard Esteban's voice countless times since they'd met back in Chalk Port, but he was still surprised by its power, strong enough to knock a man down through the sheer force of sublime sound. Esteban's healing songs were strong but also gentle. This one had the commanding beauty of an ocean or a tornado or a look from a woman with fierce eyes and magic in her hands.

Archer barely held onto his bow and arrow and his tree branch as the song rippled outward from Esteban. It wasn't even directed at Archer, but its reverberations traveled through the ground, the tree, the pit of his stomach. The men down on the road wouldn't know what hit them.

The voice magic rolled over Larke's retainers like a tidal wave. They ducked instinctively, though only sound had actually touched them. The song would disorient them, leaving their minds unbalanced and their senses reeling.

Esteban deepened his tone, and the effects changed from confusion to fear. Terror rippled through the caravan as the men covered their ears and frantic whinnies burst from the horses, only to be swallowed up by that petrifying sound. The song blasted them, wrecking their nerves, ruining their resolve. It was as destructive as any curse, even though it left their bodies untouched. Every note, every beat, every turn and cadence conveyed to these men that death was coming for them.

The horses were the first to bolt, a dozen animals trying to flee at once. Some riders managed to keep their mounts under control, but others were even more scared than their horses, and they gave the animals their heads, allowing them to run where they wished.

As some men succumbed to Esteban's music-induced terror, others ran toward the trees where Archer and Esteban were hiding. They'd realized the threat was coming from that direction, and they were making a desperate charge, trying to take down the hidden sorcerer before he hurt more of their comrades. Archer swallowed as the men drew nearer. He had to defend Esteban, even if that meant striking down those brave soldiers. He'd brought the voice mage into it. He'd brought all of them into it.

He began to pick his targets. He drew back his bowstring, sighted, released. There was a twang and a thud, again, and again.

The vibration of the bow and the thump of arrows slamming into bodies made their own music, which Archer felt more than heard. One by one, frightened men fell to his arrows. He tried to close his eyes to their faces, even as he closed his ears to Esteban's song, but he knew some of those men. They had protected him on long rides through the countryside. They had laughed at his youthful jokes. They had served him, pledging to give their lives for his family. They were fulfilling those vows, charging up the ridge, forcing him to shoot—and each arrow felt as if it were striking Archer's own body.

More arrows found their targets. More men dropped like stones on the road. One got caught in his stirrups as he fell, his horse too mad with fear to care. The animal charged back down the canyon, dragging his dying rider with him. Archer released another arrow to put the man out of his misery.

The chaos didn't last long. The surviving soldiers regained control of their horses and formed up around the carriage. Lord Larke's face was no longer visible through the window. Archer didn't think he could shoot an arrow into that face anyway, and he was relieved he didn't have to make that choice. He pressed a shaking hand against the tree trunk, staring at the men scattered across the ridge, his arrows protruding from their bodies. It had happened so quickly—going from swearing to do anything to save Mae to shooting men he knew. He felt as if he were descending into a pitch-dark well with no way of stopping.

Then the carriage door opened, and a new face appeared. Another man had been riding in the carriage with Lord Larke, a well-dressed, portly fellow Archer recognized as Croyden, his father's loyal voice mage. Archer shouted a warning to Esteban. Despite looking like a country gentleman, that mage was powerful, well trained, and fully licensed.

Croyden stepped down from the carriage and strode across the rocky ground, the soldiers falling in around him. He pulled back the sleeves of his fine purple cloak, revealing the tattoos covering his fleshy arms. He drew in a breath, and the counter-attack burst from his throat and spun toward the trees.

Esteban's tone changed in response. Croyden's attack crashed into a fortress of sound. Undeterred, he catapulted notes at the ridge with increasing ferocity. Esteban's lips curled, and he answered the attack chord for chord.

The two mages fought, shouting and singing death at one another. The song of one voice mage was sublime enough. The dueling duet of two voice mages was on another plane altogether. It was as if demons and gods and beasts were roaring at each other from the heights and depths of their dominions.

Archer nearly forgot his arrows as the cacophony shook the leaves from the trees and made the earth tremble. He could see—and hear—why mages had to be licensed and subject to such strict rules. Their powers unchecked could rip apart the fabric of the world.

Archer tightened his grip on his tree branch as the mages shook the mountain to its roots. Few mages were as powerful as Esteban, but Croyden held his own, undaunted by the magical barrage. Archer hadn't realized he was so strong.

Suddenly, Croyden bared his teeth and howled like a wolf, targeting Esteban's tree. The attack rattled the elm so hard Archer feared his friend would be shaken loose.

Esteban had a death grip on the trunk, but his aged hands were slipping. His voice became hoarse. The attack had gone on for too long. They needed to distract Lord Larke for as long as possible, but Esteban couldn't keep singing forever under those conditions.

Archer pulled another arrow from his quiver and nocked it. He sighted along the slim wooden shaft. He would only have one shot. Croyden could slay him with a word if he figured out which tree he was in. One shot or Esteban would fall too.

Croyden's lips and ears bled from the assault of sound, but he refused to back down. He was slowly overwhelming Esteban. Archer didn't want to kill the man simply for fulfilling his duties, but he had to protect his team. He found his target, drew back, breathed, released.

The arrow struck true. Croyden toppled to the ground. Silence echoed through the canyon.

For one heartbeat, Archer allowed himself to believe they might succeed in their quest after all. Then the large stone door at the end of the canyon swung open, and thundering footsteps shattered the sudden quiet.

Reinforcements poured out of the doorway—a dozen soldiers, two dozen. More than Archer could shoot with his remaining arrows even if he wanted to. At their head rode two people he'd never seen before—a man and a woman, both with straight backs and severe expressions. The man had large owlish eyes, and the woman had dark frizzy hair. Both carried satchels across their saddles, and their hands were dripping with a multitude of colors.

"Archer!" Esteban shouted, his powerful voice strained thin. "That's—"

The rest of his words were lost as the entire ridge exploded, throwing Archer from his tree. A pinwheel of white light swirled across his vision. Then everything went dark.

CHAPTER 22

B riar repeated the strokes for the curse on the tunnel wall
again and again, her fingers tingling with magic. Yellow
ochre, umber, green earth, carbon black, carmine, umber,
brown ochre, lead white, carmine, yellow ochre, bone black,
carmine. Over and over she painted a gray-brown mountain
pierced by a nimbus of fire. As she finished each curse with a
flare of red at the center, the mountain rumbled, and a stretch
of stone fell into dust.

Some of the rubble disappeared with each blast, a tricky
addition to the curse using yellow ochre and carbon black—
one of several modifications Briar had made to the standard
demolition curse. It kept the tunnel from filling up with stone
dust as she worked. Even so, there was precious little air to
spare. She worked in silence, only speaking when she needed
to confirm the route with Jemma, who crouched behind her
with a candle lantern.

Briar's back ached from bending over in the tunnel, and her
eyes were grainy from the dust. The smells of linseed oil and
candle wax were suffocating. She felt as if she hadn't seen the
sky in a year. Her paints were becoming congealed and dirty.

She had to close all the jars tightly before painting the final stroke in each curse, slowing her progress through the mountain.

Earth-deep rumbling sounds indicated a fight had begun at the stronghold's entrance. So far, no one knew they were there. The usual guard patrols would cover the woods where the tunnel opened, but the excitement in the ravine was keeping most of the soldiers occupied. Nat kept watch among the juniper trees at the tunnel entrance in case someone happened by unexpectedly.

Briar would have preferred Nat's company in the tunnel over Jemma's. The older woman had directed Briar's course into the mountain with confidence, but she made a taciturn companion. Briar still wasn't sure why Jemma objected to her so strongly. She hadn't said much at all to Briar since Archer had kissed her.

"Okay, get ready for another one," Briar said, closing her jars and preparing the final stroke.

Jemma adjusted her red shawl over her nose and mouth without speaking.

Holding her breath, Briar painted the final swatch of carmine. There was a loud crack, and the painting began to eat into the stone, its colorful maw swallowing dust and breaking off larger rocks, which fell to the floor. She hadn't found any magical protections so far. Hopefully she wouldn't hit a magical barrier when she reached the inner shell of the stronghold. She couldn't fracture it without the marine-snail purple.

When the curse had cut as far into the stone as possible, Briar wiped the dust off her face with a scrap of canvas, climbed over the rubble, and prepared to paint it yet again.

Jemma clambered after her then set down the candle lantern and produced a water skin from her saddle bag, holding it out without a word. Briar accepted it gratefully and took a large gulp, the dust turning to mud in her throat.

"We'd better check on Nat soon," Briar said, wiping a drop of water off her chin. "I want to know what's happening out there."

"I'll go." Jemma took back the water skin and returned it to her bag, but instead of heading down the tunnel, she frowned at Briar for a long moment, the candlelight flickering in her deep-blue eyes. "Do you know who he is?"

"Nat?"

"Archer. Have you figured it out?"

Briar hesitated, wondering whether to reveal how much she had guessed. "He's Lord Larke's younger son, isn't he? Tomas is his brother."

"Very good." Jemma didn't smile. "I always thought you were sharp."

"He knows too much about the Larke household," Briar said. "And he hasn't really hidden the fact that this mission is personal. No one gets people riled up like family." She twirled her paintbrush between her fingers. "I've heard the names of Jasper Larke's sons before. He was called Ivan, right?"

"You know a lot about the powerful families of this kingdom."

Briar met Jemma's gaze steadily. "I lived in Barden County, remember?"

Jemma glanced at the paint smearing Briar's hands, and Briar flinched, resisting the urge to hide them from view. She doubted Jemma had started the conversation out of friendship. She turned to the wall and began the curse again. Yellow ochre, umber, green earth, carbon black, carmine, umber, brown ochre, lead white, carmine, yellow ochre, bone black, carmine.

"So why did Archer leave home?" she asked as she worked, magic swelling and shivering in her hands.

"He saw how Jasper Larke's hatred for Lord Barden corrupted him," Jemma said. "Larke would happily ruin his entire county to prevail over his rival—if they weren't already impoverished by his draconian taxes." She paused. "And Jasper is cruel. Tomas suffers from corruption of a different sort, but neither lord is what you'd call noble. Archer became disillusioned with his family and tried to wash his hands of them by becoming an honest thief."

It fit with almost everything Archer had told her about himself. He'd sworn he was neither prince, nor duke, nor long lost king. The Larkes were barons. And he had a noble streak, one that had nothing to do with fine breeding and education, but he had been drawn back into his family's affairs.

"I take it Tomas getting Lady Mae pregnant changed things?"

Jemma nodded. "Archer and Mae Barden both summered in High Lure in their youth. Archer struck up a friendship with her, hoping to bridge the divide between their two houses. He thought the younger generation could heal the old wounds."

Briar dipped her paintbrush in a jar of brown ochre. "Were they courting?"

"They got on well, but she never looked at him the way she looked at his dashing older brother when he visited the city to make sure Archer wasn't getting into too much trouble."

"So Tomas never would have gotten close to Mae if Archer hadn't done it first."

"He feels responsible for her and for that child," Jemma said. "But he also sees the potential if the two households are united. He wouldn't condemn anyone to a life with his brother, but he could still serve that function himself."

Briar wiped her brush and switched to the jar of lead white. "I don't understand."

"Don't you?" Jemma asked quietly. "Archer intends to marry Lady Mae and raise the child as his own."

The tunnel became very still. White paint dripped onto the stones at Briar's feet. That would explain why Archer had gone to such lengths for Mae, why he had resisted kissing

Briar for so long. If the way he'd finally pulled her into his arms was any indication, he'd been wanting to for a while. She pictured him striding toward her, reckless, intense. *Stop. That's not helping.*

She frowned at Jemma. "Why are you telling me this?"

"Because I don't want you to get the wrong idea," Jemma said. "That kiss back there ... Archer got swept up in the moment. You shouldn't think it means anything beyond that. Archer has a greater mission, one that could heal this land of the damages the Barden-Larke rivalry has caused, and he would raise a better son than his brother to steward both counties in the future."

Briar lowered her brush and turned to Jemma, feeling that old destructive impulse rising up. The mountain seemed to tremble in response. "Are you telling me to stay out of the way of this grand destiny?"

"I'm telling you to stay away from Archer," Jemma said. "I've warned him you're dangerous, but he doesn't listen to me."

"He hired me because I'm dangerous."

Jemma snorted. "I'm not talking about your ability to destroy wood and stone. You have the power to offer that boy exactly what he has always wanted. He envies freedom. His quips about his horse and his bow and the open road are sincere. You broke away from your past, and you are tempting him to run even farther from his."

"That sounds like his decision not mine."

Briar returned to her work, refusing to be intimidated. But as she painted the mountain with the nimbus of fire, the aroma of linseed surrounding her, she thought she smelled dry thatch and wood smoke, too, heard laughter and fiddles and drums. The image collapsed before it could form.

"Archer won't abandon his duties," Jemma said. "He set out on this mission to restore his family and change the way they treat their people. He could do such good for this land. Don't make it harder than it has to be. If you care for him at all, walk away."

The ground rumbled beneath them, above them. Somewhere on the mountain, the fight was escalating. Somewhere, Archer was risking his life to atone for his brother's sins. Briar had known Archer and Mae had history, possibly romantic history, but she hadn't fully understood they had a future too. Still, she resented that Jemma was telling her rather than Archer himself.

"What's your stake in all this?" she asked. "You worked in the Larke household. You were Archer's tutor or something, right?"

"I'm his mother."

Briar's hands jerked, paint smearing on the wall. The response seemed to have slipped unbidden from Jemma's lips.

"You are never to repeat this." Jemma stepped closer. "Archer himself doesn't know."

Briar turned slowly to face the older woman. Only the lantern stood between them, illuminating Jemma's silver-and-blond hair, the same shade of blond as Archer's.

"How is that possible?"

"I worked as a clerk for Jasper Larke. He took advantage of me." Jemma's voice was calm, matter of fact. "He kept my little boy—born right here in Narrowmar—just in case anything ever happened to his firstborn. His wife was already sickly then, unable to have more children. I swore to keep it secret to keep my position in his household, first as a clerk then as a tutor for his sons. I was willing to live in the home of my attacker if it meant I could see my child grow up. When Archer ran away, I was only too happy to follow."

Briar released a breath, the exhalation echoing through the tunnel. "Why haven't you told him?"

"I meant to when I caught up with him a few months after he left Larke Castle," Jemma said. "But I worried he would go after his father in a rage and get himself killed. He controls his anger much better now than he did in his youth. But the longer I waited, the harder it was to explain why I hadn't told him earlier."

"Does Lew know?"

Jemma adjusted her red shawl. "Lew knows I had a child before I met him, but he thinks it died at birth. I am only telling you because I believe you will do the right thing."

Briar blinked. "You do?"

"Yes." Light flickered across the lines in the older woman's face. She sounded sincere, and it caught Briar off guard. People had rarely counted on her to do the right thing.

"Whatever awful things are in your past," Jemma said, "I believe you really are trying to be good. This is one of the ways you can show it. Mae is a sweet girl, and I believe she and Archer can raise a child who will not continue his father and grandfather's legacy. They can change what it means to be a Larke."

"And you want bigger things for Archer than a life of crime."

"He deserves better than this," Jemma said. "I think you see it too."

Briar didn't answer. Jemma's revelations tumbled through her mind like stones in an avalanche. She understood what Jemma wanted for her son—and why Briar didn't fit into that plan—but she didn't know if Archer shared her ambitions. Did he really plan to marry Lady Mae? He had seemed to mean that kiss. On the other hand, he'd held back when he'd had other opportunities to kiss her. Was it because he had a different future waiting for him?

Her heart sinking, she looked at the other woman, seeking confirmation, reassurance, even sympathy. Fierce resolve showed in the set of Jemma's mouth—but there was pain in her gaze too. This woman had sacrificed so much for a child who didn't know her. Unsure what to say in the face of that pain, Briar turned back to the wall and opened her jar of carmine paint.

"I'd better go check on Nat," Jemma said after a minute, her voice betraying just a hint of emotion, like the beginnings of a sore throat. "I should check the tunnel's length anyway. We'll need to turn left soon."

"I'll keep going here. Tell Nat he's a hero."

Jemma didn't leave right away. "Will you be okay?"

"We have a job to do." Briar kept her eyes on her work, on the meticulous shape of the curse. "We'll worry about the rest of it later."

Jemma still didn't move. Briar knew what she was waiting for.

"I will keep your secret. I promise."

"I'll be right back."

Leaving the lantern on the ground, Jemma hurried back up the tunnel. Her stride sounded confident as she traversed the treacherous path. Briar heard Archer in that stride, heard the truth of Jemma's story as the darkness swallowed her.

Briar sighed. Archer and Jemma had been on a mission before she'd met them, and it would continue long after she left. Perhaps she had been foolish to think she might have a part in his life. She would finish the job she had been hired to do, and then it would be time to move on.

She painted the final strokes of the curse a bit bigger than before, hoping to accelerate her progress. Her fingers had gone numb from the magic, and she felt the beginnings of a sore throat, too, the beginnings of a heartache. She wanted to be done.

The usual cracking and rumbling began as the curse ate into the rock, scattering dust and rubble at her feet.

Suddenly there was a distant boom she felt more than heard. An explosion far larger than the others shook the mountain. Briar lurched sideways, clinging to the tunnel wall as the earth shuddered. The candlelight flickered wildly.

A hairline crack appeared beneath her fingers. It spread, widened, reaching to the ceiling. The stone was cracking all around the tunnel.

Briar threw herself at the curse eating into the stone in front of her, willing it to work faster. A terrible rumbling sounded overhead. She pressed against the curse, flinging more paint to push it just a little bit farther.

The tunnel began to collapse around her, snuffing out the light. Briar strained against the magical image she could no longer see, her hands slipping on the oil paint, scraping against the stone.

Then the cursed wall gave a shudder and crumbled before her. She broke through the rock into an open space and tumbled to the ground in a pile of dust.

CHAPTER 23

When Archer opened his eyes, Esteban was singing. At first, he thought the fight must still be going, but the song didn't have the violent timbre he remembered from right before he'd lost consciousness. This song was rather pleasant. Unfortunately, at the same time Archer realized that, he noticed he was in a great deal of pain. The location of the pain was indiscriminate, as if his body were one giant throbbing welt.

He tried to lift his head and groaned. "What happened?"

Esteban paused in his song. "You broke your back falling out of the tree."

"What!"

Esteban planted a hand on Archer's chest to keep him from moving. "I have fixed the worst of it already. Now, will you allow me to finish healing your lacerations as well, or would you like Lew to sew them up for you?"

"Continue."

Esteban gave a delicate cough and resumed singing. As his voice poured over Archer, the pain receded, and a dull itching sensation replaced it as his torn skin stitched back together. Soon even that discomfort faded, along with Esteban's melody.

"Finished?" Archer asked as the mage fell silent.

Esteban didn't answer, and Archer feared he'd suffered some other ailment Esteban didn't want to tell him about. Perhaps one of his limbs had been severed when he'd fallen out of the tree or half his brains had ended up outside his skull. But the older man was simply very tired. He ran a gnarled hand over his face and slumped down beside Archer.

"You will live," he rasped. "At least long enough to face the next assault."

Archer sat up carefully, attempting to get his bearings. He and Esteban were alone in a shallow hollow. It looked entirely different from where he had climbed the wych elm to ambush his father's carriage. Fallen trees surrounded them, and piles of rocks were strewn about, some steaming as if a fiery volcano had thrown them skyward. The ground had peeled back, uprooting shrubs and loosening the earth for a hundred yards. The setting sun further altered the landscape.

"What *happened*?" Archer repeated.

"Do you remember attacking the caravan?"

"I thought we were winning." Archer rubbed the back of his neck. His pain might be gone, but the events were still hazy. "I killed their voice mage, but then some riders came from Narrowmar, and at their head ..."

Archer pictured dark eyes in proud faces, hands dripping with paint.

"Curse painters," he said. *Briar's parents.* He had dared to hope they hadn't stuck around after punishing New Chester. It was a wonder his father had kept them on if their services cost as much as Briar said. Jasper Larke was famously stingy.

"I have heard of those two," Esteban said. "Donovan and Saoirse Dryden. Mages across the kingdom, licensed or not, speak of them in hushed voice at their firesides. The Drydens work outside the law, believe themselves above it. Some still seek their services, though their help does not come cheap. I didn't expect to find them all the way out here."

"I did," Archer said. "Briar recognized their work in New Chester."

Esteban frowned. "She has some link to them, then?"

"You could say that."

"So my initial suspicions were correct. I had begun to think she … no matter." Esteban cracked his knuckles, looking resigned and maybe even a little hurt. "Can we assume she has already done away with Jemma and Nat and she is even now making sure Lady Mae will remain imprisoned until her child is born?"

Archer blinked. "What are you talking about?"

"Briar. You implied she's in league with these dark mages. I thought she must have had unusual teachers. I suppose she was placed in our group to betray us."

"No, she left them," Archer said. "She cut ties with those two. She'll help us fight them if it comes down to it."

Esteban went quiet, and Archer heard all the skepticism he needed to in the silence.

"You truly believe she is with us by coincidence?" Esteban asked at last.

"Yes, I do," Archer said stubbornly, though he understood Esteban's wariness.

They had all kept secrets upon secrets buried beneath more secrets. It was plausible that Briar had joined his crew in order to sabotage them, but could her pain when she'd described her work with her parents have been faked? Could she have lied about her desire to use her dark magic for good, which had so inspired Archer?

"I hope your trust in her is warranted," Esteban said gruffly, as if sensing Archer's doubts. "It will almost certainly be tested before the night is over." He glanced up at the setting sun. "We cannot remain here, but I've had no word from Lew."

Archer felt a tight pinch in his chest that had nothing to do with his fall from the tree. "Think he's hiding on the other side of the ravine?"

"I hope so. Lew is not equipped to face those curse painters, but he should have the good sense to remain hidden." Esteban got to his feet slowly, his joints creaking. "The Drydens know we're here now, but more importantly, they know *I* am here. My reputation is also spoken of with fear at certain firesides."

Despite his brave words, Esteban swayed. The fight and the healing song had taken too much out of him. His face was paler than usual, and his hands trembled. Archer leapt up and offered him an arm. He was grateful to be whole, but he wondered if Esteban should have saved his power instead of wasting it on healing him.

He helped the older man over to where the trees were still standing, the autumn leaves blown off them as if by a fierce wind. Esteban had only managed to drag Archer a little way from the ravine after they were flung from the trees.

"What will it take to defeat the Drydens?" Archer asked when they reached a more sheltered spot in the woods.

Esteban pursed his lips. "A variety of spells that require more time than we have and more power than I have left, at least without rest."

"Can we keep them busy while Jemma and Briar finish their task?"

"If you wish to scream in the face of impossible odds, then yes," Esteban said dryly. "We can keep them busy."

"They don't know Briar is here," Archer said. "I reckon we have the advantage."

Esteban snorted, but he didn't try to argue. He sank down to sit against a tree trunk, looking as tired as if he'd been running for three days. No matter what he said about screaming in the face of their odds, Archer didn't think Esteban had a whisper of power left in him. They would have to finish their task without magic—at least from Esteban.

Archer refused to contemplate the notion that Briar had been working with her parents all along. He had to believe children could choose a different path than their parents', a better path. He had to believe a son wasn't always doomed to repeat his father's mistakes.

His own father had made plenty of mistakes. Perhaps it was time they had a chat about them. Archer grinned. "Sit back and rest as much as you need, Esteban. I have an idea."

CHAPTER 24

B riar rubbed the dust from her eyes, coughing until her shoulders ached. Blackness surrounded her, as oppressive as a weight on her shoulders. At first she feared the debris from the tunnel collapse had blinded her, but she was simply in a very dark room, and her lantern had gone out.

She scrambled to her feet and felt around the mess of stone and dirt behind her. Huge rocks blocked the tunnel entirely. She couldn't get to it without cursing the whole mountain open again—and possibly bringing it down on her head. Hopefully Jemma had made it out to where Nat was keeping watch before the tunnel collapsed. Regardless of their fate, Briar was on her own—inside Narrowmar Stronghold.

She checked on the paint jars in her satchel, relieved to find most of them intact. Only one jar had broken open, though she couldn't tell which color was seeping through the canvas bag.

An eerie quiet filled the darkened space after the ruckus of the collapsing tunnel. She must be in one of the unused rooms at the back of the stronghold. She hadn't expected to be there without Jemma to navigate. She had no choice but to move forward.

She crept along the wall, the stone smooth beneath her hands, seeking an opening or corner that might indicate where she was. As her eyes slowly adjusted to the dark, the outlines of the space began to emerge, like a rough charcoal sketch. The room was large and rectangular, perhaps a former banquet hall or a training area. She grimaced. It could just as easily be a storeroom or a dungeon or an especially large privy. She wished she had a candle.

The sound of distant footsteps reached her. They were muffled, as if coming from inside the wall, or from a nearby corridor. Sure enough, her fingers soon met the scratchy wooden plane of a door. She pulled back, hoping the owners of those feet wouldn't come inside.

The footsteps drew nearer, accompanied by two male voices.

"… see what they did? The whole damn mountain rolled up and tried to make a run for it."

"Reckon they got the voice mage?"

"I'd be shocked if they didn't."

Briar winced. Were those men talking about Esteban? And were "they" who she feared they were? She inched closer to the wooden door.

"They still out there?"

"Aye. They're with Lord Larke. He wants us to bring the little one to his quarters."

"And the mother?"

"He doesn't much care about her."

"Poor girl. She's not much older than my daughter—and with a daughter of her own already."

Briar bit her lip, holding in a gasp. The two men passed the door at that exact moment—but they didn't enter. She remained motionless as their footsteps continued down the corridor outside her hiding place.

"Don't let his lordship hear it, but that son of his deserves to be castrated for using that young lady as he did."

"Aye, and after all that trouble, the baby turned out to be a girl. His lordship still doesn't have his heir."

"He could give it all to the little thing anyway. That would make a change, eh?"

"I'd rather follow a girl child than Lord Tomas."

"Aye. But that ain't up to folks like us."

The voices faded as they got farther from Briar. She waited until they were almost out of hearing range, then she used a gray curse stone to spring the lock on the door. She hurried down a dimly-lit corridor after the two men, trusting them to lead her to Mae.

Any misgivings Briar might have had about continuing the mission alone no longer mattered. The baby had already been born. The time for stealth had passed. If Briar didn't rescue Mae, she wouldn't survive the night—and the child might not either.

Briar followed the two men along the stone corridor as quietly as she could, holding her paint satchel carefully so the jars wouldn't rattle. Alcoves appeared at regular intervals in the walls, some with sculptures and some without. Twice she jumped when especially lifelike statues leered at her unexpectedly. Sweat crept down her face, mixing with the dust. Fortunately, the men ahead of her didn't encounter anyone else until they turned into a narrower torchlit corridor, where another pair of guards stood before a wooden door at a dead end.

"His lordship wants to see the baby."

"Yes, sir." One of the guards saluted and turned to unlock the door.

It's now or never. Briar grabbed a red curse stone from her bag and tossed it in the center of the corridor. There was a bang and a bright flash of light. The four men whirled around, reaching for their weapons in unison. Briar was already running toward them, drawing sleep stones from her pocket.

"What in the lower—"

Briar collided with the first man, his sword only halfway out of its sheath. She hooked one arm around his neck and stuffed the curse stone directly into his mouth. He dropped like a rag doll, and Briar landed hard on top of him.

The others gaped at the girl covered in dust who'd tackled their companion. She touched another curse stone to the nearest hand she could reach, and a second man slumped to the ground, snoring loudly. She shoved the stone down the neck of his shirt to keep him unconscious, praying it would stay against his skin.

The others finally recovered from their shock at the appearance of a stranger in their impenetrable fortress. One took off down the corridor, shouting for backup. With no time to think, Briar seized a black curse stone and threw it as hard as she could. It hit the retreating guard in the back of the neck.

He swore and clamped a hand over the wound, already gushing blood. The curse had cut deep and swift. He stumbled, frantically trying to hold in his lifeblood. There would be no stopping the bleeding.

Briar shuddered at his panicked gasps—which quickly faded to gurgles. She hadn't wanted to kill anyone, yet five minutes after entering Narrowmar Stronghold, she already had blood on her hands. Could she never stop?

Quivering with shame, she faced the final guard. He was young, and he looked wide-eyed and nervous and far too much like Nat. Briar searched her pouch full of stones, trying to find another sleep curse. All she had were cutting stones and explosives. Death curses, always death curses.

The young guard overcame his surprise at her sudden appearance and advanced with the careful steps of a practiced swordsman. He had seen her incapacitate three men in a matter of seconds. He must know she wielded dangerous magic, but he held his blade steady, daring her to advance.

Briar shook the bag of stones, searching for the nonlethal ones. She'd had more blues than this before. Where were they?

The guard drew nearer. She would have to use a cutting stone. She would have to condemn another innocent young man to bleed to death. No matter how hard she tried, she still piled ruin upon ruin. With a sob, she drew a black stone from the bag.

Then the door behind the guard opened, and a young woman in a pink dress slipped quietly into the corridor, a heavy clay pitcher in her hands. She was plump with golden curls and a pale, determined face. She moved stealthily, and the guard didn't notice her.

The girl caught Briar's eye and gave a slight nod. Briar made a sudden threatening movement, keeping the guard's attention on her. He drew in a breath, preparing to strike. Before he could, the young woman took a resolute step forward and smashed her pitcher over his head. The guard dropped to the ground without so much as a groan.

"I hope you're here to rescue us," Lady Mae said, facing Briar over the unconscious bodies of her captors. "He was the nicest one."

CHAPTER 25

Archer crouched among the rocks and splintered timber above the ravine, watching his father speak to Briar's parents. Lord Jasper Larke was taller than both of the Drydens, with broad shoulders and thick brown hair showing a hint of white at the temples. He always dressed impeccably—in the burgundy of House Larke today—and his gaze was hard, focused on what he wanted no matter how it affected the people around him.

Revulsion curled through Archer at the sight. He avoided thinking of Lord Larke as his father as much as possible. Most of his team didn't know his true identity, and he couldn't afford a slip of the tongue. He pretended his childhood in Larke Castle had been a dream—a nightmare, really—but as he watched from the ridge, Archer couldn't help but remember the many years he'd spent calling that man Father.

From the outside, Jasper Larke was a respectable member of the nobility, a baron who controlled one of the larger—albeit more remote—counties in the kingdom of Lure. On the rare occasions that he visited King Cullum's court, he was treated as an honored guest. The other gentry didn't see his cruelty. Jasper took pleasure in exercising control over his servants and retainers with no regard for fairness. And he believed firmly in his and his family's innate superiority.

Archer had first seen it in action when he was eight years old and he and the kitchen boy had set a pig loose in the Larke Castle banquet hall as a prank. In the ensuing chaos, a tapestry had caught fire and several valuable vases had been shattered. Archer had owned up to the stunt, insisting the whole thing had been his idea. Instead of punishing Archer, as he'd deserved, his father had taken out his rage on the kitchen boy. He'd beat the lad so badly that his skull had cracked, and he'd never been the same bright, good-natured person again. Larke had given the boy's family a handful of silver pennies and warned Archer to choose worthier companions in the future.

Larke treated everyone except his sons as inferior beings. He'd been cruel to Jemma, making demeaning comments anytime they'd crossed paths, though Archer knew she was smarter than all of them. He took advantage of the humble folk who worked his lands, levying the highest taxes in the kingdom and ignoring their pleas for a reprieve. The county barons were supposed to offer protection in exchange for labor, leadership in exchange for sweat and blood, but Jasper Larke didn't uphold his end of the bargain. Archer had seen nothing to suggest his brother would either.

Tomas cared only for sword fighting and chasing women. Archer had tried to talk to him about reforming their father's practices when he became the lord of Larke County, but Tomas had just stared at him as if he'd sprouted three heads, each uglier than the last. Tomas accepted their father's superior attitude wholesale, and he turned a blind eye to their father's cruelty.

Jasper's behavior had worsened after Archer's mother had died. At age eighteen, fed up and restless, Archer had run away. He'd had lofty plans for a life of heroism that would set him apart from the other Larke men—plans that had failed within a week. Highwaymen had robbed him of every ounce of gold he'd saved up for his escape, leaving him to wander the wilds, starving and ill-equipped to do anything about it. Finally, he'd stolen from a family of honest farmers. Then he'd kept stealing.

The wide world was harsher than Archer had expected without the aid of his father's name and fortune. He'd turned to thievery to make his way and wound up having a knack for it. More importantly, he got a taste of freedom outside his father's dominion, and he never wanted to go back.

As he grew more successful, he tried to focus only on the wealthiest targets who wouldn't be unduly burdened by his actions. He knew he wasn't *good* exactly, but he tried to treat his partners in crime fairly, and he was never cruel. It was still a far cry from the nobility he'd once dreamed of showing, and despite his best efforts, he had been drawn back into his father's world.

Jasper Larke must have danced for a week when he realized the strategic advantage Tomas had handed him through his indiscretion. Larke loathed Lord Barden deeply, and Mae and Tomas's child would be Barden's only heir as long as Mae didn't have more children. Tomas had never shown much aptitude for leadership, but his child would have Larke blood and a Barden inheritance. It was little wonder Larke had hired the terrifying Dryden couple to keep the child under his control.

Archer surveyed the ravine, where broken trees and broken men littered the ground. He couldn't defeat the curse painters, but he might still give Briar, Jemma, and Nat time to get Mae out of the stronghold. He would count that as a victory—even if it meant handing himself over to his father. It was better than shooting more of his men.

The sensation of descending into a pitch-dark well lingered in Archer's gut. It wasn't right to make other people pay the price for his and his family's actions, but there was another way.

Instead of continuing to take lives, Archer could give his up—at least the one he'd hoped to live.

Larke and the curse painters had finished instructing the retainers who were caring for the injured. They turned their backs on the carnage and headed toward Narrowmar's great stone door. Archer couldn't delay any longer. Bidding a final farewell to his freedom, he took a deep breath, climbed onto a large boulder, and began waving his arms over his head.

"Ahoy there! Your prodigal son has returned! Did I miss the action?"

His father's eyes widened in shock, and the color drained from his face. It was rather gratifying.

Lord Larke recovered quickly, lifting a hand to placate the curse painters, who were reaching for their brushes. His guards brandished their weapons, too, but none moved to attack their lord's younger son. For a moment, they all stared at each other across the rubble.

"Shall I come down there?" Archer called.

Larke looked as if he wanted to say no, but after a swift glance at the curse painters, he ordered his retainers to stand down and beckoned Archer with an impatient wave.

Archer hoisted his bow on his back and scrambled down the sloping side of the ravine, plastering on a wide grin. "I sure am glad to see you, Father. I was hunting in the woods nearby when I heard the commotion."

Larke's face could beat a statue in a staring contest. "Hunting."

"That's right. When I saw the mess here, I was afraid you were hurt, but it looks like your new friends have the situation well in hand."

"They do." Larke cast a tense glance at the curse painters. He looked embarrassed at his son's sudden appearance—or that he hadn't seen it coming. Lord Larke knew of Archer's exploits—as he'd communicated when he offered rewards for every member of the team except Archer—but he clearly hadn't expected him to walk up to Narrowmar's front door. "Where are your ... hunting companions?"

"Gone," Archer said. "I believe they met some of your men in the woods."

"I see." Larke's mouth tightened. He wouldn't question Archer further. He wouldn't want these powerful mages from High Lure to know his second-favorite son had fallen in with miscreants. Archer was gambling on his father's pride to keep himself and his friends alive a little longer.

"I don't think we've met." Archer turned to the curse painters, preparing to stall them, and recoiled from their gazes. He had seen hints of darkness within Briar, mere flickers of her destructive capabilities amidst everything else that made her *her*. He'd expected to find hints of humanity in her parents after hearing of the joy they'd taken in their young daughter and her work. But in the intervening years, the Drydens had scoured away anything but the darkness.

The woman was beautiful, with a crown of wild hair like Briar's and eyes that burned with black fire. She had an energy about her, incendiary and passionate. The man looked almost studious, with patrician features and elegant hands, but there was a cruel turn to his mouth and a soulless sort of intensity in his gaze.

"This is Saoirse and Donovan Dryden," his father said, a muscle working in his jaw. "They are here on important business from the king. Why don't you wait in my chambers until I have time to hear about your recent activities?"

"There's no need to send your son away," said Briar's mother. "Perhaps he has some insight into what happened on the ridge."

"Insight, Mistress Dryden?" Archer asked.

"You appeared soon after the voice mage ceased his song."

A specter of a smile crossed Saoirse's lips. "Very soon. Perhaps you saw something?"

"You mean heard something?"

The woman's smile vanished.

Archer swallowed, hanging onto his grin as if it were the edge of a cliff. "I just thought, since he was a voice mage, it would make more sense for me to *hear* rather than to s—"

"Please excuse my son's insolence." Lord Larke gripped Archer's shoulder hard, his eyes blazing with barely controlled fury. "He cannot always tell when it's appropriate to speak."

"On the contrary," Saoirse said, "I should like to hear what he has to say. Wouldn't you, darling?"

Donovan was staring at Archer as if he were a strange insect —one he was planning to take apart leg by leg. "I am sure it will be an enlightening conversation."

"I'll help however I can," Archer said. "Shall we go inside for a drink? I wouldn't mind taking off my boots in front of the fire in your sitting room, Father."

Larke gave Archer a severe look warning him not to offend the curse painters. Archer smiled blandly back. Little did Larke know the Drydens had also been forsaken by a child with a conscience. Perhaps they could commiserate when all was said and done. More importantly, his father would never send for Mae while Archer was in the room. He couldn't possibly hide the schism in his household then.

The Drydens clearly intimidated Larke, and there were currents of tension between the three of them that Archer hadn't yet figured out. The longer he kept them talking, the longer Briar and the others would have to finish the job.

At last Larke sighed. "I could do with a stiff drink myself. Shall we?"

They approached the stronghold's entrance, and the white-haired old captain who commanded the Narrowmar garrison met them at the large stone door. His burgundy uniform was neat but faded, and his back curved with age. His eyes were as clear and sharp as ever, though. He eyed them all with obvious disapproval. Archer had never particularly impressed the fellow, but it was the curse painters who received his starkest glowers.

Interesting. Archer might be able to use that.

"A moment, my lords," Donovan said before Larke and Archer could enter through the broad doorway. "The stronghold gates have two curses laid upon them. The first will kill instantly unless we invite visitors inside by their full names. The second ensures that no one who crosses this threshold may exit the mountain without our permission." He looked at Archer then. "Unless they wish to die painfully."

"That's very thorough of you," Archer said. *So Mae can't leave through that doorway.* Briar's tunnel might be the only way out for all of them.

He bowed, flourishing his hands as if ushering the man inside. "Please, won't you invite me into my own ancestral halls?"

Donovan cocked his head to the side. "Your full name, if you please."

"Ivan Archibald Larke. That's *Lord* Ivan Archibald Larke."

The curse painters entered the fortress, ignoring the old captain's glare. He watched them like an old guard dog—chained up and unable to stop an intruder from crossing his yard.

The curse painters spoke quietly to each other as they arranged jars and brushes along the floor. An intricate pattern of stars and moons was painted all the way around the entrance, including across the ground and over the lintel, as if stepping through the doorway signified stepping into the dark night of the lower realms. How much purple paint would it take to break *that* curse?

"Where did you find such friendly curse painters?" Archer

asked his father while they waited for the Drydens to work their magic.

"Do not trifle with them," Larke said through clenched teeth. He was clearly annoyed at having to wait outside the door like any other visitor while the curse painters added his name to the design in intricate swirling letters. "They are exceedingly powerful. I've gone to great personal expense to secure their services."

"Why is that exactly?"

"Play the fool if you must," Larke said. "You know about my guest, or else you wouldn't be here. Her father will try to retrieve her if he realizes where she is."

"And ignore the king's orders about your fun little rivalry? Surely only you are brave enough to do that."

Larke looked as if he wanted to strike Archer. It wouldn't be the first time. Archer tensed, waiting for the clenched fist, the raised hand. He felt young, as if the years and bravado he'd built up were being stripped away, even though he was as tall and strong as his father.

But Larke didn't try to hit him. Instead, his broad shoulders hunched. "I couldn't let Barden get his hands on the child. I had no choice."

Archer quirked an eyebrow. "Did you have a choice when you gave a bunch of illegal mages control of Narrowmar?"

"They won't be here long," Larke said, not sounding entirely convinced. "I only need them until—"

"It is done," Donovan Dryden announced. "All but the final stroke."

He dipped a brush as tiny as a bundle of eyelashes in a jar of pure-black paint, the deliberate precision of his movements so like Briar's. One by one, Donovan called out the names of Lord Larke and his surviving retainers, adding little black symbols on the doorway as he invited each man across the threshold. He saved Archer for last.

"This will be painful if you gave a false name," he said. "The effects would be even more fascinating than if someone were to cross this barrier without permission." His voice became animated, as if he were discussing an interesting phenomenon that had nothing to do with real people and real pain. "If you are impersonating another, now is the time to say so."

"That's the only name I've ever had," Archer said.

Larke sighed. "He is definitely my son."

"Very well." Donovan fixed Archer with an unblinking gaze, making a chill creep down his spine. "You have my leave to enter Narrowmar, Ivan Archibald Larke."

Archer glanced up at the sky. It was growing dark, and the stars had begun to flare to life, mirroring the curse on the door. If he entered Narrowmar, he might never see those stars again, but the others were counting on him, Briar and Mae and the child she carried. He crossed the threshold.

CHAPTER 26

L ady Mae ushered Briar into her prison chamber, leaving the guards where they lay, and pulled the door closed behind them. Briar took in the austere room at a glance—a small table, one chair, a narrow cot.

"This door wasn't locked?" Briar asked.

"It usually is. I heard the click, as if they were about to come in. When the door didn't open, I went out to investigate." Mae's eyes widened with excitement and fear. She looked younger now that she no longer wielded a water pitcher against her captors. "Did my father send you? How many men are with you?"

"I'm alone," Briar said. "I got separated from my friends. Are you well enough to leave this place tonight?"

"Tonight?" Mae eased herself down onto the chair. Her cheeks were as pale as her pink gown, and her belly still looked large. She must have given birth recently indeed. "As in now?"

"Yes," Briar said. "Where is the—"

Before she could complete the question, she heard a little sound, like the sneeze of a kitten. Then the distinct, piercing wail of a newborn filled the room.

"Oh, dear. The commotion must have woken her." Mae hoisted herself up again and hurried to a box resting beside the cot. Blankets lined the rough wooden sides. Mae reached into them and lifted a tiny, squalling baby into her arms.

"It's all they had," Mae said, nodding at the box. "We're making do, aren't we, dear heart?" She cooed at the baby, already seeming comfortable with the swaying, soothing motions of motherhood. But when she looked up at Briar, her eyes looked slightly frantic.

"She came early," she said with a sort of terrified awe. "I thought I had three weeks left, but here she is, already three days old."

"Three days?" Briar wished she had a healer's training—or a voice mage's power. She had no idea if it was even safe to take a baby outdoors when it was only three days old.

"Can you help us?" Mae asked. Her expression darkened, going from fearful to murderous with lightning speed. "Lord Larke wants to take her away from me."

"I'm going to get you out," Briar said quickly. "We made a tunnel into the stronghold. Part of it collapsed, but I think I can break through at another point. It will take time. Can you keep her quiet until we're safe?"

Mae gave an unsteady laugh, and Briar was alarmed to see tears springing up in her eyes.

"Sometimes I can get her to fall right to sleep, but sometimes *nothing* works. I know women do this all the time, but I didn't expect it to be so hard!"

"Uh, it's all right," Briar said. "Don't cry. Um, I might be able to do something that will help, but I need you to trust me." She would never risk using a sleep stone on a three-day-old baby, but she might be able to paint a smaller, gentler curse onto the baby's blankets. "I ... I don't think it will hurt her."

"I don't even know you!" Mae held the tiny baby to her chest, curving around her as if she could put the child back inside her body for safekeeping. She seemed to oscillate rapidly between fear and feral, protective anger.

"Archer sent me," Briar said.

"I don't know any archers."

"Lord Larke's son, the younger, nicer one."

"Ivan?" Mae asked. "Ivan is here?"

"He's outside, creating a diversion," Briar said. "I've been traveling with him and a woman named Jemma, his ... tutor."

"I remember him speaking fondly of a Jemma." Mae still didn't sound convinced. "How do I know it's really him out there?"

"He has blond hair and dark eyebrows and the most piercing blue eyes you've ever seen," Briar said impatiently. "He's brave and kind, and he's a terrible dancer and a great shot with a bow."

Mae's eyes narrowed mistrustfully. "Maybe I should wait here."

"He's intelligent, and he's tall, and he'd do anything for his friends." Briar's tone sharpened. "He'd do anything for *you*, Mae, and we really don't have time to stand around talking."

Mae bit her lip. "I don't know how far I can walk."

"We just need to get out of the mountain." Briar hadn't expected she would have to talk Mae into her own rescue. Shouldn't the girl be grateful rather than suspicious? "We have horses waiting. Sheriff—that's Archer's dog—is guarding them for us."

"*Sheriff* is with you?" A sudden grin lit up Mae's features. "Why didn't you say so? Let's go!"

Briar blinked in surprise as Mae spun into action. She swaddled up the baby then herself, using the nonbloodstained coats from the guards sleeping outside the cell door. She was like quicksilver, changeable and passionate, but determined once she decided to do something. Briar helped her retrieve the coats, making sure the sleep stones stayed in position. They wouldn't have much longer before someone came to see why the guards hadn't returned with the baby.

"We need to find a large banquet hall in the eastern passage," Briar said as they finished bundling up the baby. Jemma had described the place, which sat on the outer perimeter of the fortress. Briar hoped to use it to connect to an earlier point in the tunnel and hopefully save some time. She would drill all the way out of the mountain from Mae's cell if she weren't certain she would run out of paints before she made it halfway. "Do you know the one I'm talking about? The East Hall?"

"I haven't exactly been allowed to explore." Mae pulled a guard's burgundy coat over her pale dress and tucked her golden curls beneath it. "They've kept me locked up in here ever since the curse painters arrived."

Briar went still. "The curse painters?"

"They're two scary art mages who have taken over security from the captain," Mae said. "He used to let me walk where I pleased as long as a guard accompanied me, but they put a stop to that."

Briar clutched a paintbrush in her fist. So her parents were still there. She had hoped they might have moved on after securing the stronghold. Why had they stayed? Protecting the entrance of a remote fortress wasn't nearly as stimulating as the jobs they preferred to take. What else could Narrowmar offer them?

Briar shook her head. There would be time to worry about that later. "Let's just hope the curse painters keep busy for a little while longer."

She opened a jar of blue smalt to put the baby to sleep then hesitated, flinching at the thought of wielding her dangerous magic against such a tiny, innocent thing. But their options were severely limited. "Remember I said I could do something to help her sleep?"

Mae clutched her baby closer, the suspicion returning in a flash. "Yes."

"And that Arch—Ivan sent me in to help you, and he trusts me?"

Mae tightened her hold on the baby. "Yes ..."

Briar held up the jar of paint and her smallest, most delicate paintbrush. "Are you ready to test that trust?"

CHAPTER 27

Archer stalled his father and the curse painters as much as possible on their way down the main corridor of the stronghold. The passageway, a remnant of the original mountain fissure, had veiny walls reaching upward to a ceiling well out of range of the torchlight. The place smelled of mildew and boot polish, just as he remembered.

The stronghold was busier than Archer had ever seen it. The men of the Narrowmar garrison buzzed with excitement over Esteban's attack, their voices echoing through the broad corridor.

"He sang twenty men to their deaths, I hear."

"I heard something about arrows of fire."

"That's a load of dung."

"I swear it on my left knee."

The walls hadn't seen that much action in a hundred years. Many of the men traversing the halls were new recruits, their uniforms almost as fresh as their faces.

"Think more of the bleedin' hedge wizards are lurking out there?" asked a particularly youthful soldier as Archer and the others passed.

An older man at his side grunted. "I've met enough magic makers for my lifetime. What with those—"

"Shh!" The young soldier gestured urgently. "They're right there."

The curse painters paid no attention to the clamor. Archer listened for hints of what was happening to his team, hoping to find out if the cursed tunnel had been discovered. Unfortunately, the soldiers tended to fall silent when they realized the two curse painters were nearby. What had the Drydens done to make the men fear and respect them so quickly? Archer wasn't sure he wanted to know.

The curse painters didn't acknowledge the soldiers at all, and they barely listened when Lord Larke tried to engage them in polite conversation. Donovan and Saoirse moved in tandem, disconcertingly in tune with one another. Though they obviously weren't blood relatives, they looked alike. It was something about the way they carried themselves, the way their hands moved, the twin fires burning in their eyes.

Archer couldn't imagine what it must have been like for Briar to grow up with those two. Their self-assurance would be intimidating for anyone, much less their own child. Rich men and nobles tended to fear losing their power, but the curse painters were utterly confident in theirs. Nothing could take away their ability to instill fear in others—and they knew it.

Half a dozen soldiers marching down the corridor squeezed aside to let them pass. Archer searched for familiar faces among them and found none. Why had his father hired so many fighting men? Defending Narrowmar didn't require that many soldiers. Was he up to something else besides stealing Mae's child?

"How long do you plan to stay here?" Archer asked him.

"That's none of your concern," Lord Larke snapped.

"Isn't it? You'd think you were getting ready for a siege."

Larke's mouth tightened, and Archer wondered if he was onto something. "You don't think Barden could really reach the ravine without—"

"Later." Larke stopped at his chamber door and muttered, "I need that drink."

Archer frowned, a chill creeping down his spine. If this wasn't just about Barden and Mae, what else could his father have in mind? Insurrection? Surely not. Still, the idea made him uneasy. A man could get away with a lot in the outer counties if he had the right resources. His father was nothing if not ambitious, and he currently had a rather powerful pair of sorcerers on retainer.

Before Larke could open the door to his sitting room, the Drydens stepped smoothly into his way.

"Pardon, my lord," Donovan said. "We have been using your antechamber as a studio in your absence, and it is cluttered with canvases and other tools of our trade."

Larke's jaw tensed. "Is that so?"

"Indeed. It might not be the best place for us to talk."

"We have had the East Hall cleaned up," Saoirse said. "Perhaps we can speak there."

"Oh, yes," Donovan said. "It contains some excellent examples of the ancient stone craft. It's a shame it isn't often used. Let us go."

Archer felt a stab of panic. He'd suggested the sitting room because it was close to the front of the stronghold. He needed to keep his father and his new friends away from Mae for a while yet.

But Donovan and Saoirse set off down the corridor without waiting for a response.

Larke's face turned as red as a poison oak rash. He was *not* happy about his space being commandeered or his hired mages dictating their movements, but he managed to keep his voice polite as he caught up. "You mean the chamber at the end of the eastern passage? Very well. As I recall, it has a rather fine fireplace."

Donovan inclined his head. "I have never seen finer."

"Wait!" Archer shouted.

"Yes, Lord Ivan?" Saoirse looked back at him.

He scrambled for an excuse. "Isn't … isn't it nicer to chat in a more intimate setting?" If he remembered correctly, the East Hall was far too close to where they had planned to open their tunnel. At the end of the main corridor, two passages branched deeper into the mountain, east and west. Mae was most likely being held down the eastern passage. "Maybe one of the rooms in the western—"

"Nonsense." Larke's voice was a whip crack. "The East Hall it is."

Archer had no choice but to follow. After being ordered around by the curse painters, his father would never put up with Archer disrespecting him too. Why was he tolerating those two? There *had* to be more going on there than the procurement of a Larke-Barden heir. Jasper Larke wanted something from the Drydens. How could Archer use that to keep them away from the tunnel?

Saoirse glanced over at Archer with a faint smile. He grinned toothily back, praying the others had already gotten out of the stronghold. With luck, they were meeting up with Esteban and Lew in the forest. At least they wouldn't be in the East Hall itself.

They approached the fork at the end of the main corridor, where a stone gargoyle stood sentry between the two branching passageways. Water spewed from the gargoyle's mouth into a wide stone basin. A freshwater spring bubbled up from beneath the mountain there, one of the reasons Narrowmar had withstood every siege in its history.

"I heard this place was built by mages like you," Archer said, slowing to examine the gargoyle and the basin beneath it. "Is that true, Mistress Dryden?"

"Not curse painters," Saoirse said. "Stone crafters, sometimes known as stone charmers. They are exceedingly rare. We have not managed to find one in over ten years."

"What do you do when you find one?" Archer asked.

She ignored the question, trailing her paint-smudged fingers in the water basin. "Narrowmar is the finest example of stone craft in Lure and all the surrounding lands. We have yet to see its equal."

"Is that why you're here?" Archer asked.

"We were hired to protect this place," Donovan said. "You ought to be pleased we are guarding your inheritance."

"He is pleased," Archer's father said smoothly. "Though Ivan does not stand to inherit Narrowmar. That will go to my eldest son, Tomas, and his son after him."

"Oh yes." Saoirse looked up from the water, a strange light dancing in her eyes. "His son."

Archer didn't understand why she suddenly looked so gleeful. It didn't matter. Mae and the heir she carried would soon be out of reach of both the Drydens and the Larkes. He imagined her emerging from a mountainside tunnel, holding her belly, surrounded by Jemma, Nat, and Briar. They would race through the forest, find the horses and the others, take to the open road. They would be free, as long as Archer could distract these three a little longer. He grinned at the stone gargoyle the Drydens admired so much, already feeling a hint of relief.

Then they turned down the eastern corridor—and abruptly found themselves facing Briar and Mae, who had just entered it at the other end.

Briar was covered in gray dust, and she wore pure determination like armor. Mae was wide-eyed and pale, clutching a bundle of burgundy cloth in her arms. Only a few dozen paces separated them from Archer and the others.

The two girls stared at the curse painters and Lord Larke with looks of twin shock. Which was nothing compared to the shock on the faces of Donovan and Saoirse Dryden.

CHAPTER 28

Briar's parents had never been slow to react before, but she was clearly the last person they expected to find attempting to steal their prisoner. Their astonishment gave her the tiniest edge. She used it.

She plucked a black curse stone from her pocket and hurled it as hard as she could at the distinguished man with thick brown hair standing between her parents. It struck his forehead, cutting deep. Briar was already reaching for her paints.

"Run," she hissed to Mae.

"But—"

"Go! Get as far away as you can."

With a frantic gasp, Mae clutched her baby tighter and ran.

Briar yanked paints indiscriminately from her satchel and began daubing rough lines on the floor. Her parents had turned to look when the curse stone struck their companion—Lord Larke presumably. He was bleeding heavily, crimson streams dripping onto the collar of his fine coat. Briar's father reached for the man to try to stop the bleeding.

Her mother advanced toward her, eyes blazing with cold

fire. She had a paintbrush in her hand, and her lips were pulled back in an angry rictus.

Briar painted faster, using her largest brush to streak umber and carmine across the stone, counting each stroke. *Four. Five. Six.*

Her hands shook, making her work sloppy, and her fingers burned with magic. She had to finish the design before her mother reached her. Footsteps drummed down the corridor, counting down like a clock.

Eight. Nine. Ten. The rough image of a volcano took shape, its mouth pointing down the corridor. Someone said her name like a curse.

Briar glanced up to check how far away her mother was as she prepared the final strokes, dipping her brush in carmine lake. That's when she saw Archer running after Saoirse Dryden, as if he could stop the legendary mage with his bare hands.

Panic seized Briar. If she finished painting the volcano, the curse would strike Archer with just as much force as it struck her mother. She didn't want to hurt either of them, but her mother was almost to her, eyes alight with the particular rage of betrayal. Briar's hands felt as hot as a blacksmith's forge.

Archer sprinted after Saoirse. He wouldn't catch up in time.

"Do it!" he shouted. "You have to!"

Briar tightened her grip on her paintbrush. He was right. Blocking the passage and stopping her mother was their only chance to escape.

Saoirse was almost to her, the brush in her hand dripping bone-black paint.

"Hurry, Briar!" Archer bellowed.

Twelve.

Briar painted the final stroke. The painting exploded.

A wave of pressure hurtled from Briar's position, blasting right into Archer and her mother. Both of them flew backward, sliding the length of the corridor. Chunks of stone broke away from the ceiling and rained down on them. A plume of acrid smoke filled the air.

Briar lurched forward a step, ears ringing, but Mae was going the other way, running as fast as she could under the circumstances. She and the baby weren't safe yet. They didn't deserve to die. Briar had a job to finish.

Not daring to scrutinize the carnage left by her curse, Briar caught up to the young mother and baby and pulled them through the nearest doorway. They ran full speed across a room cluttered with bunks and open-mouthed young men. The soldiers' barracks. Briar paused to throw a handful of red exploding stones in their midst. Then she and Mae burst out the other side into a broader corridor. Briar remembered Jemma telling her the large barracks had entrances on the eastern and main passageways. She turned left, and they headed toward the front of the fortress.

They couldn't go back through the tunnel. Briar would never be able to curse her way to a clear section before her parents caught up. But she might have enough of a head start to blast straight through the front door before they recovered from her last curse.

"Was that Ivan?" Mae demanded as she struggled to keep up with Briar. "What did you do to him?"

"He'll be okay," Briar said. *Please, let him be okay.*

The torches flickered as they ran past, and their footsteps echoed around them, announcing their progress. Briar breathed in smoky air and linseed oil and ash. She had to get Mae and the baby girl out of Narrowmar before she worried about what she had done to Archer and her mother.

Thanks to the tiny curse on her blankets, the baby remained asleep as they charged down the corridor. Armed and uniformed men rushed by them, running toward the big explosion. They weren't looking for escaped prisoners, and they didn't glance at the bundle in Mae's arms. Still, it would only take one soldier to raise the alarm. Briar and Mae ducked into alcoves and empty rooms whenever they could, which slowed their progress. How long before her parents came after her? They would surely use their nastiest curses to punish her for daring to stand against them.

Mae's steps were becoming labored. Briar didn't know how long it took to recover after having a baby, but it had to be more than three days. There was nothing she could do about that at the moment. She just had to get Mae and the baby out the front door, then Esteban could heal whatever ailed the young mother.

If Esteban had survived. Briar didn't know how Archer had ended up with her parents and the tall, distinguished man she assumed was Lord Larke. What if the rest of the team had already been killed?

Nothing you can do, she reminded herself as she pulled Mae through a doorway to allow another group of soldiers to run past.

The soldiers were streaming toward the explosion site now, but once word spread that Mae had escaped, they would comb through every room in the fortress.

Briar pressed her ear to the door, listening to the footsteps receding and the shouts echoing from deep within the stronghold. Her pulse raced, and sweat dripped down her back as she waited for her moment.

She was about to charge back into the corridor, when Mae grabbed her sleeve. "Wait! Could you use this?" Mae held up a jar of purple paint.

Briar whirled around, taking in the room they'd ducked into to avoid the last group of soldiers. The large, richly decorated chamber was filled with paint supplies, brushes, canvas, ground-up pigments, vats of linseed oil, detailed sketches of future paintings. Her parents must be using the room as their studio.

Hardly daring to believe her luck, Briar took the purple from Mae and began stuffing her satchel with as many additional paints as she could carry. Mae helped, balancing a few small jars on top of her sleeping daughter and slinging another satchel over her shoulder. Briar found several containers of the marine-snail purple that had given her such trouble. Of course her parents would have plenty of the rare shade. Her father was obsessed with studying the unravelling of magic.

"What do we do now?" Mae asked.

Briar blinked at her trusting expression. She wasn't used to people looking to her for leadership. "I think we're close to the exit," she said. "When we get there, I'll hold off the soldiers and curse painters as long as I can. You get outside and run until you can't run anymore. My friends will find you and help if I can't."

Mae nodded. "What if they don't?"

Briar hesitated. What if they were all dead? Nat and Jemma and Lew, even Esteban. They had begun to show her what a family could be like. She couldn't accept that they might all be gone, but Mae was right. If they *were* dead, she would be helpless out there, no matter how fiercely she wanted to protect her child.

Briar cast about for another idea. "Do you remember a village called New Chester?"

"Yes, it's a day or two south of here." Mae scowled. "*He* took me through there." She looked as if she was ready to crack heads with a water pitcher again. She apparently didn't have any lingering affection for her erstwhile lover.

"You can hide there, and none of the people will bother you," Briar said. "Stay until you're well enough to travel. The place is under an enchantment, but you'll be safe enough."

"What about Ivan?"

"I'll go back for him after you're safe," Briar said. "I promise."

Mae gave her a considering look then nodded. "Do you have enough paint?"

Briar patted the satchel weighing down her shoulder. "With all this, I could bring down the mountain."

Mae flashed a quicksilver grin. "Good."

They gathered their precious burdens and listened at the door. When the corridor was clear, they slipped out of the room full of paints and began their final sprint. In a few minutes, they would cross the threshold of Narrowmar's only door.

CHAPTER 29

The old captain stood before the great stone door, running a hand over his sword hilt. The burgundy leather wrapped around the grip had begun to crack.

The captain had never shirked his responsibilities. Even in the dark days after his wife left, when he'd questioned his commitment to the forgotten mountain and a liege lord he rarely saw, he had kept his watch. When vile sorcerers had come to the mountain with their talk of art and pain, he'd stayed, ignoring his aching bones and his seething conscience in the name of duty. He *was* the stronghold of Narrowmar, and he refused to forsake his guard.

Until a frightened girl dashed toward him with a baby wrapped in swaddling clothes. Lady Mae looked desperate and terrified and determined, as she had when she pushed out that tiny little girl in a rush of blood and water. She had been valiant despite her captivity, despite the cruelty of the Larkes and the malevolence of the curse painters. Now, with her damp curls plastered to her face and a bundle in her arms, she ran as if there was still hope of escape, as if she might one day walk beneath the sun with wildflowers in her hair. At the sight of her wide-eyed determination, the captain's resolve wavered.

He realized that he didn't care if he was stripped of his honors and exiled for the rest of his days. Mae and her child were innocents. They didn't deserve to be kept beneath the mountain, subject to the machinations of mages and lords. The captain had always followed orders, but he saw at last that keeping his duty wasn't worth the cost.

He ordered the two soldiers with him to go inside the guard station to the right of the main door. They looked at him questioningly but obeyed. As soon as they were gone, the captain stepped into Mae's path. A wild-haired girl skidded to a halt at her side.

"Stop!" he said. "There is a curse on the door."

"Who are you?" asked the wild-haired girl.

The captain waved off the question. "If Lady Mae walks across that threshold, she will die instantly."

The strange girl scanned the doorway, her large, luminous eyes taking in the pattern of stars and moons. There was something familiar about those eyes.

"He's right," she said, turning to Mae. "This is a powerful barrier curse."

"Then we're trapped?"

"Not if I can help it." The girl reached into a satchel at her side and pulled out a jar of purple paint. The glass glinted in the torchlight.

Mae's arms tightened around her baby. "Are you going to tunnel through the walls again?"

The captain grunted. "Tunnel?"

The other girl shook her head. "There's no time for that, but if I can unravel this—"

Quick footsteps sounded behind them. A group of soldiers advanced up the corridor toward them. The old captain recognized the broad-shouldered young man leading them and grimaced. All this was *his* doing.

Mae's face had gone milk white. "What do we do?"

The other girl had the jar of paint open in her hand, and she was scrutinizing the curse on the door. "This is complicated," she muttered. "It'll take ages to—"

"We don't have ages!" Mae said. The soldiers were getting closer, their broad-shouldered leader shouting commands.

The wild-haired girl touched the stone doorpost where the names of everyone in Narrowmar had been scrawled among the celestial lights. Some had flourishes beside them. Mae's didn't.

"Names," the girl whispered. "The curse painters demanded everyone's names for this curse, didn't they?"

The captain nodded, keeping his attention on the approaching soldiers, unsure what they would do when they closed the distance. He had always imagined he would die defending the door from enemies on the *other* side. "No one can leave without their permission."

The girl wiped a smear of sweat and dust from her forehead. "Have they done the baby?"

"The baby?"

"After she was born, did they scribe her name on the wall?"

"She doesn't have a name yet," Mae said.

"Okay. Give her to me, then."

Mae's eyes flashed. "What?"

"There are two curses here—one to keep people out and one to keep specific people in." The girl screwed the lid back on the jar of purple paint and dropped it in her satchel with a clink. "I came in through the tunnel, which is why I didn't fall to the first curse. My name and the baby's are not held by the second curse. I can get her out of the way then use some more dramatic curses to fight them off."

"You want to take her?"

269

"Larke will never let her go if he gets his hands on her."

The old captain didn't know exactly what was going on, but he had to agree. Jasper Larke was a ruthless man, and he'd proved willing to hurt women to serve his own ends. The captain had seen it before and—to his shame—he hadn't spoken up. He had protected a powerful man's interests instead of defending the woman he had hurt. No more.

"Give her the babe, lass." The captain put a hand on his sword, which he'd rarely drawn except in training. "I'll look after you until she returns."

Mae gave a ragged sob and handed the still-sleeping baby to the other young woman. It was a marvel that the child could nap through all the commotion.

"You get her to safety," Mae said fiercely. "Don't come back."

The wild-haired young woman gave her a searching look, then she nodded. Clutching the baby tight to her chest, she took a deep breath and stepped across the threshold. For a moment, the captain feared they had been wrong.

The girl paused, swaying on her feet. Then she peeled back the blankets and bent her head over the baby. She looked back at Mae and the captain. "She's all right! It worked." Then her eyes widened, her lips parting.

And the captain noticed a red-tipped sword had suddenly appeared, sticking clear through his back and out the front of his chest.

CHAPTER 30

Briar gasped as the old captain was stabbed from behind. Mae screamed, leaping back as her would-be protector fell to the ground. She teetered at the threshold, nearly falling across it. Then she pitched the other way and crawled away from the fallen captain and his murderer.

The newcomer was broad-shouldered and young, with a mop of thick brown hair and a barrel chest. Briar didn't wait to learn more. She wrapped her arms tighter around the baby and ran.

It was pitch-dark outside, and rocks and boulders rose out of nowhere to trip her. Clouds had gathered overhead, blocking out the starlight. Despite her unsteady footing, Briar ran like she had never run before, pure terror driving her onward. She had faced her parents. She had risked crossing the most complex barrier curse she'd ever seen. Worst of all, she now had a very fragile, very fresh baby in her arms.

So she ran, with nowhere to go, no one to help her. She could be the only member of her team left. Archer wouldn't come to her aid with his knack for knowing which way to go, his certain kind of vision. He was under the mountain, knocked down by her curse. If he still lived, he wouldn't escape that fortress unless Briar's parents willed it.

Briar winced at the thought of that burst of power she'd hurled across the corridor. Her father had been far enough away to avoid the blast, but her mother and Archer...

Did she really have to paint such a powerful incendiary? She could have painted a border that would put her pursuers to sleep if they crossed it. She could have created a flashbang to divert their attention while Mae escaped. Why had she turned so quickly to one of the deadliest curses she knew? What was it inside her that allowed her to unfurl such destruction when a simple stop curse would do the trick?

You know the answer.

She gritted her teeth, trying to push down the little voice whispering to her like the deadly hum of a voice mage.

You wanted to show them, didn't you? You wanted to prove you are more powerful than even they dreamed you could be. You've been practicing that curse, that blast of destruction, for far too long, imagining their reactions when they saw it. Well, congratulations. You sure showed them.

Briar wanted to scream at the voice, to deny the assertion that some part of her wanted to shove her power back in her parents' faces. She refused to admit she had become exactly what they'd always wanted her to be.

She ran on through the night, getting farther from Narrowmar, farther from what she had done. She wanted to go back, to see if she really had rained down death in that corridor, but Archer and Mae would never forgive her for putting the baby in jeopardy to save them. Running away was the right choice, but that didn't stop the tears that flooded her eyes, blurring her surroundings.

Briar stumbled, catching herself before she fell on top of the baby. The satchel of paints swung heavily at her side. She needed to stop, or neither of them would survive the night.

She slowed, blinking her eyes clear. The ravine looked different, as if a great fist had punched into the middle of it, making the ground ripple like struck flesh. The trees on the ridge were ripped up and scattered, their broken branches rising like skeleton fingers. That must be where Esteban had ambushed Lord Larke. There was no sign of him.

Briar scrambled toward a pile of ripped-up logs partway up the side of the ravine. She dropped to the ground behind the rubble, hiding from the men her parents would surely send after her. She sat in the darkness, attempting to slow her racing heartbeat and recover her strength. Clouds gathered overhead. A storm was brewing.

How far did she have to go to find safety? New Chester was more than a day's journey away. Mae and Archer would be long dead by the time she deposited the baby and returned. Her heart stuttered, rebelling against the idea. She couldn't lose him. They were barely getting started.

Then she heard a sound like the sneeze of a kitten. She raised her head and found herself looking into the wide blue eyes of the wide-awake infant. The baby stared at Briar, and Briar stared back.

She looked perfectly healthy with a pink face and a fuzzy shock of blond hair. Briar was relieved the tiny little sleep curse hadn't hurt her, even though it hadn't lasted long. The baby made a gurgling, mewling sound, still staring at the person who had carried her away from her mother. Briar felt a delicate flicker of hope, a moth wing fluttering against her cheek. Then the baby filled her lungs and began to wail.

"No," Briar said desperately. "Please don't cry."

The baby cried louder.

"Please be quiet."

The sound was piercing, echoing around the ravine, getting louder with each breath. Briar had never been more terrified of anything in her life. She looked around frantically for something to soothe the child. Nothing but rocks and uprooted trees surrounded her.

"I don't know what you want." She tried humming, but it came out more like a wail of her own. "Please, little baby. I got you this far. I need you to work with me."

Her pleas had no effect on the baby whatsoever. It was probably hungry, and she couldn't do anything to fix that. She would have to curse it to sleep again, though she feared she wouldn't be able to make the curse small enough in the dark. As the baby cried louder, Briar buried her face in the blankets and began to sob. This was a disaster. They were going to be caught, and all their efforts, all the sacrifices that Archer and Mae and the team had made to get the little girl out of Larke's clutches would be wasted. Briar had tried to do something good, and she had failed. She couldn't keep from destroying things. She couldn't save the tiny, innocent being. She couldn't be anything other than her parents' daughter.

The sound of movement reached her over the baby's cries, rocks skittering away beneath heavy footfalls. Briar lifted her head, teeth bared, preparing to make one final stand—and found herself looking directly into a wrinkly face covered in slobber.

"Sheriff!"

The big dog whined and began licking all over her face. He switched to the baby next, showering affection on the tiny creature that would almost fit inside his mouth. The baby broke off crying, hiccupping softly, and stared up at the dog.

"What are you doing here, Sheriff?" Briar asked. "You're supposed to be with the horses."

Sheriff pulled back and gave her a reproachful look.

"You're right. What am I saying? I'm so happy to see you."

Briar wrapped her free arm around the big dog's neck, wanting to cry again at the thought that she'd thrown a curse straight at Sheriff's master and friend. How would she explain to him that Archer was lost? But the dog reminded her she wasn't alone. She had joined a new family, and she wasn't ready to give up on them yet.

"Sheriff, I need you to take care of something for me."

The dog looked up at her curiously. She pretended not to see the skepticism in his gaze as she explained what she wanted him to do.

CHAPTER 31

When Archer opened his eyes, he was severely disappointed Esteban wasn't there to sing him a healing lullaby. Every inch of his body hurt, and he feared he'd broken his back for the second time in two hours—and maybe his head too. There had to be limits to how many times that could happen in a day.

He struggled to sit up, and no one moved to help him, mage or otherwise. Dust, smoke, and groans of pain filled the corridor. It took Archer a minute to realize most of the groans were coming from him.

His father sat on the ground a dozen paces away, his face covered in blood from a gash in his forehead. He was surrounded by his soldiers, who were making a group effort to stop their lord from bleeding to death. The blood that also ran in Archer's veins leaked out beneath their hands.

Archer wanted to run before the men realized he was awake, but first he had to stand, and that seemed like a lot to ask right then. He prodded his dust-covered body, trying to assess where the damage was. The answer seemed to be everywhere. Again.

His back didn't appear to be broken this time, though, and he managed to stagger upright and prop himself against the nearest wall to get his bearings. A massive crater split the stone floor not far from him, where Briar's curse had erupted.

Briar.

The details were coming back to him. Archer, his father, and the Drydens had walked right into Briar and Mae in the eastern corridor. Briar had reacted the quickest, diving to the floor to paint the curse that had taken out half the corridor. Mae had run for it. Archer had been too busy being blasted off his feet to see which way she'd gone.

He remembered Briar's sorrowful eyes right before the blast, though. She'd seen him running toward her and decided to finish the curse anyway. Good for her. He'd had some idea of tackling Saoirse before she reached Briar and Mae, but Briar's curse had taken care of the threat handily—and had possibly destroyed several of his internal organs.

Let's worry about that later, shall we? Archer needed to determine what had become of the curse painters. Donovan had been closer to Archer's father, but he wasn't in the crowd fussing over the lord. Saoirse had been right in front of Archer. He rubbed his dusty eyes, wondering if she'd gotten past the curse and reached Briar after all. A jolt of fear went through him at the thought of losing Briar. She wasn't even really *his* in the typical sense, yet the idea of anything happening to her hurt as much as all his injuries combined. He pressed a hand against the crumbling wall, trying to summon the energy to seek out those horrible painters before they found her.

Then an object Archer had taken for a lump of fallen stone moved. There was a faint moan, and a pair of dark eyes opened. Dust sifted through thick, curly hair matted with blood. Saoirse Dryden was lying beneath a pile of rubble.

Archer staggered over to the woman and dropped to his knees at her side. Saoirse looked as poorly as he felt. He brushed stone dust from her face, some of it clinging in the lines in her forehead. She looked at him, her fierce eyes dulled with pain.

"You're ... you're here with her, aren't you?" she mumbled. "Arrived same time ... not a coincidence."

"That's right," Archer said. "I'm with her."

Saoirse's mouth twisted in a sad smile. "Clever girl."

"I think so too."

Saoirse didn't seem fully aware. Archer examined her injuries, wincing at their extent. She was hurt badly. The metallic odor of blood mixed with a hint of oil paint and burned flesh. Archer moved some debris off her body, trying to make her more comfortable. He didn't want the woman to kill his friends, but he couldn't let her die in his arms either. How would Briar feel if the curse she'd painted killed her mother?

Saoirse touched his sleeve. "Is she ...?" She drew in a pained breath, and blood bubbled at her lips. She must be bleeding badly inside. It would take a voice mage to save her. As far as Archer knew, her husband was the only mage left in the fortress—wherever he was—and all he could do was destroy.

Saoirse tried to speak again. "Is she ...?"

"What was that?" Archer leaned closer to the woman then grunted as the movement sent agony through his gut.

"Well."

"I'm sorry," Archer wheezed. "I didn't catch that."

"Is ... she well?"

"Your daughter?"

Saoirse blinked, perhaps too hurt to nod.

"Yes." At least he hoped she was.

Saoirse's hand dropped away from his sleeve. He continued talking, hoping to keep her with him a little longer—or at least to distract himself from his own pain. "In fact, she's better than well. She has a new life, and she's trying to be good ... or at least better than her parents." He winced as another stab of agony jolted through him. "You know how talented she is, and she has this powerful need to do what's right, even though a huge part of her just wants to blow things up. It's incredible to see her fighting against the cards she's been dealt, choosing to walk a difficult path no matter how many times she has failed."

Saoirse's eyelids fluttered rapidly, and more blood bubbled from her lips. He couldn't tell how much she could hear or how much she cared. Briar had told him her parents didn't bother with good and evil, but even they had to look at a young person fighting against injustice, though the battle seemed hopeless, and feel a little bit inspired.

"How can I help you, Mistress Dryden?" Archer asked. "After everything you made her do, I still think Briar wouldn't want you to die."

"Sweet ... briar." Saoirse drew in a rattling breath and blinked rapidly, her lashes tinted gray with dust. Then she whispered, "Good." And her fierce eyes closed.

Archer put a hand on her forehead, where the warmth was already fading, and wished her redemption in the next realm.

The commotion around his father had calmed. Jasper Larke was covered in bandages, though the bleeding didn't seem to have stopped entirely. Briar's curse stone had worked its magic, but Larke wouldn't allow such a thing to slow him.

"Where is the Barden girl?" he demanded. "She must not escape."

"The curse painter went after her," one of his retainers said. "She won't get past that door anyway."

"I want that child," Larke said. "I'll give you to the curse painters if she escapes."

"She won't, sir."

Archer rolled away from Saoirse's body with a pained grunt and began to crawl, dragging himself away from his father. His job wasn't done yet. His father's cruelty was different from that of the Drydens, but Archer couldn't let him get away with it. Larke would spread his influence over half the kingdom if he controlled the Barden heir, and it would be Archer's fault. He had to keep fighting a little longer.

CHAPTER 32

B riar marched on the gates of Narrowmar, her satchel of paints bouncing at her hip, a thick horsehair brush clutched in her hand. The air smelled of char, sawdust, and upturned earth, remnants of the earlier battle. A chill wind whipped through her hair, cooling the sweat on her brow. A storm was building over the mountain.

Despite everything she had been through that night, Briar felt lighter and more energetic now that she no longer carried such fragile cargo. She had left the newborn baby nestled on a bed of branches, the massive dog standing watch. Lady Mae might kill her for taking that risk, but the baby was probably better off in Sheriff's care than in Briar's. He, at least, didn't seem afraid of hurting the delicate little thing.

Briar saw no sign of the rest of the team as she neared the stronghold. Their efforts at infiltration and diversion had failed, and the night had swallowed them up. She was the only one left who could challenge the fortress. This time, she didn't intend to sneak through the back.

She planned her curses as she approached the stone door, etching out the shapes and colors in her mind in meticulous detail. She wasn't going to unravel her parents' work or fight them curse for curse. They'd had plenty of time to prepare additional defenses while she'd carried the baby away, but she was done playing by their rules. It was time to show her parents a curse painter could do more than harm.

With a little help from the Law of Wholes, she was going to rip open that mountain without shedding another drop of blood. Master Winton's house back in Sparrow Village had shown her how. She had planned out a subtle curse to weave into the cracks between the siding boards and eat away at the pitch—then a quick slash had turned the carefully threaded curse into absolute demolition. There were cracks in stone, too, and after tunneling through the mountain, she understood them well enough to put them to use.

The wind picked up, howling up the ravine as Briar reached the pale-gray wall at the front of the stronghold. Dark clouds amassed quickly in the night sky, and the scent of rain hung in the air. She didn't have much time before the storm broke.

Ignoring the stone door and its elaborate protective curses, Briar studied the broad wall, which had been built across a natural fissure to form the stronghold long ago. It was a stone charmer's work, one of the finest examples in the kingdom, formed as an extension of the mountain itself, but that didn't mean it was faultless.

Briar took a deep breath and laid a hand on the pale-gray stone. Her fingers tingled, almost to the point of pain. She was tired, but she hadn't reached her limit yet.

She opened a jar of umber and began to paint.

Archer was pretty sure he had cracked several ribs. That would explain most of the pain. He had cuts on his face, too, lacerations of the normal, clotting variety. He should be pleased about that. He had always thought a few scars would make him a more convincing outlaw.

But despite his best efforts, he couldn't be glib. As he lurched down Narrowmar's torchlit main corridor, it was difficult to believe he'd ever claimed to care for nothing but his dog and his bow and the open road. Archer cared a great deal, for his team, for his friend who had been ill used by his brother and kept captive by his father, for the girl who could slay him metaphorically with a look—and literally with a flick of her paintbrush.

Deep within the mountain, Archer once again felt like young Ivan Larke, who had been trapped within the walls of his station and his father's name, who'd thought he lacked the power to change anything around him. Despite the callous household he'd grown up in, he cared about the people under his father's dominion, those who had suffered, those who had been treated unfairly. And now Jasper Larke was trying to grab more power, no matter who got hurt along the way.

Ivan Archibald Larke had had enough. He'd once raged ineffectually against his father, his anger righteous but weak. He'd run away from his family's name and legacy, believing he couldn't change them. But after traveling with Briar and seeing the way she tried to use her dark power for good—albeit with varying results—he knew he could do better. He might never leave that mountain, never walk free on the open road, but he was his father's son still, and he could right at least one of his wrongs.

He had put a patch on his youthful rage before. Now it had returned, but new-forged, focused. He let his new wrath drive him down the corridor, propelling him through the pain in his body. It wasn't enough to be angry. He had to stand up and fight.

The stronghold reverberated with the shouts of men and the pounding of footsteps. They were searching for the missing prisoner in every chamber and exclaiming about a tunnel. If Mae and Briar had decided to go out the way they came in or hide instead of trying to leave through the cursed doorway, it wouldn't take the soldiers long to find them. He wondered what had become of Jemma and Nat. They were all supposed to be in there together.

Archer stuck to the main corridor, and no one challenged his right to be there. The torches flickered as he hobbled past, marking his progress toward the front of the stronghold. That was where Briar and Mae had been headed when he'd seen them last, so that was where he would start.

As he neared the end of the main corridor, he spotted Donovan Dryden crouched by the stone door. A full selection of paints lay before him, and he was embellishing the curse on the threshold. Beside him loomed a familiar pair of broad shoulders topped by a mop of thick brown hair. Archer's steps faltered. It was his brother, Tomas.

The firstborn Larke son watched the curse painter work, a sword in his hand, blood dripping from the blade. Archer hadn't expected Tomas to remain in Narrowmar for the birth of his child after delivering Mae there. He had washed his hands of her months ago, casting aside his responsibility and leaving Archer and their father to clean up his mess, as usual. Archer clenched his fists. Tomas was so frustrating. He bumbled through life with a smile on his face, not noticing how much damage his carelessness caused.

Archer stopped ten paces from the door, eyeing the blood dripping from Tomas's blade. His brother never cleaned his weapons promptly either. The owner of the blood sprawled on the ground between Archer and the pair, the old captain who'd kept Narrowmar faithfully for decades.

Archer didn't understand why Tomas would kill the captain. He'd been their father's man for decades, as much a part of Narrowmar as the great stone door itself. Whatever the reason, the captain's sword was still in its sheath at his belt, its hilt wrapped in burgundy leather.

Archer checked the corridor behind him to make sure no one was coming then studied the weapon. Dare he reach for it? Tomas was the better swordsman, and Archer was injured. He didn't fancy the idea of stabbing his brother in the back, but what if he could take out Donovan while he was occupied? Would his death break the curse on the door?

Before Archer could lunge for the sword, the curse painter turned.

"I know you're lurking in the shadows," Donovan said. "Take heed, for there is an incendiary curse in place between us. You will not live long enough to slay me."

Tomas looked up, his blunt jaw slackening in surprise.

"Ivan? What in all the realms, high and low, are you doing here? This is my brother, Master Dryden. Why would he slay you?" Tomas gave a hearty guffaw, and Donovan shot him a derisive look. He'd clearly figured out whose side Archer was on.

Tomas wore a stupid grin on his handsome face. It was inconvenient really, having a handsome brother. "When did you get here, Ivan?"

"Earlier this evening." Archer leaned casually against the wall, grunting at the pain in his ribs.

"Have you seen Father?" Tomas asked.

"He's bleeding badly from a curse," Archer said. "Can you help him, Master Dryden?"

"Healing is not my area of expertise. I was hired to protect this keep and its inmates, and that is precisely what I'm doing." Donovan resumed his work on the doorway, adding vermilion streaks among the stars and moons. "Is Saoirse on her feet yet?"

"Not yet." Archer didn't elaborate.

The curse painter was too focused on his work to realize something was amiss with his wife. It was a testament to their combined strength that it didn't even occur to Donovan that Saoirse hadn't survived their daughter's curse. Archer didn't want to be anywhere near him when he learned the truth.

Had Briar and Mae found a way past the door's curses, or were they still somewhere inside Narrowmar? They'd never escape with Donovan in their way. Archer was running out of time to help, but he'd only have a chance against Donovan if he took him by surprise.

Could the curse painter be bluffing about the incendiary curse on the floor? Archer glanced at the body a few paces from him—and the sword at its hip.

"What happened to the captain?" he asked Tomas, striving for a casual tone.

"He betrayed us," Tomas said. "He tried to help Mae escape. Can you believe it? We got to her first, though. She's in the guard station just here."

Archer looked up. Torches flickered on either side of the guard station door, which was located to the right of the stronghold's entrance. It was too far. He'd have to deal with Tomas and Donovan before he could get to it.

He took a step toward his brother. "Why can't you let her go?"

"It was father's idea, bringing her here." Tomas shrugged, his sword loose in his hand. "I find her tiresome."

"If she gives birth to a boy—"

"Yes, but she didn't, did she?" Tomas said. "I was right all along."

Archer frowned. "What are you talking about?"

"The baby. It was a girl."

"She already had it?" Panic bubbled up in Archer's belly. He was too late. The baby wasn't supposed to come for weeks yet.

Suddenly it didn't matter what happened to Archer or to his family. If they had killed that innocent child, those callous bastards would get what was coming to them. Archer dove for the old captain's sword.

At the same moment, outside, Briar finished painting her curse.

As Archer's hand closed on the burgundy-wrapped hilt, the mountain gave an almighty lurch, as if it were being slammed hard against the earth. There was a great cracking sound, and the entire front wall of the stronghold began to disintegrate. Rocks fell with a deafening roar, pummeling the ground, collapsing the cursed doorway as if it were made of paper. Archer threw up his arms to protect his battered body, smelling a whiff of linseed oil and smoke. Then the billowing dust snuffed out the torches and covered everything in darkness.

CHAPTER 33

T he impenetrable fortress fell like a wooden house.

The earth shook with teeth-cracking intensity as the rocks crumbled. Briar's curse targeted the whole front of the stronghold, slicing off a layer of stone three feet deep. Thick gray debris choked the air and scattered across the ground. The veins of the mountain opened, exposing its secret interior to the air. The gaping wound revealed a cross section where the main corridor had been built into the ancient fissure. The front of the fortress wasn't as much a part of the mountain as it had seemed. Briar's curse had found a way through the cracks and broken the barrier into pieces.

She crouched on her hands and knees, ears ringing, hands quivering from the magic. The curse had used unprecedented quantities of power. The destruction alone was enormous, and she'd added a verdigris flourish to make the wall fall outward as it collapsed. If Mae was still near the front of the stronghold, she should be okay, and with the cursed doorway obliterated, she should be able to walk right out.

Actually, Briar hoped Mae would run. It wouldn't be long

before Larke's men recovered from their surprise and poured out of the stronghold like wasps from a broken nest.

The dust gusted, not quite settling in the breezy weather, and Briar coughed into her sleeve. Droplets fell here and there, hints of the rainstorm to come. Briar knelt to outline another curse on a flat stone protruding from the road, hoping to hold off the coming swarm. Her hands shook badly. She must be approaching the absolute limits of her power. She had never fully tested those limits. The destruction was already greater than she'd ever thought she could produce. She wasn't sure whether to feel proud or frightened of her capacity.

Keeping an eye on the gaping hole exposing the stronghold's main corridor, she switched deftly from yellow ochre to blue smalt. It wasn't her most beautiful work, but she'd had lots of practice painting quick and dirty curses recently. This one would put someone to sleep who walked across it without needing to touch their skin. She hoped it would hold off a few of the soldiers while she and Mae escaped into the darkened woods above the ravine.

Thunder rumbled in the distance. The smell of rain sharpened, cutting through the thick dust. Briar painted quickly, praying the storm would hold just a little longer. *Hurry up, Mae. I still need to find Archer.*

But the first person to stumble out of the wreckage was the broad-shouldered young man who'd killed the old captain. He brushed rubble out of his thick brown hair, blinking at the carnage. There was something familiar about his long-fingered hands and the shape of his high forehead. He looked a little like Archer and a lot like the older man who'd been with her parents earlier. That must be Tomas Larke, the source of all the trouble. The Larke heir had an uncommonly handsome face and a confident stance that said he knew how uncommon his looks were.

Tomas didn't notice Briar, and she was grateful for the semi-darkness, though it made painting more difficult. She worked faster, switching from blue smalt to azurite. Then another figure emerged from the ruined fortress, and Briar's hands slipped, smudging the paint.

Archer. Relief surged through her. He was alive. She hadn't killed him. Battered and bleeding, he was on his feet and fighting still.

Their eyes met across the carnage.

"Hey! You there!"

Briar froze. Tomas had spotted her too. He took a step forward, his features turning ugly at the sight of the paintbrush in her hand.

"Did you curse my fort, you evil—"

"Don't touch her!"

Archer lunged toward his brother, waving a sword. Tomas gaped stupidly at him, only just raising his own sword in time to block the attack.

The brothers traded blows, steel ringing loudly against steel. Archer's movements lacked their usual energetic quality. He was injured, and he wouldn't last long when Tomas figured it out. Briar gripped her paintbrush tight enough to bend it.

Suddenly, Tomas stumbled over some debris and exposed his neck, and Briar felt a surge of triumph. But Archer didn't take advantage of the opening, holding back from a fatal blow. He wasn't trying to kill his brother, only distract him. Tomas was angry, though. He bellowed wordlessly, his attacks becoming more ferocious by the second. Archer struggled to meet each strike, and steel clashed in the night.

Raindrops landed on Briar's face, reminding her to hurry. Finishing her painting would help Archer more than having an anxious spectator. She needed to incapacitate Tomas, though she resisted the temptation to make the curse lethal. She'd had enough of death for one day. Maybe for one lifetime. She completed the shape of a moon over a quiet lake on the slab of stone and added the final flourish.

"Archer!" she shouted. "Get him over here!"

Archer jabbed clumsily at his brother's toe then dashed toward her. Tomas followed close on his heels.

"Don't touch it," Briar called as Archer drew nearer.

He didn't seem to hear her. He lurched straight for the curse, his brother in hot pursuit. Briar shouted his name, and Archer jumped aside at the last possible moment, clearing the painted stone in a single bound.

Tomas didn't react as fast and ran right over the painting. He collapsed in a heap.

"Got him!"

Archer staggered back to kneel beside Briar and dropped the sword in the dirt. "That was close. I'm a worse swordsman than I am a dancer."

"Are you okay?"

Archer prodded a lump on his temple. His dark eyebrows were singed. "Been better."

"I was afraid you were ... that I ..." Her voice caught in her throat, and for a minute, they just looked at each other across Tomas's prone form, the weight of their last encounter heavy between them.

Briar opened her mouth to apologize for blasting him off his feet at the same time as Archer said, "Don't worry about that curse. You did the right thing."

Briar grimaced and dropped her gaze. "I hope so. Here, help me move him."

They adjusted Tomas's position so he wouldn't lose contact with the cursed stone, Archer grunting at the effort. He didn't seem to be moving very well with his injuries. It was a wonder he'd lasted as long as he had against his older brother. He might be willing to sacrifice himself for Lady Mae, but Briar wished she hadn't been the one to hurt him. And there had been other people in the line of fire.

"Archer, my parents—"

"Your father was just here," Archer said quickly, glancing around the ruins of Narrowmar's façade. "Didn't you see him?"

"No." Briar's hands knotted around the strap of her paint satchel, scanning the rubble for any sign of her father. If he'd survived the wall's collapse, he could be hidden somewhere, painting a worse curse. "What about my mother?"

Archer hesitated for a beat. "Unconscious," he said.

Briar nodded, still searching the ruins. "Did you see Mae?"

"She was in the guard station near the door."

"She must be here somewhere, then." Briar seized Archer's hand. "You're hurt. Wait here."

"Not a chance. We have to find her baby too," Archer said. "Apparently, it has been born."

"One step ahead of you," Briar said. "The baby is safe."

"Then all we need to do is find—" Suddenly Archer's hand was ripped out of hers. He flew backward ten feet and slammed hard onto the ground with a sickening crunch.

Briar whirled around, scanning her surroundings. Nothing moved but shifting dust, raindrops, a breath of wind.

Her father was near. She didn't know how he'd gotten a curse to throw Archer like that, but it had to have been done at close range. She reached for her satchel, needing to act before he finished his next curse.

Then an incredible force slammed into her too. Briar landed on her back, the impact jarring her teeth. Storm clouds roiled darkly above. She struggled to draw in a breath—and failed. She tried again, and again. At last, the night air flooded her lungs.

She rolled onto her side, groaning at the ache in her head. She had landed twenty feet from where Archer lay sprawled and motionless. Blood trickled from his ear. He didn't get up.

No. Not now. Not when we're almost safe.

Briar sat up, searching the rocks for the hidden mage. Her paint satchel had split open, spilling colors across the dirt.

Movement flickered to her right. She rolled to the left as a large chunk of rock hurtled out of the darkness toward her. She glimpsed the rough curse painted on its side before it struck the spot where she'd been lying and shattered into a million pieces.

"Father, wait! Won't you talk to me?"

Her father's heated voice cut through the darkness like a knife. "You forfeited your right to talk when you betrayed us."

Another rock soared through the air. Briar rolled sideways, feeling the breath of its passing on her cheek. It crashed down, shards of rock scattering like stardust.

"I didn't mean to." Briar scrambled to her feet. She still couldn't see where he was hiding. "I just wanted to leave. I didn't know breaking the curses on the house would bring the voice mages down on us."

"And when you attacked your mother, what excuse have you for that?"

"She would have killed me!"

"I wish she had."

Whether her father's words were true or not, they did their job. Briar froze, her limbs refusing to obey, and the next attack scored a direct hit. A cursed stone crashed into her, and her arm cracked at the impact.

Pain screamed through her, but that mattered little compared to what her father had said. She had spent a year hiding from her parents, but she didn't want them dead, and until then she hadn't thought they truly wanted her dead either —only back in their power. She remembered how they'd leapt forward to scrub her cheeks clean when she'd painted stars and moons on herself as a little girl. She'd thought they cared for her in their own way. She had underestimated the extent of their anger.

Another stone punched into Briar's thigh, and she collapsed to the ground. That time the pain was enough to provoke her into action, to awaken her self-preservation instincts. Her paints had spilled from her satchel and scattered across the ground. She stretched for anything she could use, fingers twitching, fighting through a haze of agony.

But then despair filled her up like water in a glass.

Her family hated her. They wouldn't forgive her betrayal. No matter how many little acts of goodness she performed, she had already hurt too many people. She would never make up for what she had done. Why was she even trying?

Vaguely, Briar recognized the effects of a psychological curse. Anxiety. Despair. She couldn't fight it. Her father must have something of hers, something with enough resonance left to affect her. She remembered how the people of New Chester had stared into their drinks, unable to pull themselves out of their spiraling gloom.

She felt utterly isolated. She deserved it. She destroyed everything.

Tears blurred her vision and raindrops fell onto her spilled paints. The colors smeared, slipping away from her. She couldn't fight it. The anxiety of the curse smothered her, cutting much deeper than the physical pain. Briar curled into a ball, unable to counter the terrible power of her father's curse.

Then, out of the corner of her eye, she saw Archer raising his head. Despite his injuries, he was still trying to fight, trying to reach her. He had something in his hand. Something that shone purple inside a glass jar. He rolled it toward her across the damp, cracked earth.

Briar reached for the jar with her unbroken arm, summoning the last of her strength. It spun toward her, a slow wheel, her final hope. Her fingers closed on the jar. She had no paintbrush, no tools of the trade she had learned from her parents, from the mother she had attacked and the father who was trying to suffocate her with despair.

She cracked the jar open on the stone and dipped her fingers in the rare purple hue. She remembered the stars and moons on her cheeks, her parents ordering her never to curse her own skin. But as her father's curse deepened her despair, she had to try something, anything, to fight him off. So she began to paint an unravelling curse on her own body. She looped the design around the eyes she shared with her father, beneath her mother's nose, across her own sunburnt cheeks. She spread patterns down her neck, her broken arm, her chest.

The anxiety and despair receded a little, allowing the physical pain to return in earnest.

Nearly delirious with agony, Briar continued scrawling the curse onto her skin, using every drop of the precious pigment. She painted by instinct, the creative rush hot in her hands. Mages never cursed their own bodies, but what else could she do when it was her own flesh and blood causing such pain?

The painting taking shape on her skin was different from a typical unravelling curse. It was a new creation. She couldn't see it, but she imagined it looked like waves curling across a beach, spreading sea foam, fragmenting the sand. She swirled the paint, following the contours of her skin as if it were a shoreline.

She sensed the design nearing completion. Just before she smeared the final stroke, she looked at Archer, his broken form splayed on the ground. Though it must hurt him to move, he lifted his head and held her gaze for a blazing moment. He nodded, giving her one last burst of strength.

She closed her eyes and completed the final stroke, dabbing a line of rare purple across both eyelids. The despair shattered, releasing a rush of pure liquid hope. The curse was broken.

Briar opened her eyes. A dog-sized stone was flying toward

her, about to deliver her father's final blow. She flung up her purple-coated hands to protect her face—and the stone stopped at her palms. It hovered for a moment, cursed rock brushing oil paint–slicked skin. Then it fell.

Briar drew in a shocked breath. The ambulatory curse must have broken the instant it touched her skin. The unravelling curse was still working.

Another stone flew out of the darkness. She raised her hands, and that one stopped too. Wonder filled her. She'd never seen anything like it.

Her father began to hurl stone after stone at her. As the cursed rocks reached her cursed skin, they fell to the ground, cracking open at her feet. Droplets of purple paint mixed with the sparse rain and the stone dust.

Donovan tried other attacks—waves of pressure, blasts of fire, nightmares formed of smoke and fear. Briar's painted skin unraveled each curse, snuffing out each burst of power. She didn't feel the heat and force, the intended terrors. A few strokes of the purple hue were enough to unravel most curses. Covered in it, she was untouchable.

Briar's head spun at the possibilities her discovery opened up, but she still needed to stop her father's attacks. She wasn't sure how long the unravelling effect would last—and the rain was falling harder.

Shouts rose over the sounds of the curses. Larke's men would be pouring from the stronghold at any moment. Briar's limbs shook, and she barely stayed upright. She couldn't fight the soldiers and her father at the same time.

Something moved in the darkness. She limped forward, weaving through the rubble as well as she could. A particularly large pile of stone had fallen into an approximation of a door-way. The lintel was still in a single large piece, scrawled with the remnants of a powerful barrier curse. That was where the

CURSE PAINTER

movement had come from. Her father must be hiding behind it.

Briar hobbled sideways and found Donovan crouched among shattered stones and assorted jars of paint. He looked up at her, brush poised to scribe another curse. She saw curiosity in his eyes, a hint of admiration.

"Remarkable, Elayna Rose," he said. "I've never heard of someone cursing their own skin to unravel the curses thrown against them." Donovan studied the patterns she had scribed on herself, analyzing, memorizing. She knew he would take apart her discovery stroke by stroke, trying out variations with Briar's mother. He was a student of his art more than anything else. "We must examine this further," he said eagerly, as if he hadn't been breaking her bones and hurling his magic at her moments ago.

"You said you wished Mother had killed me," Briar said. Her throat hurt from inhaling so much dust, and her voice sounded creaky and thin.

Her father waved his paintbrush impatiently. "Nonsense. You will return with us, of course. We must explore the implications of your discovery. I hope you remember the stroke order."

Briar blinked at him. The purple paint dripped into her eyes, stinging like tears. Then she understood. Her father had been bluffing when he'd said he wished she'd been killed. It was a spoken curse designed to unsettle and distract her.

"Stand still and allow me to attempt a few more curses on you," her father said, opening up a jar of crimson lake. "Do you feel anything? I should very much like to know how long these effects last. Let's try an incendiary."

"Stop," Briar said.

Her father looked up.

"I'm not working with you."

"Nonsense. You are a Dryden. You've had your rebellion, but it is time to return to the work you were born to do."

Briar swallowed, wishing her voice sounded stronger. "I'll decide how to use my own power."

Donovan raised an eyebrow, his owlish eyes glinting in the light from the ruined stronghold. Then he picked up an emerald-green scarf that had been lying on the fallen lintel, one Briar had often worn to hold back her frizzy hair at home. She remembered her mother wrapping it around her head with nimble, paint-stained hands. The scarf was dripping with paint now—azurite and precious ultramarine. That was how her father had placed the despair curse on her. He had been carrying a part of her with him all that time, and he'd used the Law of Resonance on it to crush her with hopelessness.

He held up the scarf, azurite paint dripping from emerald silk, and lowered his voice. "I can make you accompany me."

Briar stared at her father, looking into the face of what she was, what she had come from. And instead of the old destructive urge, she felt a profound sense of calm.

"No," she said. "You can't." With the purple curse on her skin, he couldn't force her to do anything. For as long as it lasted, she was free.

"You could be extraordinary," her father said. "It will never happen if you squander your talent in your youth."

"I can live with that," Briar said.

"Elayna—"

"You can't make me go anywhere or hurt anyone." Briar met his gaze steadily. "Try it."

Donovan's elegant hands tightened around the scarf. He understood. He no longer had power over her. His art had failed him, and in his eyes, she saw a hint of fear.

Suddenly, torchlight flooded the ruins, and shouts filled the stormy air. Fighting men in Larke burgundy charged out of the stronghold, looking for whoever had destroyed their fortress. Briar reached automatically for her satchel, but it had split open when her father hurled her across the ground. She had no way to fight those men.

Then hoofbeats thundered toward her from farther up the canyon, and people shouted in familiar voices. Half a dozen horses charged out of the darkness, their hooves shaking the earth. Lew rode the leader, with Nat close beside him. The two brawny outlaws drew their weapons and bellowed war cries as they charged Larke's men—all of whom were on foot. Jemma rode close behind them, wielding her cudgel, red shawl flying. Esteban followed, barking rough spells in a strained and exhausted voice to hold back the swarm of soldiers. He held the reins of two additional horses, saddled and riderless.

Briar gasped in relief. She was no longer alone. Her friends were there.

Donovan reached for his paints, about to attack the newcomers.

"Don't move." Briar hobbled forward, placing herself directly in front of her father. He couldn't wield his curses against her. She would hold the line against him, stopping his violence with her cursed flesh. She could take the power her parents had given her—along with her own invention—and use it to stop them from doing harm.

So, with her broken bones aching and the rain falling harder by the minute, she stood up to her father, no longer bound by her family's curse.

Archer was pretty sure his body had stopped working at last. He could barely raise his head a few inches off the ground, and when he did, agony ripped through his broken form.

But it didn't matter, because Briar had done it. She had painted a curse to dampen her father's power, and now she had him trapped among the ruins of what had once been the strongest fortress in the kingdom of Lure. Even better, the team was there to save them all.

They arrived in a rebellion of shouts, punctuated by thundering hooves and the strangled song of a very tired voice mage. Lew. Jemma. Nat. Esteban. They got there just in time to hold back the Larke soldiers trying to emerge from the dark confusion of Narrowmar. The clash of their weapons was sweet music to Archer's ears.

Donovan and Briar looked as if they had been turned to stone, though lightning could strike between them at any moment. Neither knew Saoirse was dead. Donovan couldn't find out until they were long gone from there. Archer wished Briar never had to find out.

The curse painters ignored the commotion as the outlaws tried to stuff the soldiers back into the stronghold, pushing them toward the exposed main corridor. More men were jammed in the narrow space, unable to wield their weapons properly against the team.

Archer needed to get back on his feet and fight with his friends, but his body wasn't cooperating. He twitched helplessly, feeling as if he were locked in the stocks again, this time with fewer rotten vegetables and more broken bones. The others fought on without him, working to hold back the horde long enough to secure an escape route.

But they were forgetting someone. Archer tried to call out to Jemma, but he couldn't speak through the blood collecting in his throat. Then a familiar face appeared in the gaping wound that had once been a fortress, next to the main corridor where the guard station had been. Looking frightened but resolute, Mae Barden crept out of Narrowmar at last.

She moved carefully to avoid drawing the soldiers' attention and skirted around the curse painters, no doubt sensing she wanted no part in their battle. Dust matted her golden curls, and blood stained the hem of her pink dress. She spotted Archer lying on the ground, and a cry escaped her lips.

Archer smiled hazily as she started toward him. Maybe the mission was a success after all. Then Mae stopped as abruptly as if she'd walked into a wall. She stood still for a moment, looking at something on the ground.

She bent down and picked up a sword, its hilt wrapped in burgundy leather. Archer had left the dead captain's sword beside his unconscious brother. That was what Mae was staring at so intently—Tomas, Archer's careless, jovial brother. She hefted the sword in her pale hands.

"No." Archer's words gurgled through the bubble of pain. "Don't, Mae."

If she could hear him, she paid no attention. She tightened her grip on the sword, looking down at the man who had seduced and discarded her, who had turned to his ruthless father to clean up after his indiscretions. Who, through his irresponsibility, had threatened her life and nearly ended their illicit child's.

Archer understood what Mae must be thinking, but Tomas was still his brother. They'd endured their father's cruelty together, and even though Tomas had made selfish choice after selfish choice, Archer didn't want him to die. He reached out to the friend whose life he had saved, unable to speak above a whisper, and pleaded with her not to kill his brother.

But Mae didn't hear him. She raised the sword over Tomas's body. Her face twisted with passion, a mix of hatred and betrayal and sorrow. She had always been quick to laughter and quick to anger. She hurled herself into every pursuit, whether it was friendship with the son of her father's enemy or a love affair that had always been doomed. Archer hated to see her in anguish, but vengeance wouldn't help—and it would change her forever.

Mae let the sword fall.

The blade clanged like a bell against the stony ground and clattered to rest a few feet away from Tomas's still-sleeping form.

Archer dropped back, lacking the strength to hold up his head any longer. Mae had spared Tomas's life despite how much grief he had caused her. There was still room for mercy in the cruel world the Larkes had created. Archer drew in a rattling breath. If there was room for mercy, there was room for change, and hope.

Then Mae was kneeling beside him, carefully touching his body, feeling the extent of his injuries. He couldn't feel much himself anymore. He couldn't hear much either, or see, now that he thought about it. Archer's world faded to a muted buzz and skittered out of reach.

CHAPTER 34

B riar listened to the cacophony as her friends held back the soldiers. Relief flooded her body. The rain was falling harder than ever, and the paint on her skin would wash away soon, but the arrival of the others would give her time to escape. It was almost over.

Lew and Nat fought the soldiers among the rubble, using their brawn for all it was worth. Esteban and Jemma gathered up Archer and Mae and hoisted them onto the spare horses. They left a mount for Briar and charged back up the ravine.

"Hurry, lass!" Lew shouted. "We can't hold them much longer."

Briar backed away from her father, ready to dive in his way if he tried to curse Lew and Nat, but he slumped, as if his daughter's opposition had drained his strength.

"Mark my words, Elayna Rose," he said as she turned and limped to the waiting horse. "You will return home when you realize this world cannot match the family calling."

Briar didn't answer. She pulled herself into the saddle with her good arm, whimpering as she jarred her broken bones. Her ambulatory curse was still painted on the pommel, a reminder that she had the potential to do vast and interesting magic that was entirely separate from her family's dark work.

"Ready!" she shouted to the remaining members of her team. Lew and Nat pulled back on their mounts, allowing the soldiers to pour forth from Narrowmar, and they charged into the rain-drenched night. With a flick of the reins Briar followed, praying her father wouldn't curse her as she fled.

She caught up with Lew and Nat just as they rode past Esteban, who had paused in the center of the ravine. He opened his mouth to shout a final spell to hold off their pursuers. It sounded like a good one, full of destruction, but Briar didn't look back.

⁂

They regrouped at the broken statue beyond the ravine. Jemma, covered in dirt. Mae, the rain plastering her curls to her forehead. Esteban, a black shape crumpled in his saddle. Lew, with assorted cuts and bruises and a bloody rip in his vest. Nat, a makeshift sling around his neck. The squall of a very irritated baby came from beneath his patchwork coat.

"I found her with Sheriff," Nat reported. "He almost bit my hand off, but I told him you'd want me to take her."

Mae rode close by Nat, checking to see that her baby still had all her fingers and toes. Sheriff barked, weaving through the horses' legs to stay close to Nat and the baby.

"You both did well." Briar was beginning to feel lightheaded from the pain in her arm. She wanted to take shelter beneath the statue's giant legs, but they weren't safe so near Narrowmar. "Are we riding all night?"

"We can rest in New Chester," Jemma said. Her clothes were dirty and torn, but she had emerged from the tunnel unscathed. "Esteban can't heal anyone until he has a long sleep."

The voice mage clung to his saddle, swaying dangerously. That final spell had taken a lot out of him after a long night.

"We thought you were done for when the mountain collapsed," Lew said, drawing his horse closer to Briar. "Did you get Lord Larke?"

Briar hesitated. "I don't think he'll bother us for a while." In truth, Jasper Larke probably wouldn't survive the wound from the black curse stone unless he found a voice mage. She hadn't seen what had become of Tomas after she'd put him to sleep.

Archer himself was in no condition to ask about his father and brother. He had been slammed to the ground, first by Briar in the tunnel then by her father. The brutal blows had taken their toll.

Briar was afraid to get close to him and see the extent of his injuries. Jemma and Lew fashioned a litter to transport him, but they couldn't do much to make him comfortable. He lay unconscious in the sling, his face covered in cuts, his skin swelling from internal bleeding.

"Can't you fix him?" Nat asked Esteban as they prepared to set out into the forest.

The voice mage was barely awake. Jemma moved forward to tie him to his saddle so he wouldn't fall off his horse.

"I have done ... more ... can't."

"Don't speak," Jemma said. "When you get your strength back, you can try again."

She finished the knots on Esteban's saddle then mounted her own horse. She, too, could barely look at Archer, but her back was straight and her eyes were resolute as she led the way into the darkness.

They had a somber ride away from Narrowmar. The sparse pines rose above them, not thick enough to protect them from the rain, and the sloping ground was wet and perilous. After an hour, they left the woods for the road to avoid jarring Archer's litter more than necessary. Briar held out hope that they would encounter a traveling voice mage along the way, but the road remained empty.

They stopped to rest in the small hours of the morning, making camp beneath the dripping pines. Nat and Jemma managed to find enough dry wood for a small fire. Lew laid Archer beside it, wincing as the flames illuminated his bruises. They were dark and swollen and still spreading.

Esteban tried twice more to sing Archer back to health, but his powers were utterly spent. He wheezed and gasped, unable to produce a single note of magic. Archer had killed Larke's voice mage, Croyden, the only other person nearby who might have had a chance at healing Archer's body. Esteban mumbled an apology, struggling to hold up his head on his scrawny neck.

"It's not your fault," Lew told him gruffly. "We all did the best we could."

They had hoped making camp would give Esteban time to recover, but Archer was fading fast. His breath became a slow rattle. Jemma and Lew sat with him, whispering soberly to each other. Briar didn't have to eavesdrop to know they didn't think he would live to see the dawn.

Jemma wore a stoic expression as she pressed a wet cloth to her son's forehead. She whispered in his ear, perhaps telling him the secret she had kept for his entire life, but he was beyond hearing. The others huddled beneath the pines, unable to revel in their successful mission as their leader lay dying.

"Can *you* do something?" Mae pleaded with Briar, her daughter swaddled up tight in her arms. "You're so powerful."

"I'm not," Briar said. "I've tried to heal before. It doesn't work."

"He can't die, not because of me."

"It was for both of you." Briar started to reach out to the baby then pulled back, clutching her injured arm. "And for everyone Larke would have hurt if he'd used your baby to expand his dominion. Now, you can return to your father's house, or take your daughter and leave this kingdom forever."

Mae hugged her baby closer, tears spilling onto the blankets. "Please try something."

Briar couldn't tell her no, even though she knew it was futile. Mae looked at her with too much trust and desperation.

Briar approached Archer's broken form, her leg protesting every step. Jemma moved aside to give her space.

Archer was covered in the age-worn cloak they had stolen from Mage Radner in Mud Market, one arm resting atop the faded fabric. The cloak wasn't quite thick enough to hold off the chill in the air. Archer shivered, his face pale beneath the bruises.

Briar sat in the dirt beside him, her saddlebag of spare paints clinking as she set it on the ground. She only had a few colors left, but even if she had every hue of the rainbow, she didn't know a curse in the world that would hold off the slow march of death.

She took the paints out anyway and began a design on the sleeve of Archer's shirt. The soft scrape of the horsehair brush whispered in time with Archer's death rattle. Tears dripped down Briar's cheeks, tinged with purple, but it was no use. No tears or paints could bring him back from the brink.

"Archer," she whispered. "You probably can't hear me, but I want you to know you did well. We saved Mae. We saved the baby. She's beautiful. Sheriff is already in love with her. She's going to adore the forest and the open road too."

Briar sniffed and felt Sheriff nudging her arm. She made room for him to lay his head gently in his master's hand.

"Do you remember the day we met?" Briar whispered. "You saved me too. I was too mad about my cottage to see it then, but you gave me a chance at a different life. You gave me freedom and hope and ... so much love. I don't know if you loved me specifically, but the love you showed your team and your friends and even your family, it wrapped me up like a blanket, and I can never thank you enough for that."

Sheriff gave a low whine, as if to echo the ache in Briar's heart. Archer's breathing was slowing. The bit of paint on his sleeve had no power to save him. It was just a pretty picture of a cottage in the woods, with a large dog beside it and a bow resting by the door.

She brushed her fingers over the painting, wishing she could conjure that scene into being. The oil paint smudged slightly at her touch. She let her hand fall onto the rough cloak covering Archer's chest, the one they had taken from Mage Radner to carry her paints way back in Mud Market.

Briar sat up. Sheriff raised his head, looking at her with mournful eyes. Was it possible?

Briar held her breath, not wanting to let the others know there was even a glimmer of hope lest it fade. She dipped her brush in a jar of verdigris and began a new design. She worked one-handed, more by feel than anything else. She painted along the hood of the cloak, telling the story of what they had been through in the weeks since she'd seen her little cottage burn. She painted a voice mage with his words full of fire and power, painted the long road they had traveled since then. She painted the scene all the way across Archer's chest, planting it on the rising and falling planes, scribing it above his heart and down the other side of his body where the cloak rested. The well-worn, treasured cloak that had belonged to a powerful voice mage.

When it was done, Briar wrapped her arm around Sheriff's neck and waited. She watched the painting rising and falling on Archer's chest, praying that the rise and fall wouldn't stop, that the cloak still had a resonant connection with the mage who had worked so hard to earn it, that the curse would be in place for just long enough.

The others had gathered around as the fire burned low.

They must have watched Briar paint the cloak over Archer's body, perhaps thinking it was a funeral ritual only she understood. They kept watch, knowing it wouldn't be long. Her face still wet with tears, Briar didn't dare tell them what she had done.

She waited. Sheriff seemed to sense something was going on because he tensed beside her, waiting, waiting. Then she heard the voice. It came from so far away, she would have thought it was an insect if she hadn't been listening for that sound, but she heard it, and she knew what it was. The voice grew from a low buzz to a whine to a scream. The others looked around, trying to figure out where the noise was coming from.

Then Mage Radner plunged out of the cloudy sky, wearing nightclothes and shouting an angry tirade at the curse that had picked him up and carried him across half a county to Archer's side.

In other circumstances, Radner might have broken the curse before it had carried him far, but he was too shocked at being wrenched out of his bed and into the air, and Briar's magic was too strong.

The voice mage landed in a heap on the other side of Archer's still-breathing form. Briar leapt up at once, ignoring the pain in her leg. She seized the voice mage by the scruff of the neck—Sheriff chewing on his elbow to reinforce her authority—and ordered him to speak healing words faster than he had ever spoken them in his life. Radner was too confused and scared to argue.

Then the words were pouring forth, healing, restoring. Briar might not be able to heal herself, but she could drag forth hope by the scruff of the neck to save the man she loved. The spell filled the camp, sonorous and life-giving and strong.

Then Archer was opening his eyes and sitting up, and everyone was crying—everyone except Radner, who was grumbling about what Lord Barden and the sheriff would have to say about his most undignified treatment, but he had the good sense not to try to fight the curse painter who had flown him there.

All that mattered to her was that the magic had worked.

Archer's eyes flew open. Loud and joyous sounds surrounded him, but he couldn't quite make sense of them. Something had called him back from the brink, something he didn't fully understand. His friends' faces bobbed around him like cattails in a stream, and a large tongue was covering his hand in slobber. Amidst the commotion, all he could see was Briar.

Purple paint streaked her hair, and every color of the rainbow covered her shirt. As she looked at him, the most delicious sense of wellness filled his body. She was a healing song in his ears, a crackling fire in his blood.

He sat up, a cloak sliding down from his chest, and pulled Briar toward him. The others crowded in to hug him and slap his back, but he paid no attention to them, intent on the woman in his arms. Briar pressed her cheek against his chest, smudging the paint covering his shirt, and for a moment, all they did was breathe in time with one another.

Then he tipped her face up, her luminous eyes meeting his.

"Thank you," he said. "And I do."

"You do what?"

"Love you, specifically."

A smile broke across that paint-smudged face, and Archer wondered if he had died and gone to the higher realms after all. Briar's eyes held deep wells of sadness, wells that might never be empty, but at last, joy flowed there too.

T HIS STORY ENDS WITH A PROMISE. It was a solemn
promise, the kind made in a breathless, joyful moment.
This promise saw a young man named Archer clasping the
paint-smudged hands of a young woman named Briar and
offering her his world, such as it was, and in return, she
promised him her heart, such as it was, every smudged, hopeful
piece of it.

ABOUT THE AUTHOR

Jordan Rivet is an American author of swashbuckling YA fantasy and post-apocalyptic science fiction. She has written eighteen books across five worlds and doesn't plan to stop anytime soon. Originally from Arizona, Jordan lives in Hong Kong with her husband.

www.JordanRivet.com
jordan@jordanrivet.com

ALSO BY JORDAN RIVET

FANTASY

Duel of Fire

King of Mist

Dance of Steel

City of Wind

Night of Flame

The Watermight Thief

The Thunderbird Queen

The Dragonfly Oath

The Spy in the Silver Palace

An Imposter with a Crown

A Traitor at the Stone Court

SCIENCE FICTION

Wake Me After the Apocalypse

Meet Me at World's End

Seabound

Seaswept

Seafled

Burnt Sea: A Seabound Prequel

THE THREE LAWS OF CURSE PAINTING

The Law of Wholes

A curse applied to an object can affect that object in its entirety regardless of whether the pieces are intact.

The Law of Proximity

A curse applied to an object can affect any person who comes in direct contact with that object except the original painter.

The Law of Resonance

A curse applied to an object of emotional significance can affect a person from a distance. The stronger the emotional connection, the stronger the curse.

GUIDE TO PAINT MAGIC

Color	Magical effect
White	Cloaking
Lead-tin Yellow	Illness
Yellow Ochre	Decay
Brown Ochre	Fragmentation
Umber	Destruction/Collapse
Reds:	Incendiary:
Vermilion	Fire
Crimson	Heat
Carmine Lake	Explosion
Greens:	Ambulatory:
Malachite	Movement
Verdigris	Flight
Green Earth	Falling
Blues:	Psychological:
Blue Smalt	Sleep
Azurite	Anxiety
Ultramarine	Illusions
Indigo	Nightmares
Purple	Magical Unravelling
Bone Black	Death
Carbon Black	Binding